Emy Moon

Emy Moon

By

Murphy Gordon

Sawmill Publishing
6444 East Spring Street, Suite 215
Long Beach, California. 90815
Orders: www.sawmillpublishing.com

Second Edition, first printed 2004

Cover art and chapter illustrations by Diane Lucas

Printed In the United States of America

Hardcover ISBN: 978-0-9749915-9-7
Paperback ISBN: 978-0-9749915-8-0

ACKNOWLEDGMENTS

With much gratitude to my family and my many friends for encouraging me to write this novel.

Seeds

THE RICHLY INTRICATE TAPESTRY of History is woven one thread at a time. It is only from the perspective of time, when the tapestry can be viewed from a distance, that the connection between each individual thread becomes clear. Without that perspective, the individual threads that make up the fabric of History are nothing more than the pedestrian pattern of daily life; yet without the individual threads, each in its exact and proper place, the pattern of the fabric would be forever altered.

Four hundred years ago, the light from a full moon shone bright upon a new land as a seed from a mighty oak was sewn. Thrown to the ground, the seed thrived. Nurtured by the rich, untouched soil, nature, over untold millennia, had instilled in the tiny seedling the timing of its first sprout, the height and rate at which it would grow, and when it would cease to exist. Subtly, and without swerving from the plan of its life cycle, the young oak entrenched itself in the soft black earth. Grappling and clinging, the life-sustaining roots deepened and flexed, giving the new oak strength and permanence.

Threads upon threads.

One of those threads arrived at approximately five o'clock on the cool, blustery morning of April 27, 1762, when the cry of a newborn female child sliced through the silence of a sleeping Colonial village.

Her name was Lucille Killgrew.

One year later, in 1763, King George the Third ascended to the throne of England and claimed its vast Empire. With the costly French and Indian War still to be paid, King George turned desperately to the American Colonies. Life in the Colonies grew increasingly difficult under the double yoke of unjust taxes and unfair laws.

In 1774, the first Continental Congress formed in Philadelphia, unifying the Colonies with a common resolve. In that same year, Benjamin Franklin, who had been unable to convince the King to ease his harsh taxes on the Colonies, returned home from England.

Rioting and unrest ushered in the year of 1775. The New Year also ushered in the thirteenth birthday of the girl named Lucille Killgrew.

Without the perspective of time, threads are nothing but a tangle of strings, each weak and insubstantial. But the loom of History was already hard at work, and as the shuttle continued its slow but steady magic, a vital part of the tapestry was beginning to take shape and texture.

And by the time it all was finished, the strong, mature oak's roots would cross the paths of both Lucille Killgrew and another young girl who would follow after her.

Chapter One

The MacAllisters

Los Angeles, California

STEPHANIE MACALLISTER unconsciously began to rub her thumb back and forth over a small tear in the arm of her seat as she watched the controlled anarchy of the tarmac from her airplane window. She didn't want anyone to know she was nervous about flying—especially her brother, Randy. Even though he was a year younger than she was, he could really be a pain when he wanted to be—which was almost all the time.

"You know, Steff, I read this story the other day," Randy said suddenly, poking his head up over the back of her seat. His voice cut through her thoughts like a dull meat cleaver, rusty and caked with God-knew-what. It was so unexpected that she jumped slightly and sucked in her breath. For just the briefest moment, she clung to the forlorn hope that Randy hadn't noticed, but when she looked up at his crooked grin and saw the sparkle in his bright blue eyes, she knew that *he* knew!

She sighed deeply and resigned herself to spending the next five hours—and three thousand miles—as the target of her brother's teasing and baiting.

"You would have loved that article," Randy continued, after just a short pause. "It was about these people who lived through a plane crash. At least some of 'em lived through it. The lucky ones died…"

"Dad," Stephanie whined. "Can't you shut Randy up? Please?"

Stephanie's father didn't look up from the brochures he was reading.

"Randy, leave your sister alone," he said in his "I'm not listening" voice, the one he always used when he wasn't really paying any attention to what anyone was saying.

"The survivors didn't have anything to eat for weeks… until they finally started eating—each other!"

To emphasize the words, Randy poked his finger between the seats and jabbed Stephanie in the ribs. But she tried to keep a straight face. She was determined not to let her brother know that he was bothering her.

She concentrated hard on making her voice sound tired and bored.

"Wow! I'm amazed."

"Really? Amazed that people would eat each other?" Randy said, making his voice sound sinister.

"No," said Stephanie. "I'm amazed that you can read."

Randy snorted but continued hovering over his sister, probably making faces at the top of her head, but Stephanie didn't look back to find out. Finally, he sat back down and kicked the back of her seat once—hard.

She smiled, knowing she had won that round. Then she leaned part way over her father, who was sitting in the middle seat next to her, and looked into her mother's face. Her mother's eyes were closed, and for just a moment, Stephanie wondered if her mother might also be a little afraid of flying. For some reason, that thought made her feel better.

"Can't I go to Europe with you and Dad, please?" she pleaded. "I promise I won't get in the way. You'll hardly even know I'm there."

"That's true, and do you know why? Because you *won't* be there," her father said, still not looking up from his brochures.

Stephanie's mother turned her head slightly, but her eyes remained closed.

"Your grandmother is expecting the two of you," she said. "And besides," she continued, opening her eyes and taking her husband's hand, "a second honeymoon just wouldn't quite be the same with kids along."

Stephanie saw her father and mother exchange knowing smiles. Stephanie was only thirteen, but she knew what those smiles meant—although she did her best not to think about it.

With a sigh, Stephanie settled back in her seat and resigned herself to the fact that it was going to be a long flight—and an even longer summer, stuck in some tiny flyspeck of a town with just her grandmother and the brother from hell to keep her company.

Dear God, why is this happening to me? She whined silently. *Please, just let me survive the next five weeks.*

With a sudden jerk, the plane's engines thundered to

life, and the huge machine began to inch away from the gate. Stephanie closed her eyes tightly and squeezed the armrests involuntarily.

Scratch that, God, she thought. *Just let me survive the next five minutes!*

What Stephanie did not know, what she could not possibly have known, was that she was embarking on more than just a dreaded holiday with family she hadn't seen since she was six. From the moment her parents had decided to take their second honeymoon and had arranged for the kids to stay with their grandmother in the tiny New England town of Mayfair, a whole series of inevitable events had begun to be added to a complex tapestry that spanned more than two hundred years—a tapestry that would soon bind the lives of Stephanie MacAllister and Lucille Killgrew together in the wondrous cloth of History.

"Ladies and Gentlemen, Captain Peterson here. We're next in line for departure, so sit back and relax. Our flight is about to begin."

Chapter Two

The Killgrews

Hampshire, Massachusetts

April 27, 1775

Dear Emy,
I awoke this day at an early hour, for it is
my birthday and the excitement of it fills me
so. I pray Father returns to mother and I. He
promised. Guide him safely home.
—Lucy Killgrew

THE WINTER SNOWS HAD finally gone and nature was beginning to breathe new life into the land. Once again, as in eons past, the new world was coming alive with the sounds and smells of spring. The rich black earth of the neatly furrowed soil lay in stark contrast to the multi-colored greens of the surrounding landscape. It was the end of April 1775, and though she didn't know it at the time, it was also the year of Lucille's greatest adventure and her destiny's fulfillment.

Within Middlesex County, the village of Hampshire was situated near the coast, two days' ride north of Boston. There were, in that year, eighty-five homes surrounding the Common and the Meeting House. Beyond the village lay the individual fields where each resident raised and harvested their crops.

Over the years, after the French and Indian War, with confidence in themselves and in their future, Hampshire had increased in size. The more adventurous farmers had begun leaving the towns and villages, moving westward, into the wilds of Massachusetts. Alone, and without the immediate protection of the community, these hardy souls carved out their futures—and the future of a new nation— through backbreaking work and raw courage.

The Killgrew farm was just a few minutes' ride north- west of the Hampshire Common. The fertile land they had cleared stretched out beyond the white oaks and tamaracks and was the pride of the Killgrew family. On each side of the gate leading to the Killgrew home stood an oak tree; one tree larger than the other. Over the years, the roots of the larger oak had become exposed, and it was to this tree that neighbors, or Reverend Moore, when he came for supper, would tie their animals before walking the narrow path that led them past a grove of smaller trees and then to the door of the Killgrew's white two-story house.

The vestibule in the entrance of their modest home led either to a stairway or through one of two doors. The main floor consisted of two large rooms, separated by a large fireplace, with a hearth on each side. The room to the right of the vestibule was the main hall, used by the family for cooking and dining. To the left was the parlor and occasional sleeping room.

Up the narrow stairway were two sparsely furnished bedrooms, each with its own small fireplace. Small, but cozy, the bedrooms were simple, each containing a bed and an oak dresser. On the wall by each door, a group of pegs held several articles of clothing.

It was through one of the windows on the first floor that the yellow light from the burning hearth and two oil lamps cast the silhouette of a young girl upon the ground outside. She had been keeping a daylong vigil at that window, perched upon a narrow bench, anxiously awaiting the arrival of her father.

With the setting of the sun, and the rising of the moon, what little warmth there had been during the day now surrendered to the cold evening air. Inside, the steadily burning fire had temporarily taken away the chill of early spring. The scent of pine inside the house was now being replaced by the warmth and smell of the evening meal.

The silhouette belonged to Lucille Killgrew, but her parents, and all the people who lived nearby, simply called her Lucy. She wasn't like most of the other young girls in the area. She had the spirit of an unbroken colt and a thirst for learning and, although she never told anyone, Lucy secretly wished she had been born a boy. More than anything, she wanted to be able to ride, hunt, and be treated like the community treated the young boys.

On several occasions, she had been seen riding the back roads of Hampshire at a full gallop in her handmade buckskin riding breeches. No one, man or boy, could out-ride Lucy Killgrew. It was as if she were one with her horse. Their speed and grace was freedom in motion, and it was a freedom that Lucy loved—at least, until she was seen riding with such abandon by her father, or worse, by one of their neighbors.

These were times when women had to know their place, and though society dictated that her father punish Lucy for such unheard-of female behavior, Lucy could sense the love and pride her father felt for her, even as they talked about setting her punishment. She could see it in his eyes and hear it in his voice, and no matter how many times he punished her, or how many times she received tongue-lashings from neighbors, Lucy's father never denied her the use of her horse or took away her riding breeches.

Lucy was a beautiful girl of thirteen who, unlike the other girls of Hampshire, preferred breeches to dresses. Lucy was slightly heavier than average; however, that only seemed to add to her strength. At first, the other young ladies teased her, but after several of them had tested both Lucy's temper and strength, the teasing stopped. Whether in breeches or a dress, Lucy's tomboyish beauty still turned many a young man's head, and her fierce independence gained the respect of boys and girls alike.

Over the years, Lucy had grown tall, and now she stood a little over five feet two inches tall. Her hair was as black as night and thickly curled; her tanned face wore a look of determination, yet there was always a light of compassion shining in her large brown eyes.

Her parents were proud of having a daughter who was healthy and able to endure the hard and serious life of a Colonist. Because of the poor medical and sanitary conditions of that time, many children—especially newborn children—failed to survive. In the Killgrew family, Lucy was the only surviving child of the three her mother had brought into the world. An only child, especially the child of a farmer, had many responsibilities. She rarely had time for children's games, and now, with her father gone, it was her duty to help her mother run the farm.

Among the many chores she had to perform was to split wood for the fire and care for the few animals they had. Early in her childhood, her father had taught her to master the oxen; thus, the straight furrows that she cut deep and true into the fields of the Killgrew farm were a testament to her skill.

Inside the house, Lucy also helped her mother cook, clean, do laundry, and the thousand other chores that women generally performed.

Furthermore, she developed another talent early in her life. With a skill equal to most men of the time, Lucy could use a musket. From the time she was a very young girl, her father had taught her everything he knew about using a pistol and musket, much to the dismay of her mother. However Lucy's father understood that, in the wilds, skill with a long rifle was not only important for hunting but also for providing protection against animals and some- times, even against other human beings. As it turned out, her father's guidance had been well worthwhile, because, now that he was gone, it was Lucy's marksmanship that provided most of the meat for the table.

Most of the children in Colonial America were taught the ways of farming, but very few were taught anything else. Lucy's mother, however, was an educated woman, and she taught her daughter to read and write. It was knowledge that Lucy truly treasured. Her parents always tried to have pen, ink, and paper for their daughter to use in expressing her thoughts, and on many occasions, Lucy could be found off in some corner of the house or a field, recording the day's events in her journal.

Her notes often included conversations with her best friend, Emy Moon. At the age of three, Lucy had named the full moon Emy. No one knew why she had chosen that particular name or why she had developed such a continued fascination with the moon, but it didn't matter—in time, everyone accepted Emy.

To Lucy, the changing phases of the moon represented Emy's coming and going. Emy was in her fullest splendor during the full moon, and it was then that Lucy believed she had Emy's complete attention. It was also then that she would speak to the moon and, as any young child might do, make wishes upon it. Over the years, Emy became Lucy's trusted confidant and provided a way to explore her innermost thoughts and deepest feelings.

Lucy's mother had been born Nancy Collins and was raised in Plymouth, where her family had lived and worked since arriving from England more than a hundred years earlier.

Nancy's father owned a shipping supply company, and he had grown wealthy as his business prospered. His daughter grew to become a beautiful and gentile young woman who eventually caught the eye of a young frontiersman named Tom Killgrew. Tom had come to Plymouth to serve as an escort to several Commonwealth officials who employed him as a guide for their excursions into the backwoods of New England.

One day, Nancy was leaving her father's office when she noticed Tom approaching from the opposite direction. As she slowed her pace, Tom did the same. Not being a shy man, Tom struck up a conversation with her, which led to a yearlong courtship and their eventual marriage.

With what little money Tom had saved and a generous wedding gift from Nancy's father, Tom and Nancy purchased a small tract of land and built a modest home in nearby Hampshire.

Tall and slender, Nancy was a beautiful woman. The

long auburn hair that showed from under her hood swayed back and forth as she walked. Her complexion was fair, and her eyes were hazel. However, years of living on a farm in rural Massachusetts had changed Nancy. She had become a strong, independent woman, capable of doing almost any kind of farm work, and it was a strength that she passed on to her daughter. Her once delicate hands had become calloused. Her delicate, porcelain-like face had become hardened by the sun and wind, but the harshness of rural life had not diminished her beauty. In spite of the hardships, she was always a gentle, loving mother and faithful wife.

Lucy turned from the window to face her mother, who was busy preparing supper.

"Why hasn't Father come yet, Mother? He said he would be here for my birthday, and today *is* my birthday. Oh, Mother, he must come. He simply must!"

Nancy was bending before the fireplace, stirring the large black pot that hung above the crackling fire. She looked at her daughter and said, "Lucy, you've been sitting on that *settle* and asking me that same question all day. Your father will be here if he can, you know that. But don't get your hopes up. Your father has much weighing on his mind."

As her daughter slowly turned back toward the window, Nancy's mind continued to swirl, threatening to race out of control. She fought hard to harness her thoughts, focusing on one fact that thrilled her, yet sometimes made her feel as if she was slightly set apart—the deep love that existed between her husband and their daughter. She thanked God every night for that love. At the same time, though she hated to admit it, even in the privacy of her secret thoughts—she sometimes felt a twinge of envy, theirs was a special bond of which she was could never quite be a part.

Her thoughts made Nancy laugh silently at herself. *Just listen to me! I should be ashamed for thinking such things—today, of all days.* In her heart, she knew that only one thing was truly important at this moment. She prayed that Tom would return safely to both of them.

Nancy was well aware that the situation in the Colonies had changed since what had happened at Lexington and Concord a few weeks ago, and she was concerned for her husband's safety. Nevertheless, Nancy would not allow herself to dwell on the dangers her husband now faced. She, instead, tried hard to occupy her time and mind with other things.

Above the fireplace's large hearth was the heavy mantel-tree, from which a number of pots and Lucy's musket hung on pegs. The empty pegs next to Lucy's Fowler rifle would hold Tom's own weapon and saber when he returned. On the side of the hearth, recessed into the stone, was the oven that Nancy had used that day to bake enough bread for the week. As the logs cracked and snapped, Nancy stood and placed her hands on her back and stretched, in an effort to loosen her aching muscles.

The soft glow of the fire seemed to transform Nancy's hardened features back into the soft, radiant image of her former self. As she stretched, Nancy's hair curled from beneath the hood she wore, brushing down along her cheeks and resting on her shoulders.

While she didn't tell her daughter, Nancy, in anticipation of his return, was wearing a special dress that Tom had always favored. She gazed into the orange and yellow flames as they licked the blackened side of the large kettle. Within the dancing flames, she could almost see the face of her beloved husband.

Memories, like water over a broken dam, began to

flood over her, but it was a flood she welcomed. She had held back those memories far too long, and it felt good for the torrent of feelings and emotions to finally be set free.

As she looked into the fire, she could clearly recall the day Tom had come running into the house to the sound of the church bell ringing in the distance.

"This is it, Nancy!" he had shouted, rushing to the hearth. "It's finally happening."

"What? What do you mean?" Nancy had asked, though she knew full well the meaning of his words. Her heart had been filled with dread that morning—a dread that she knew would never completely leave her for the rest of her days.

Grabbing his long rifle from above the manteltree, Tom had hurried across the room to the small cabinet where his powder horn and shot were kept.

"Lexington!" he responded. "The British have fired on our men at Lexington!"

Her husband might have said more at that moment, but Nancy's mind had stopped listening. She simply could not bear to hear any more, couldn't allow herself to think about the horror of what was about to happen.

The loud crackle of a log snapped Nancy out of her reverie—but only for a moment. The flood of emotions, too long held back, was too strong to stop just yet. She turned her gaze from the fire to the empty vestibule, and the floodwaters engulfed her mind once again.

"I have to go," Tom had solemnly told her that day, looking deeply into her eyes.

His eyes had told her that all he really wanted to do at that moment was to be lost in the depths of her own eyes forever, but then he turned and said, "You know I don't want to go, but it's something I *have* to do."

Even as she choked back her tears on that day, Nancy

had told her husband that she understood what he was saying—but she had lied. There was no doubt that she had honestly tried to understand, and that she desperately wanted to understand but no matter how hard she tried, the only thing she had truly understood that day was that the love of her life would soon be leaving; furthermore it was also possible (though she had pushed the thought as far away as she could) that he would never return.

The evening of Tom's departure was also a night she would always remember. She had awakened many times that night and lay in the darkness with tears streaming down her face, until she cried herself to sleep once more.

The next day, she had walked through her chores as if in a dream. Nothing seemed real. Everything had happening so quickly. One instant, she had been holding her dear Tom tightly, vowing never to let go—and then, in the next instant, he had been on his horse, preparing to leave.

As time went by, she prayed often for the nightmare to end, so that she and Tom could once again hold each other in a loving embrace. But day after day, the nightmare did not go away, and she had begun to believe, in spite of herself, that life would never be the same again.

"Good-bye, Tom. Please be careful," she had said through her tears as her husband turned his horse to the south.

"I'll return to you soon; I promise," he replied, hesitating for a moment, apparently feeling the need to explain his reasoning once more. "This was bound to happen, you know. We all expected it. You understand, don't you, my love?"

Nancy had nodded her understanding but said nothing.

His horse had danced impatiently as Tom Killgrew

bent down to kiss his wife one last time. Then he bent low, swung Lucy up to the saddle, and kissed his daughter good-bye.

"You take care of your mother, Lucy," he had said, embracing her tightly.

"Will you be back soon, Father?" Lucy had asked.

"I'll be back as soon as I can. I promise."

"Promise me you'll be here for my birthday."

"Well, Lucy, I will promise you this: If it's at all possible, I'll be here for your birthday."

He had then set his daughter back on the ground, placed his tricorn hat on his head, and without looking back, spurred his horse and rode away.

With his cape fluttering behind him and his saber rattling against the saddle, Tom Killgrew had ridden southward toward Boston, slowly disappearing down the long, dusty, tree-lined road. With tears rolling down their faces, Nancy and Lucy had finally turned and walked back into the house, without saying a word.

In the fireplace, the pot began to rattle and hiss, breaking Nancy's concentration. For the moment, the flood was stemmed. Releasing the emotions that she'd been holding back all these hard, lonely weeks had done her good. She reached into the fire, removed the large bake kettle from the hearth, and carried it to the table.

"Lucy, come away from the window. It's time for supper."

"Can't we wait just a few more minutes, Mother? I just know he's going to come."

Seeing the love and trust in her daughter's eyes almost broke Nancy's heart. She sat down at the table, closed her eyes, and pictured her husband, not as she had last seen him, but as she imagined him to look at this very moment.

"Tom," she prayed silently, "come home to us. Please, come home."

She almost believed that Tom could somehow hear her thoughts, just as she was certain that she sometimes felt his.

Whenever Nancy pictured her husband, the first thing she remembered were his eyes—large, laughing, and hazel green. There was a genuine depth in those eyes, and they had seen a great deal of this new land. Tom had spent his entire youth as a hunter and trapper, roaming the forests east of the Appalachians, all the way up into the wilds of Canada.

She remembered, too, his ready smile, which seemed to bathe his entire face in a warm, happy glow. His clean-shaven features had been hardened by the elements. His face, covered with deep narrow lines appeared to be chiseled from granite.

Tom was tall, six foot two inches in his stocking feet. His body was wiry and muscular. He wore his shaggy hair slightly long, and a few strands of gray were just beginning to adorn his temples. He preferred large, loose-fitting shirts and buckskin breeches. Having spent most of his life in the woods, he had the instincts of an animal and the cunning of an Indian.

Early on, he had taught Lucy everything she would need to know to live alone in the wilds and survive. Once, over Nancy's strong objections, Tom took Lucy, who had just celebrated her tenth birthday, on a ride deep into the woods.

Handing her only a knife, a length of twine, and a piece of flint, Tom had left his daughter alone for a day and a night to fend for herself. When Tom had finally brought Lucy back home, she was filthy from head to toe, but she had trapped and eaten a rabbit and had made a hearty stew from wild herbs and vegetables she had foraged from the woods. Lucy told her mother that it had been the greatest experience of her life, and in spite of herself, Nancy had been almost as proud of her daughter as Tom had been.

Unlike some other frontiersmen, Tom never hunted for sport, and he taught Lucy never to kill except when necessary for either protection or food. Tom believed that all life was sacred, and he made sure his daughter felt the same way.

Nancy opened her eyes and again looked into the fire, remembering how much her husband loved to dance. His big feet and large hands made him look clumsy and awkward—until he hit the dance floor, where he suddenly became as graceful as flowing water. The thought of Tom gliding across the hardwood floor made her smile.

Finally, with great effort, Nancy pushed aside her memories of Tom, heaved a long sigh, turned her attention once more to her daughter, who was now almost a grown woman at thirteen, and wiped a tear from the corner of her eye.

The glow of the moon rested on Lucy's face as she moved closer to the window. The warmth from within the house, coupled with the cold night air outside, had caused a heavy mist to build up on the widow pane. Lucy cleared away the moisture with the palm of her hand so she could look out at Emy Moon. As tiny streams of water trickled from between her fingers, she closed her eyes.

"Please, Emy, please," she said. "Guide my father safely back home."

Then, over the sound of the crackling fire, Lucy thought she heard a faint beating sound. Lucy's world suddenly narrowed, until nothing else existed except that sound. Then she realized it was the pounding of approaching hoof beats. Lucy's heart began to race, her cheeks flushed with excitement. She turned her head and looked at her mother, who was now standing, straight and still, listening, not making a sound.

"He's coming!" Lucy said under her breath, not daring to say the words out loud. "He's coming. Oh, thank you, Emy. Thank you."

Her hand was still pressed upon the windowpane, her fingers pressed together. She slowly spread her fingers apart, one by one, to reveal the figure of a rider approaching in the moonlight. The man was tall and muscular, and Lucy saw him bend low in the saddle to avoid an overhanging tree branch. When he straightened, Lucy could tell who it was, even from that distance.

"It's Father! Mother, come quickly, it's Father! He did come. I knew he would!"

In an instant, Nancy was standing next to her daughter, her hand on Lucy's shoulder. Even though Lucy could not take her eyes off her father for even a moment, she reached up and squeezed Nancy's hand, feeling her mother's relief washing over them both.

In the moonlight, Lucy could see how big and strong her father was. No man could ever take his place. His long shadow, cast by the full moonlight, stretched from the gate all the way to the door. For the rest of her life, Lucy would never forget that vision.

"Thank you, Emy," she whispered again softly. "Thank you for bringing Father safely back to us."

And then, in an instant that was laced with magic, her father suddenly was standing in the doorway, with cold air swirling into the vestibule from behind his back. The serious look on his face gave way in an instant to joy at the sight of his family.

Lucy ran to him with outstretched arms, crying, "Oh, Father! Father! You've come home!"

He smiled and pulled his daughter close, lifting her off the floor. He kissed her cheek and then swung her onto his right arm, embracing his wife with the other. Father and husband had come home at last.

"I'm so glad you came, Father."

"Tom," said Nancy, "you should have seen her, sitting by that window all day long, looking, and waiting."

Tears streamed freely down Nancy's cheeks. She buried her face deep in Tom's chest and breathed deeply, savoring his smell—a scent she loved more than almost anything else in the world.

"All of our prayers have been answered," she said softly. "You're home. Thank God, you're home again."

The three of them held each other tightly for a long time, as if they were afraid to let go—afraid they'd lose everything if they did. Then Tom unhooked his saber, removed his coat and cocked hat, and hung them on the wall pegs. Under his long coat, he wore an old, faded military waistcoat.

With a surprised look, Lucy asked, "Don't you have a uniform like the British?"

"No, Lucy. We wear what we have," he replied.

"Will we be victorious in this fight, Father?" she asked. "Against the Redcoats, I mean."

"Lucy!" her mother said in a scolding tone, "Let your father be. He just walked in the door."

"Thank you, love," Tom said. "It's good to see you both again. You can't imagine how much I've missed you."

"Come, Tom. Eat. You must be starved."

"That's true enough," he said as they sat down to a meal of corn biscuits and rabbit stew.

When everyone had finished eating, Nancy pushed away from the table and stood.

"I'll be right back," she said.

Leaving the room, she walked up the vestibule stairs to their bedroom.

Tom watched his wife disappear, and then turned to Lucy and said, "Well, young lady, how does it feel to be thirteen?"

"I'm not quite sure, Father," Lucy said with a slightly puzzled look. "I suppose I feel older, but, at the same time, I wish we could all be together again and have things just the way they used to be. Do you remember, Father?"

He sighed heavily and said, "Oh, yes, Lucy, I remember."

In a few moments, Nancy came back downstairs and walked toward the table, carrying a cloth-wrapped package. Tom smiled, slapped his knee, looked at his daughter, and said, "That's right! You're a young woman now, Lucy, and being the distinguished age of thirteen, we, that is, your mother and I, thought you might like to have this."

Nancy handed the package to her daughter.

"What is it?" asked Lucy.

"Well, darlin', why don't you open it and find out?" her father replied. "Your mother and I picked it out special when we were in Boston more than a year ago, before all the trouble began."

"And it's been awfully hard keeping it hidden from you all this time," her mother added. "But your father and I thought that becoming thirteen was a special year for a young woman, so you ought to have a special present for the occasion."

Lucy's eyes widened as she slowly laid the cloth back.

"Oh, it's a dress! A beautiful dress. It's lovely!"

"And we can embroider your name on it, if you'd

like," her mother said, her eyes sparkling almost as much as her daughter's.

"Oh, I love it! Thank you, Father. Thank you, Mother!"

Lucy hugged both her parents, closing her eyes, never wanting to let this moment go.

"How about singing a song for your father now, Lucy?"

"All right, Mother."

Lucy stood up and moved away from the table, saying, "In honor of your homecoming, Father, this song is for you."

Lucy danced gracefully around the room as she sang an old song that her father had taught her when she was a very young girl, barely old enough to talk—a song Tom had heard many times during his early years in Canada.

"Un jour triste et pensif,
Assis au bord des flots,
Au courant fugitif
Il adressa ces mots:
Si tu vois mon pays,
Mon pays malheureux,
Va, Dispatch: à mes amis
Que je me souviens d'eux....

While Tom watched his daughter, his thoughts drifted back to the day she was born and to the many happy days since. He especially remembered that breeches-clad little girl who used to race her horse down the road with such skill and enthusiasm. He again felt the pride of watching his daughter command that horse as if it were an extension of her own spirit—just as he believed that Lucy was an extension of his own spirit.

Deep down, he was truly proud of Lucy, as proud as if she had been the son that he and Nancy had lost at birth. Then he smiled, knowing his family's bond was solid.

Vers toi se portera"

Lucy finished her song and as her dance ended, she gracefully spread out her arms and lowered her head in a final bow, awaiting the recognition she knew would shortly be coming.

Her mother, with hands on her cheeks, looked at her husband with pride. Turning to Lucy, she joined Tom, who was clapping his hands in appreciation as their daughter came running across the room to be swept into their embrace.

The family spent the rest of the evening in conversation, reliving fond memories, talking of happier times. Not until nearly midnight did Tom and Nancy notice that Lucy had finally fallen asleep.

"She's so happy you're home, Tom," Nancy whispered.

"I know," he said, but there was heaviness in his voice that Nancy had never heard before. "It's going to be hard to have to say good-bye again."

He then looked from Lucy to Nancy and added, "To both of you."

"Oh, Tom. When must you leave?"

He hesitated, took a deep breath and said, "Tomorrow morning."

"Oh, Tom, no!"

"I know it's hard, love, but I was fortunate to get even this short time away from the fighting. It's no longer just hit-and-run skirmishes. We've assaulted the British and we have most of them surrounded at Boston. That's where I'm bound tomorrow. Can't you see? It will be a great victory for us if we can get them to surrender Boston."

Seeing the concern on his wife's face, Tom stopped speaking and looked into Nancy's tear-filled eyes for a long moment.

Finally, Nancy sighed deeply and said, "Of course, you'll do what you feel you must. I understand that, Tom." Then she added softly, "But will Lucy?"

They looked again at their daughter, curled in front of the fireplace, happily clutching her birthday gift in her arms.

Tom crossed the floor to where Lucy was sleeping. With a special look of love on his face—a love he reserved for Lucy alone said, "Let me tell her tomorrow, Nancy. Somehow, I'll try to make her understand."

"We'd best put her to bed."

Tom bent down and gently picked up his daughter.

"Good lord, Nancy," he said, seizing the opportunity to try to lighten the mood. "Am I getting old, or is this child getting heavy? What happened to the little girl I used to throw into the air? This used to be a much easier task!"

Nancy moved quickly up the narrow stairs to Lucy's small bedroom. The bed was high off the floor, providing added protection against the cold New England winters. Nancy placed large, down-filled pillows against the wall, and pulled back the heavy blankets.

Tom had built all of the furniture in the house, with the help of Peter Bigelow, one of their neighbors. Peter's carpentry skills were legendary, and almost every home in the area contained at least one of his pieces.

"There, the bed is all ready," Nancy said with a smile. "You know, I do believe that Peter Bigelow's son Jonathan has taken a fancy to our Lucy."

"Jonathan Bigelow?" Tom asked, placing Lucy's head on a pillow. "The joyner's son?"

"Yes," Nancy said, "and if Jonathan is anything like that father of his, we had better keep a close eye on our daughter."

"What in the world could you have heard about Peter Bigelow?"

"Well," Nancy said, smiling again. "You know I'm a good Christian woman, and not given to all the gossip that most women find easy enough to spread. But, on the other hand, I'm not opposed to listening to some of it now and then."

She knew that she had piqued Tom's curiosity, but also knew it wasn't his nature to question her about such matters.

As she turned to leave the room, Nancy looked back at her husband with a teasing lift of her eyebrows, and said, "So I'll say no more on the matter."

"Well," Tom said whispering as he covered Lucy with her blankets, "all I have to say about it is that, knowing you and your daughter, I believe it's really poor young Jonathan who had better watch his step!"

Once they'd returned downstairs, Tom and Nancy shared a long, loving embrace. Trying to give no thought to tomorrow, they were determined to make each precious moment last. Before retiring for the night, Tom secured the door, and Nancy banked the crackling red embers in the hearth, so the fire could be easily started again in the morning.

Outside the house, the yellow light that had been cast outside the house from the fire and the lamps now disappeared as the house darkened. For the moment at least, all was well.

☆ ☆ ☆

Morning came quickly, and just as the sun was rising over the tops of the trees, Tom and Lucy went out to walk together in the fields. Tom was pleased to see the new furrows that Lucy had cut into the ground, deep and straight.

The morning was quiet, and Tom could hear the sound of his own breathing, interrupted only by the joyous songs of birds and the light wind that brushed softly past his ears. He bent down and scooped up a handful of rich, black earth.

"We'll need to plant as much corn as we can this year, Lucy," he said.

"I know, Father. Mother and I will plow the south section soon," said Lucy, pointing to a stretch of land that had been cleared near a small pond.

"Have I told you how very proud of you I am?" Tom said, reaching for his daughter's hand.

Lucy's heart swelled with pride. No matter how often her father gave her praise, she could never get enough. For a moment, her head felt so light that she wondered if her feet were still touching the ground. She felt more wonderful than she had felt in a long, long time. She wanted nothing so much than to preserve this moment forever, to make time stand still, so she would always feel the way she felt at this very moment! Oh, how she wanted... Her father's voice interrupted her thoughts.

"But you must understand that a plague has descended upon our country, Lucy, and we must remove it," Tom said, kneeling in order to look squarely into his daughter's eyes.

Lucy could see the pain on her father's face. At that moment, she knew that she was leaving a part of her childhood behind. And although she knew what her father was about to say, she couldn't bring herself to accept it.

"Are you talking about the British, Father?" she asked.

Without a word, her father nodded his head slightly.

"But, Father. Aren't we British?" she asked, almost pleading.

"Well, Lucy. That's a hard question. It's true that our ancestors came from England, but you have to understand: The injustices levied over the last fifteen years have forced us into the position we're in. It's a terrible thing when loyalties are divided. Freedom doesn't come easily. We're Americans now, and we will be—forever more. And as Americans, we must fight for our freedom. Do you understand what I'm saying?"

Lucy didn't want to understand. She just wanted her father. She just wanted things to be as they always had been—even though she knew in her heart that her world would never be the same again.

"But there are so many of them, and the British have uniforms, and rifles, and so much gold. How can we possibly win this fight, Father?"

"I've never lied to you, Lucy," he said. "And it's true, the British do have many men, but most of their soldiers are new to this land. We Americans, on the other hand, know every tree and every blade of grass, and what's more, we love this land—and that is a great advantage. The British have many guns, too. But their Brown Bess muskets are heavy and seldom hit their mark. The Fowler rifle I gave you is better, and my flintlock is one of Mr. Black's finest. Everyone knows his skill as a gunsmith. One of his long rifles is worth ten of theirs. And since their soldiers fight for pay, the British must use a great deal of gold to pay for them. Americans fight for something much more precious. We fight for freedom and liberty, which is worth so much more than gold."

Lucy didn't know what to say. Her thoughts were all mixed up; her emotions were swirling like dark clouds before a storm.

"Oh, Father!" she finally said. She held him as if she would never let go, while tears streamed silently down her cheeks.

"This won't be easy for any of us," Tom said, fighting back his own tears. "Every American must sacrifice if we're to win our freedom—even you and your mother."

Lucy closed her eyes and held her father tightly. She struggled to control her voice. She didn't want to make what he had to tell her next any harder for him than it already was.

"How long, Father? How long before you have to leave?"

Lucy felt her father's body stiffen.

"A few hours, Lucy. I must leave before noon."

Father and daughter continued holding each other desperately, caught up in events far beyond themselves, events which neither chose to think about at that moment.

Less than two hours later, Tom Killgrew stood beside his horse as he kissed his family good-bye.

"Take care of yourself, Tom," Nancy said softly.

Lucy quickly added, "Yes, please, Father. Be careful."

Although both Nancy and Lucy clearly remembered Tom's last departure, this one was no easier to bear. Lucy moved closer to her father to hug him one last time. When he bent down to receive her embrace, he whispered, "I love you, Lucy."

"And I love you, Father" she said.

Tom kissed his daughter on the forehead and then mounted his horse. As she watched her father ride away,

Lucy again began to sing her father's favorite song:

> *Un jour triste et pensif,*
> *Assis au bord des flots*
> *Au...cour..ant.."*

When she could no longer see her father in the distance, Lucy finally allowed her words give way to the tears she had so bravely been holding back.

Chapter Three

Bound for Glory

ASTHEWEEKSPASSED, more neighbors and towns-people were called away to take part in the Great Fight for Freedom. Ethan Allen and his Green Mountain Boys had seized Fort Ticonderoga from the British in May of 1775, capturing its heavy cannons. Small pockets of Redcoats were everywhere as the British, in an effort to draw the American forces away from Boston, raided the surrounding towns and villages. A large portion of the population still remained loyal to the Empire, making it fairly easy for British raiders to learn the names of suspected traitors.

Regardless of the turmoil, it was a beautiful day, that first of June in 1775. The land was awash with the colors of late spring, and Lucy and her mother were in the yard at the back of the house, feeding the few animals they had left.

"Mother," Lucy said quietly, trying to sound casual, "did you know that Mr. Bigelow's son, Jonathan, left to join the American cause last week?"

"Oh, my. What is a boy so young going to do in the army?" asked her mother.

"But Mother, Jonathan is almost as good with a rifle as I am," Lucy replied, this time showing more feeling. She stopped the feed for a moment and turned to face her mother, her hands on her hips.

"And Jonathan is strong and brave and— "

"And such a handsome young man," Nancy interrupted with a teasing lilt in her voice. "Wouldn't you agree, my dear daughter?"

Lucy tried hard to keep a straight face and to remove all emotion from her voice, saying, "Yes, he is." But try as she might, she couldn't hold back a smile or the blush from her cheeks.

Nancy hugged her daughter, and they both burst into laughter. Lucy could never keep her feelings a secret for long, especially from her mother. Sometimes Lucy believed her mother could actually read her mind.

It was a wonderful moment, one that neither of them wanted to end. But it did. The world was about to clamp a bony hand onto each of their hearts, and until Tom returned, their lives would never know complete happiness.

A comfortable silence settled between mother and daughter. Nancy looked out toward the fields and saw the young corn stalks reaching tentatively toward the sky, their slender green leaves dancing in the breeze.

"Lucy," Nancy said, slowly and deliberately, still looking off into the distance, and then softly added,

"I'm going to have to depend on you to do most of the harvesting if this child I'm carrying is going to survive."

For a moment, time seemed to stand still. Lucy had heard her mother's words, but she found that she couldn't move, she couldn't think—even breathing seemed to be a struggle. It was as if her mother's words had suddenly jolted her out of the real world and into another place—a place where nothing existed. But after what seemed to be a long time, her mind finally returned to reality, and Lucy turned to look at her mother with wonder.

"A child?" she said softly. "You're going to have a child?"

Nancy nodded hesitantly, as if she were afraid of how Lucy might take the news, but in an instant the two were hugging and dancing together in the middle of the field.

"A baby! You're going to have a baby!" Lucy cried. "Oh, Mother, this is wonderful!"

"I think so, too," her mother said, laughing through tears of joy. "You're going to be a big sister!"

But even that magical moment quickly passed, and the hugging, dancing, and tears of joy were brought to an abrupt end, for just as the happy pair turned back toward the house, with Lucy holding her mother around the waist, they saw three mounted riders approaching from the far side of the tamaracks. As the men drew closer, Lucy could see that two of them wore bright red uniforms. The third rider was a local man, well known to the people of the area.

"Mother, it's Lucius Coffin—and he's brought soldiers with him!"

"Lucy, get into the house—now!" Nancy whispered urgently.

Lucy recognized the alarm in her mother's voice and obeyed without a word.

Lucius Coffin was a mean man, a loyalist, who believed that the Colonies should remain under English rule. He was born into a wealthy family that still lived in England, so his roots were strong. After refusing to go into the family business and informing the family of his intention to go to the colonies to seek his fortune, his father cut him out of his inheritance. It was a bitter young Lucius Coffin who set sail on the *Lady Jane* that cool spring morning. The British trusted Coffin and often used his services as an informer. Perhaps he believed that his work in the colonies during these rebellious times would gain him the forgiveness of his family in England. Everyone in the area knew Coffin was a dangerous man, not to be trusted, which made him even more resentful.

Coffin was a small man, and while making a hasty retreat during the French and Indian War, he had run into a tree branch, puncturing his right eye. The large black patch he wore after that incident seemed to suit his treacherous nature. He had the soul of a cobra and seemed to revel in using his power to bully the defenseless.

Coffin wore a short black beard and was dressed in a white cotton shirt, black breeches, and black leather riding boots. A musket was laced to the saddle of his coal-black horse.

He was a terrible marksman and to the Americans he had always been a joke—but now that it seemed as if war with the British was imminent, there was no longer anything humorous about him.

For some reason, Coffin also had developed a special dislike for Lucy—although some might have said it was understandable. Once, when Lucy was riding her horse, racing like the wind itself, she had unexpectedly come upon Coffin as she rounded a blind bend in the road. Coffin's horse had spooked, throwing the startled little man onto the muddy ground.

A few days later, Lucy learned that Coffin had been spreading the story that she had intentionally spooked his animal by slapping it on the rump as she road by, screaming like a banshee.

Of course, it was totally untrue, and the fact that few people seemed to believe Coffin's story only increased his resentment toward Lucy. But whether folks believed him or not, from that day forward, Coffin's lectures (to anyone who would listen) concerning the need for girls and women "to stay in their proper places" would always point to Lucy as a perfect example of a "wild and insolent girl."

Lucy watched the approaching riders through the same window she had watched her father come riding up just a little more than a month ago. From her vantage point, she could see them clearly. As the men pulled their mounts to a stop a few feet from her mother, Lucy's fists clenched. She turned her head, and her eyes fell upon her trusty Fowler, hanging over the hearth.

Outside, Nancy stood her ground as the three men looked down at her in silence for what seemed like a very long time. Nancy knew they were trying to intimidate her, but she refused to speak first.

She fixed her eyes on the younger of the two Lobster-backs, until the soldier finally looked away. *They're just boys*, Nancy said to herself. She started to smile, but then caught herself, *just boys, yes—but boys with muskets!*

"Good day, mum," the older of the two soldiers said.

"Good day to you, sir."

By the insignia on his tricorn hat, Nancy could see that the soldier was a sergeant of the 38th Light Dragoons. He surveyed the farm with a practiced eye, paying little attention to Nancy. As he did, Nancy, who was standing just inside the closed gate, slowly placed the steel latch in place, locking it tightly. The low wooden gate wouldn't be much of an obstacle to mounted riders, of course, but it would slow the men down a little if the need should arise.

Nancy studied the sergeant carefully. On first impression, he seemed every bit the British gentleman. He sat straight and tall, and his keen eyes had that look of old British nobility. His face was clean-shaven and narrow. The brass plate that protected his neck, which was known as a gorget, glistened importantly in the sun.

Finally, the sergeant looked toward the house and said, with careful military precision, "You live here alone, mum?"

A thousand thoughts flashed through Nancy's mind before she responded. Her uppermost thought was, had Coffin seen Lucy, or not? Nancy decided it would be best not to be caught in a lie.

"No. My daughter lives with me," she said, tipping her head slightly to avoid the bright glare of the sun.

"Aye, that's true enough," said Coffin. "And that girl is the devil's own, let me tell you. Where might she be?" he asked, inching his horse toward Nancy.

"Well..."

"Out on some back road, riding in her men's breeches, no doubt, stirrin' up trouble," Coffin interrupted with a sneer.

Without a military escort, Nancy knew that this cold-hearted little man would never have dared to say such things to her.

"She's out in one of the fields," Nancy responded. She didn't like discussing her daughter with the likes of these men.

Lucy couldn't hear the conversation outside, but she

could sense her mother's growing anxiety, and she quickly, but quietly, moved across the room, reached up, and removed her Fowler from its pegs. Then, without quite thinking about what she was doing or why, Lucy walked to the powder cabinet, primed the rifle, then returned to the window and sat down. She again turned her attention to the scene unfolding outside, holding the Fowler in her lap.

"You won't have any objections to our having a look around the place, would you, mum?" the sergeant asked.

But from the tone of menace in the man's voice, Nancy knew that it wasn't a question.

"Well, I..."

"Where's yer man?" Coffin interrupted, looking around anxiously. "And tell me, do the men still call 'im 'captain'?"

"I don't have to—" Nancy began, but the sergeant stood up in his stirrups and cut her off by quickly raising his right arm, as if silencing a small child.

"That'll be enough, mum!" he said loudly. Then he turned to the other two men and said, "Search the house, and arrest anyone you find there. Then set fire to the house—and the barn!"

Coffin gave a yell, and said, "Aye, sir. With pleasure!"

But as Coffin began to dismount, Nancy lunged forward, reached over the locked gate and smacked the sergeant's horse on the rump.

"No!" she screamed.

The horse reared, throwing the sergeant to the ground. For just an instant, the sergeant's eyes flashed toward Nancy with a combination of surprise and white-hot anger. Then, just as suddenly, he grabbed his twisted leg and muffled a scream of pain.

The young corporal, a look of panic in his eyes, drew his pistol and pointed it at Nancy.

"You're under arrest, mum. I would advise you to hold your ground."

Lucius Coffin dismounted and knelt by the downed sergeant. After a quick examination, he looked up and shook his head.

"His leg's busted up bad. He'll be needin' some tendin'."

The corporal's attention shifted momentarily from Nancy to his sergeant. As the corporal looked away, Nancy turned and began to run toward the house.

"Lucy!" she screamed, "Get out!"

"Lucy?" Coffin said, quickly standing and turning back toward the house. "Aha! I have a score to settle with *that* one!"

He rushed toward the gate, but the small metal latch did exactly what Nancy had hoped it would do—although it only slowed Coffin for a moment. After a brief struggle with the latch, Coffin had the gate open and was racing after Nancy.

Seeing Nancy running toward the house, the confused and angry corporal raised his pistol, took aim, and pulled the trigger.

Through the window, Lucy heard a thunderous crack as a puff of white smoke billowed from the corporal's weapon and saw her mother fall to the ground.

"No!" Lucy screamed.

Her vision clouded for an instant. She saw Coffin kneel down next to her mother's lifeless body. Then, as if a life-long film had been lifted from her eyes, Lucy's vision suddenly cleared, and as it did, her mind suddenly became deathly calm.

Outside, the corporal had heard Lucy's scream, had dismounted, and was now quickly making his way toward the house. Just as his hand reached out to touch the gate, Lucy raised the Fowler to her shoulder and her trained eye sighted the corporal along the long, steel blue barrel.

The corporal was directly in her sights.

It was the same corporal who had just shot her mother.

It was the same corporal who was at this very moment rushing through the gate and running toward the house.

Lucy's mind was filled with pain and fury, and without thinking about the consequences, she took careful aim, just the way her father had taught her, and pulled the trigger.

It seemed as if the sound of the explosion from the Fowler came from miles away. The deafening sound of Lucy's pounding heart seemed to drown out even the sound of the exploding powder.

Nothing seemed real. For just an instant, before the billowing cloud of white smoke blinded her vision, it seemed as if Lucy could see the musket ball exploding in slow motion from the mouth of the rifle. She could see the ball shatter the window and saw each tiny shard of glass as it tumbled slowly outward. It was a surreal moment.

But in a heartbeat, reality came crashing back in.

The young soldier fell, clutching his chest, and then lay still.

For several seconds, the world was silent and no one moved. Coffin watched the corporal fall, and then backed slowly away from Nancy's body, moving toward his horse. He bumped into the gate, his gaze never leaving the shattered window, where Lucy was now standing, still holding the Fowler against her shoulder. Even Coffin knew Lucy's skill with a musket far surpassed his own, but still he weighed his options.

Lucy moved quickly to the door and stepped outside, slowly and deliberately. As she stepped out into the sunlight, Lucy's eyes met Coffin's—and she could see the fear on the small man's face.

Then Lucy aimed the empty rifle squarely at Coffin's chest.

"I think you'd better leave, gentlemen," she said, walking slowly toward them, showing no emotion in her voice.

Even though her heart was racing, she held her Fowler straight and sure, aimed directly at the traitor's heart.

Coffin licked his lips quickly, and his eye darted from Lucy's face to the rifle that was still strapped to his own horse. Then, suddenly, he seemed to relax, and a smile played across his leathery features.

"Don't play games with me, little girl. I'll wager your rifle's empty. No one could reload that fast."

Lucy kept her eyes glued on Coffin's face. Of course, the turncoat was right. She had to think fast.

Suddenly, she had an idea, and a sly smile crossed her face.

"The question is, sir," she said slowly and deliberately, "are you willin' to wager that this is the same rifle?"

Then, with careful precision, Lucy pulled the hammer back. It made a loud click, and Lucy held her breath, waiting to see if the turncoat would back down.

Coffin's gaze danced like a frightened sparrow back and forth between Lucy and the two soldiers lying on the ground. With a supreme effort of will, Lucy stepped past her mother's still form and approached Coffin. As she did, she raised the barrel of her rifle and aimed at a spot right between his eyes. She kept the musket positioned so Coffin could not see the empty powder pan.

A look of terror filled Coffin's face, and he backed as far as he could, until he bumped into his horse. Then he held his hands out in front of him, pleading, "No. Please, don't kill me!"

"Lucy! Don't do it!" a voice called from behind Lucy's back.

It was her mother. Her voice was weak, but still commanding. Lucy turned her head quickly, catching just a glimpse of her mother, who had raised herself to her feet once more, and was now standing, slightly crouched, holding her bloodied left arm.

Moving slowly to her daughter's side, Nancy said in a determined voice, "I don't think there'll be any more trouble here. Will there, gentlemen?"

Lucy's head spun back to face Coffin. Her eyes narrowed, and she held out one hand, palm up. The other arm still steadied her rifle, which was braced solidly against her shoulder.

"I'll take your rifle, if you please, Mr. Coffin."

With his eyes constantly fixed on Lucy, Coffin unstrapped his weapon from the saddle. Even from where she stood, Lucy could tell that his weapon was primed and ready. Coffin slowly and carefully removed the rifle from the saddle and handed it to her.

As soon as he had handed his weapon to her, Lucy threw down her Fowler, cocked back the hammer of Coffin's musket, and pointed it at him.

"So it *was* empty," he said, shaking his head and staring down at Lucy's empty Fowler. "It was empty all along. Well, I promise you one thing, little girl—I won't make that mistake again!"

Lucy pointed the rifle toward the two downed soldiers and then back at Mr. Coffin.

"Well, Mr. Coffin, just mind you don't make the same

mistake as those two."

Lucy held Coffin's rifle on him with one arm and removed the soldiers' pistols from their saddle holsters and tossed them behind her. She then removed their rifles. As she glanced at the rifles, she remembered her father's words about how much better her Fowler was than the weapons the British were using.

Coffin was becoming more and more nervous as each moment dragged by. His tongue flicked over his lips, and he said, "You know, little girl, you and your family are in for a whole peck of trouble."

Ignoring his words, Lucy asked, "What are we going to do with them, Mother?"

Nancy, still cradling her bloodstained arm, said, "Don't you worry about the kind of trouble we're in, Lucius Coffin. At the moment, I would suggest that you worry about your own skin, once the British find out that a thirteen-year-old girl took the three of you down. Now you get these two trespassing Lobsterbacks back on their horses and then get off our land!"

Coffin quickly moved to his right and helped the sergeant to his horse. Then, as Lucy continued to hold the rifle on him, Coffin pulled the younger soldier to his feet and dragged him toward his mount.

As Coffin struggled to get the wounded corporal onto his horse, Nancy said, "Let this be a warning to you, Lucius Coffin. The next time you set foot on this property, we won't think twice about placing a musket ball through your skull!"

Lucy had never heard her mother talk like that before. She stole a quick glance at her mother's face and saw that she meant every word she was saying. Lucy had always heard that people were never really sure what they were capable of doing until they were put to the test—and it appeared that her mother was made of sterner stuff than anyone could have imagined. That realization made Lucy stand even taller. From now on, no one was going to push around the Killgrew women!

Without a word, Coffin prepared to mount his horse, but just as he began to lift himself into the stirrup, Nancy spoke again.

"Leave your horse, Mr. Coffin. I think we'll be needing him."

The turncoat looked at Nancy with surprise and hatred on his face. But then he saw that Lucy had raised the rifle to her shoulder once more and was aiming the weapon straight at his heart. Reluctantly, he stepped back down and dropped the reins of his horse. Then he took hold of the reins of the other two horses and began to walk away, the two soldiers sagging in the saddles above him.

Lucy and her mother stood and watched them go. When the men had reached a coward's distance down the road, Coffin turned and yelled, "Rest assured, Killgrews, we'll meet again. And when we do, the results will be far different. That, I promise!"

Lucy moved closer to her mother, still holding Coffin's rifle against her shoulder. Only when the turncoat and the two wounded soldiers were finally out of sight did Lucy drop the weapon on the grass and spin to face her mother.

"Oh, Mother, your arm! Are you hurt very bad?"

"No, I'll be all right, Lucy," Nancy said, holding her wounded arm tenderly. "The ball passed clean through the flesh of my arm. I've seen much worse wounds than this."

Although she tried to smile, to prove to her frightened daughter that she was all right, her smile ended in a grimace of pain.

"But we can't stay here any longer, Lucy," Nancy said, turning toward the house. "That's for certain. This arm will require tending, and then we'll decide what to do."

"Right," said Lucy, helping her mother toward the house. "First, we'll take care of your arm. But what will we do then?"

Nancy said, "Then, we'll ask the Bigelows for help."

The moment she heard her mother say those words, Lucy suddenly felt totally at ease. "Yes, Mother," she said, "Jenny Bigelow will know what to do."

☆ ☆ ☆

Jenny Bigelow was a petite woman who seemed to have very little fear of anything. Her fire-red hair highlighted her fair complexion, and when she became angry, she was a formidable opponent. Surprisingly, her hospitality was just as legendary as her fearlessness. Nancy and Lucy rode to the Bigelow home that afternoon, and when Jenny heard of their plight, she freely offered to let them stay as long as they liked.

Under Jenny's care, Nancy grew stronger with each passing day. But even as her mother's strength returned, Lucy grew more and more restless, like an unbroken filly, shut away from the freedom of the wild.

Finally, after four uneventful days, Lucy could stand it no longer. She had to see what had become of their house and land. Knowing that her mother would never consent to letting her return by herself, Lucy left a note on the kitchen table, slipped silently out the front door, and mounted her horse.

She knew it might be dangerous to take the main roads, so Lucy rode toward home in the relative safety of the woods. Her common sense told her that the British probably had more to worry about at the moment than two women on a small farm in the wilderness, but Lucy was not about to take any unnecessary chances. After all, she had shot a British officer, and her mother had severely wounded another, which would surely have made them both traitors in the minds of the Redcoats.

After half an hour of riding through the woods, Lucy came upon the rise over-looking the farm. What she saw made her gasp. The house and the barn that had once stood in the clearing were gone. The smell of smoldering timbers lingered in the air. There were no animals to be seen. Everything had been destroyed. The British had certainly taken a full measure of revenge.

In the midst of her shock, Lucy quietly urged her horse forward, and with each passing step, she tried to steel herself against the pain of this injustice. It seemed so unfair, but the events of this turbulent time were forcing her to grow up faster than nature would have intended.

When she reached the gate that had once led to their house, she saw a poster nailed deep into the wood. It read:

"Be It Known: Tom, Nancy, and Lucy Killgrew are Enemies of the King. A Reward of 10 Gold Crowns Each for their Capture and Return."

She now had a price on her head! How could this be? She was only a child. The thought filled Lucy with horror.

But in a few moments, Lucy's fright began to turn into anger. Looking at the smoldering ashes of her home, her mind began to fill with hatred toward a government that could do something like this to innocent settlers.

Damn the British, she thought. If she had ever had any doubts as to where her loyalty was supposed to be, those doubts were now gone—burned away forever by the flames of this injustice.

All that remained of her old life was an oak chest that

had always sat near the hearth. To her surprise, it was slightly charred but still in good condition. Lucy carefully picked her way through the ashes, bent down, and lifted the lid of the chest. Inside were some of the family's linen and, to her delight, her new dress—the one her father and mother had given her for her last birthday.

She pulled the dress to her breast and smiled, thinking about how long ago that birthday seemed to have been, even though it was only a little more than a month ago. It hardly seemed possible.

Working quickly, Lucy made a makeshift stretcher by lashing together two sapling branches, and then secured the chest between them. She tied the end of the branches to her saddle, and then urged her horse back toward the Bigelow farm.

Because she had to travel in shallow streams and over rocky ground to avoid being tracked, it was well past sundown by the time Lucy finally managed to drag the chest into the Bigelow's front yard.

Seeing Lucy approaching in the moonlight, Nancy opened the front door of the house and stepped outside. Lucy leaped from her horse and ran to her mother's arms.

"Oh, Mother! Everything is gone! They've burned our farm to the ground! There's nothing left."

Nancy and Lucy spent most of that night crying in each other's arms. It was the saddest time Lucy had ever known.

✿ ✿ ✿

The next morning, Lucy was the first to arise. When Nancy entered the kitchen, she found her daughter sitting quietly at the table.

For a moment, neither woman said a word. Lucy had made tea, and Nancy silently walked to the stove, poured a cup, then sat at the table and looked deeply into her daughter's eyes—those eyes that were so much like her father's—and knew exactly what Lucy was about to say. She knew it as clearly as if the words had already been spoken. Even though the day had just begun, she felt more tired than she had ever felt before.

"Mother," Lucy said softly and slowly, looking down at the table, "I have something I must tell you."

Nancy reached across the table, placed a finger to Lucy's lips and said, "No. Not just yet. Please, Lucy, not just yet."

Lucy slowly lifted her head and, seeing her mother's tear-stained face, said softly, "You've always been able to read my mind, Mother."

"Yours and your father's," she said, smiling through her tears. "But knowing what the words are going to be doesn't make them any easier to hear."

As Lucy looked at her mother, her eyes filled with every ounce of love she had. She knew her words were going to cut like a knife into her mother's heart, but she also knew they were words she *had* to say.

"I'll be leaving tomorrow, Mother. I've got to find Father. Please try to understand."

"I know," said Nancy, tears streaming down her face. " But you must understand that I simply can't give you my blessing, Lucy. You're my little girl. Do you understand that? My only child. It's just too dangerous!"

But even as she said the words, Nancy knew they had no real meaning. She had known Lucy all her life, and she knew that nothing could ever change Lucy's mind once it was made up. She was as stubborn as her father—and Nancy loved them both for it!

"The British already have a price on my head, Mother. I can help you—and everyone else—more by finding Father than I can by staying here. Mrs. Bigelow can tend to your wounds until you recover."

"No! Your place is here, with me, " Nancy said, realizing the futility of her words, even as she said them.

Lucy stood up and quickly walked around the table, where she held her sobbing mother tightly in her arms.

"I can't explain it, Mother," Lucy said softly, kissing the top of her mother's head, "but I know now that I have a special place in this struggle, and I know that somehow I can make a difference. And besides," she added, trying to lighten the mood, "Father doesn't know about the baby. Someone's got to tell him!"

Nancy held tightly to her daughter and let her tears flow freely.

Nancy spent the rest of that day fighting back bouts of tears. She knew there was no way to stop Lucy from going, yet she couldn't bring herself to give her blessing.

That night, after she was sure that everyone was asleep, Lucy crept silently out of the house, carrying only a little food, some shot, her powder horn, and her rifle. Entering the barn, she quietly saddled her horse. She led the animal carefully out of the barn, and then stopped in front of the dark house. Looking up toward her mother's window, she said a silent good-bye to Nancy and the unborn baby.

Mounting her horse, she whispered, "I love you both." Then she turned toward the woods and silently rode away in the moonlight.

Lucy could not have known that her mother was awake that night, listening to her daughter moving softly through the house, gathering her few possessions, and then walking out to the barn. She couldn't have known that Nancy, her trembling hands parting the curtains ever so slightly, had watched her only child ride away, not knowing if she would ever see her daughter again.

As Nancy sat at the window, she heard someone speaking softly. It was Jenny, who was standing in the doorway of the bedroom.

"You should be very proud of that girl, Nancy!"

"Yes," Nancy whispered, looking up at Emy Moon through the lace curtains. "It seems that the two most important people in my life are now bound for glory. May God protect them both."

Jenny walked to Nancy's side, and put her arm on her friend's shoulder. Nancy reached up and took Jenny's hand and allowed her tears to flow one last time.

In the same moment, she promised herself that she would not cry again until her family was reunited—and when that reunion finally took place, the only tears she would cry would be tears of joy.

Chapter Four

Soldier-Daughter

TWO DAYS LATER, LUCY finally left the protection of the white pines that grew along the roads and felt safe enough to move out into open road. The sun was shining brightly, and she was just admiring the huge patches of white violets that lined the road when she began to sense that she was not alone. She looked up and saw three riders approaching in the distance.

They had seen her—she knew that—and there was nothing she could do but stand her ground. Lucy knew that she was close to Boston and nearing the town of Cambridge, so she could only hope that the riders were Americans.

Even as that thought crossed her mind, Lucy instinctively reached down and untethered the rifle from her saddle.

As the three men drew closer, Lucy held her horse steady by the side of the road, until they finally drew their horses to a stop directly in front of her. Lucy judged each rider to be around seventeen years old, each sitting tall in the saddle and looking very self-assured.

One of the buckskin-clad young men called out, "Where are you headed, girl?"

"That depends," said Lucy, looking directly into the young man's eyes. "Who might you be?"

"Forgive our lack of manners," the young man said sarcastically. "My name is William Ashley."

Then, pointing to the taller of his two companions, he said, "This here lanky fellow is David Weaver, and the one next to him—the one with a piece of his ear shot off—"

There was a brief pause while Ashley and Weaver snickered, and the third fellow touched his bandaged ear. Then Ashley continued, "His name is Ben White. The three of us are free Americans and Sons of Liberty, proudly servin' with Israel Putnam's Connecticut Volunteers—the best damned fightin' men in all the Colonies!"

Lucy waited while the young men gave themselves a loud cheer, whooping and thrusting their fists in the air in a show of youthful enthusiasm.

Then she asked, "If you please, sir, do you happen to know a Captain by the name of Tom Killgrew, who is serving with Mr. Knox's Massachusetts troops?"

The three young men quickly exchanged confused glances. Then Ashley said, "What's your name, girl? And what are you doin' wearin' buckskin breeches?"

"I'm the Captain's daughter, Lucy Killgrew." She paused a moment, and then added angrily, "And I would appreciate it very much if you would stop calling me 'girl'!

I'm thirteen years old, and I'll be called a woman, thank you."

As quickly as Lucy's anger had flared, it subsided. She took a deep breath, composing herself, and then looked at the three young men and asked politely, "Now, gentlemen, if you please, about my father. Do you know him?"

The young men again exchanged nervous glances, but for a moment, no one said anything. There was an uncomfortable silence, and they were clearly uneasy about what they should do next. They exchanged slight nods, raised eyebrows, and questioning looks; however, for what seemed to be a long time, no one spoke.

Then William Ashley broke the silence.

"You'd better follow us," he said, turning his horse back toward Cambridge.

The others fell in behind Ashley, and a few moments later, Lucy was riding alongside him, watching as William removed his worn and dusty cloth hat.

"I'm sorry 'bout our manners back there, little gir... miss. I suppose it's safe to tell you that your father is camped close by, and it will be our pleasure to take you to him."

Lucy's heart soared. Her father was alright! She had found him and would be seeing him soon. The thought filled her with joy, but for reasons that she didn't quite understand, she tried not to show it in front of these three handsome young Patriots. Instead, she just looked over at the young man riding beside her, nodded and smiled, but said nothing.

The four rode together for several miles along the road, saying little, passing neatly plowed fields, until they came to a densely wooded section of land. There, they left the road and entered the forest through a small clearing. Less than a hundred yards off the road the soft sounds of their horses' hooves gave way to the sounds of activity in a rebel camp.

As they rode slowly through the camp, Lucy saw men dressed in every manner of clothing...from home spun to field clothes, from grimy old uniforms to shiny new ones. The men were also of every description—young, old, rich, and poor. Lucy knew that this camp, and many others like it throughout the Colonies, was a melting pot, from which the hardened steel of a new nation would one day be forged.

After allowing Lucy time to absorb the amazing scene, William Ashley said, "It's really somethin', ain't it? There's men here who fought in the French and Indian War; there's craftsmen, clerks, farmers, and city folk. Mr. Knox's men are here, too, and Ione of Old Putt's," he said proudly, referring to Israel Putnam.

"John Stark and his men are here from New Hampshire, Mr. Green from Rhode Island, and Joe Warren is here with his volunteers. All in all, there's over sixteen thousand men spread throughout the area."

Men and boys, along with a surprising number of women and girls, were moving about, loading and unloading supplies from the carts and wagons. Lucy could hear the continuous hammering that rang out from several blacksmiths' forges, but her attention was drawn to one in particular. He was elderly and white-haired, but he was clearly very strong, and his muscular arm easily swung the huge hammer he was using to beat flat steel around a rifling die, forming a barrel that would soon become a deadly weapon in the hands of a Patriot marksman.

Off to her left, Lucy could see a tent that apparently served as an infirmary. In front of the tent sat a number of wounded men, their wounds being tended by several women as they waited for their turn to be seen by a doctor.

It was an amazing sight, but one that filled Lucy with a sense of pride she'd never known before. She rode carefully, silently through the camp, her eyes darting back and forth, searching for the familiar face of her father.

Tom Killgrew was about to enter the officers' tent when he saw his daughter. For a moment he couldn't believe his eyes, and his mouth opened in disbelief.

"Lucy?" he said softly. And then, a bit louder, he called out, "Lucy?"

Lucy turned her head toward the voice. Then her father's face lit up with a smile, and he called out loudly, "Lucy! It is you!"

"Father!" Lucy said, turning her horse toward Tom as he ran across the compound to meet his daughter.

When Tom had reached her side, Lucy leapt from the saddle and was quickly swept up in her father's arms.

"Lucy, my love! What are you doing here?"

There were tears in Tom's eyes as he hugged his precious daughter tightly against his chest.

After a long moment, Lucy pulled herself from her father's embrace, looked up at the three young men who had escorted her to the camp and said, "Thank you, gentlemen. Your kindness was greatly appreciated."

The young men smiled, and as they turned their horses to leave, William Ashley looked back at Lucy and said, "Perhaps we'll talk to you again, ma'am?"

"That would be nice, Mr. Ashley," said Lucy.

William tipped his hat graciously, and then the three young men turned and rode off once more to resume their patrol.

Tom was confused. Who was this young man to whom his daughter had obviously taken a fancy? In spite of himself, he found himself feeling slightly alarmed. After all, until that moment, he'd never thought of his daughter as anything but his little girl. Yet, looking at her now, standing in the middle of this soldier camp, she looked so much older than he remembered her. She was a young woman! All that would take some getting used to. But all that could have to wait until later Right now, there were other, more pressing, issues with which to deal.

"Lucy, you took a terrible chance coming here like this. What could have possessed you, girl? What if you'd been stopped by a British patrol?"

"I had to come Father," Lucy said slowly, hesitantly. "I have some news. And not very pleasant news, I'm afraid."

She found herself studying the toes of her riding boots intently as she spoke. For some reason, she couldn't bear to look her father in the eyes.

"Our farm...there's...there's nothing left, Father. The British came, and they set fire to it all. Everything...our home, our barn...everything's gone. Oh, Father."

With that, Lucy broke into sobs, hugged her father's neck and threw herself into his arms once more.

There was no need to say anything more. Tom had seen it happen to a hundred other Colonial families over the past few months. But there were still questions left unanswered.

Tom took hold of Lucy's shoulders and pushed her back. Then he looked at his daughter with questioning eyes and said, "Your mother? Is she all right?"

"Yes, Father. Mother's fine. She's staying with Jenny Bigelow until she..."

Lucy stopped abruptly, not wanting to upset her father even more.

But her father sensed her hesitation and pressed for more information.

"Until she what? Has something happened to your mother?"

Lucy struggled with how much to tell her father all at once. For a few moments, Lucy debated, and she decided it would be best to give her father the good news first.

Looking into Tom's blue eyes, she said, "Mother is with child!"

"Oh, Lucy, that's wonderful news!" Tom said, again sweeping his daughter into his strong arms.

They stood holding each other for a long time. Lucy wanted to let her father be able to savor the news, and Tom took great pleasure in knowing that, for these few precious moments at least, there was something in the world that wasn't beyond his control. For this brief moment, he could savor the joy of holding his daughter in his arms and think of the future.

Standing there with her father, Lucy decided not to tell him about Mother's wound. He certainly had more than enough worries on his mind already, and the news might cloud his judgment, just at the time when his country needed him most. After all, Mother was going to be all right, and there would surely be a better time to tell him. So for the moment, she decided to let her father find some joy in the midst of a world that seemed to be spinning out of control.

✩ ✩ ✩

A week went quickly by. It was the beginning of the third week of June. Storm clouds hung on the horizon, but the weather was mild and warm.

Lucy had spent that week in camp, familiarizing herself with all aspects of Rebel life. She had also had a chance to spend a fair amount of time with young Will Ashley. He wasn't as refined or as smart as her father, she had decided; but he did have a certain quality about him that

Lucy found attractive—and slightly dangerous.

But that morning, there was little time for flirting. The men were preparing to move out into the hills behind Charlestown Though she knew little about the battle plan, Lucy had heard rumors that the battle her father and the others were preparing for would be a major one. She had also heard that the success or failure of the entire fight for freedom might hinge on what happened during the next few days.

As Lucy sat at the base of a tree, engrossed in writing her thoughts into her journal that morning, her father walked up and quietly knelt in front of her.

When his daughter looked up, Tom said softly, "Lucy, there is something I must ask you to do. It's very important, and I need you to promise me that you'll do it."

Lucy closed her diary and focused her entire attention on her father's face. She could see a look of worry on his face, although he was trying hard not to show it.

Tom picked up a twig and began to draw a rough map on the ground. Then, he pointed to a spot on the map.

"This is Boston town and this is Charlestown, between these two rivers," he said. "We've already taken several key positions around Boston. Tomorrow we're going to take these two hills."

He pointed to another spot on the map.

"These are called Bunker Hill and Breed's Hill, and they overlook Boston. If we can secure these two hills, we can install the cannons we raided from Ticonderoga. Then, we can point those cannons down at Boston's harbor, and once we do that, the British will have no choice but to surrender the city."

Tom had been looking at the map as he spoke. But now, he stopped looking at the ground and looked directly into his daughter's brown eyes.

"Taking those two positions is going to mean a major battle, Lucy, and I'm going to need every man I have. But that is only one of the reasons I am giving you this task. The other, well, these are times when a trust must be earned. Mr. Black will not trust anyone else I can send. You, dear Lucy are well known to him," he said smiling. "Maybe not face to face, but I have told him all about you so many times that he will know you when he sees you."

Lucy had no idea what her father was about to say, but no matter what he asked her to do, she would gladly do it. She felt as if she were about to explode with pride that he would even trust her to help the American cause.

"You know I'll help in any way I can, Father," she said softly. "What would you like me to do?"

Tom hesitated and took a deep breath before he began speaking again. What he was about to say was more important than anything he'd ever asked of his daughter, and he was well aware of the possible danger. He continued slowly and deliberately.

"We expect the battle to last several days. That means we're going to need additional supplies—especially weapons and powder. So I'm going to ask you and Private Weaver to take a supply wagon to this point right here."

Again, Tom's attention turned to the map, where he pointed to a spot not far from where the battle would take place.

"This is Black's farm. Henry Black makes some of the finest flintlocks in the world. It was Henry who made the rifle I carry myself. He works his forge with his friend Joshua. They are true Patriots, and he has seventy-five new flintlocks completed and ready for delivery to our troops. I want you and Private Weaver to go to Black's farm and pick up the weapons and deliver them here."

Tom again pointed to the map, this time to a spot just

south of Cambridge.

For a moment, there was silence between father and daughter. Then Tom dropped his stick and took his daughter by the shoulders.

He looked directly into her eyes and said, "Lucy, this is a very dangerous assignment. If the British find you carrying those weapons, you will certainly be arrested—or worse."

For a moment, Tom looked away. But then his eyes returned to his daughter's face, and he said softly, "If you don't think you can do this, just say the word. I promise I'll understand, and I'll make other arrangements."

Lucy's emotions were swirling. She felt pride, doubt, and fear—but mainly pride.

She was her father's child, and she had never backed away from a challenge in her life, so she wasn't about to start backing down now, when her father—and her country—needed her most.

She looked deeply into her father's eyes and said, "When do we leave?"

Tom swept his daughter into his loving arms.

"I'm so proud of you, Lucy," he whispered into her ear. "So very proud."

Then he broke off the hug and said, "Stand up, girl."

Lucy rose to her feet, and then stood, straight and proud, before her father.

"Lucy Killgrew," her father said, with an air of solemn importance in his voice, "from this moment forward, you are a Private in the Colonial Army."

With that, Tom Killgrew saluted his daughter.

Lucy knew this was the most important moment of her life.

With every ounce of pride she possessed, she returned

her father's salute.

"I won't let you down, sir. I promise."

As he spoke, Lucy could hear the emotion her father was desperately trying to keep out of his voice. "Mr. Knox will give you your written orders and a coded message, which you will present to Mr. Black. He will also give you a bag containing four hundred newly minted Willow Tree Six Pence coins. Although Mr. Black and Joshua give their time and talents freely, as do most of us who fight for the Cause, Adam Black must still pay for his materials, and he requests Colonial silver."

Tom looked down at his daughter's trusting expression. Then he knelt and looked straight into her eyes, saying, "You know, you don't have to do this, Lucy."

Lucy gave her father a quick hug.

"I want to, Father. Thank you for giving me the chance to help the Cause."

With that, Lucy turned and began walking back toward her tent. Tom stood and watched his daughter walk away, shaking his head slightly in amazement. It all seemed so improbable. It seemed like just yesterday he was bouncing that little girl on his knee, and tomorrow, the fate of a new nation was going to rest partly on the young shoulders of his sweet young soldier-daughter.

Chapter Five

Stephanie

T HE CAPTAIN'S VOICE CRACKLED over the loudspeaker, announcing that they were now flying over the Grand Canyon, which passengers could see if they looked out the windows on the left side of the plane. About a quarter of the people on Stephanie's side of the plane leaned over in their seats and craned their necks to catch a glimpse of the massive canyon through the tiny windows on the opposite side.

But Stephanie's parents remained just as they were, their heads back, their eyes closed. Stephanie knew they weren't asleep, but they made no movement at all, except for the slow rhythm of their shallow, even breathing. Stephanie hadn't bothered to look at the canyon, either. She was engrossed in the latest Stephen King novel.

Randy, however, had stepped on the old lady's foot next to him in his zeal to stand and look out the windows on the other side of the aisle. For at least the fifth time in the last hour, Stephanie heard the old lady sitting next to Randy swear at him under her breath, and she found herself feeling sorry for that poor woman. After all, she knew that her brother could definitely be a pain—in more ways than one.

The book Stephanie was reading was about a girl who had become possessed by the spirit of an ancient Indian prince. Slowly but surely, the long-dead spirit was taking control of that young girl's mind and body.

Suddenly, in the middle of a sentence, Stephanie felt an ice-cold shiver pass through her body. There was just something so strangely familiar about the story. It was as if...well, as if the girl in the story could have been *her*. It was as if—

"Did you feel that?"

It was Randy's voice, coming from just behind her head, shattering her thoughts.

Stephanie jumped; she hadn't heard her brother leaning over her seat, nor had she heard the old lady next to him swear again under her breath, as she always did whenever Randy made one of his sudden and dramatic moves.

There was a tone of excitement in Randy's voice. "Did you feel that air pocket when we went over the Grand Canyon? Wow! That was really something, wasn't it?"

Stephanie sighed and closed her book, using her index finger to keep her place. Then she looked up, just in time to see Randy making a goofy face at the top of her head. When he realized that she'd seen him, he immediately put on his "innocent" look.

"No, I didn't feel a thing," Stephanie said dryly. "And isn't it past your bed time, little boy?"

Randy ignored her remark and continued, "You know what I was thinking awhile ago, Steff? I bet if a guy could get everybody to stand on one side of the plane, I bet you could get the plane to tip upside down. What do you think?"

"Hmmm," Stephanie said, shaking her head slightly. Her little brother could be so weird sometimes.

"Well, what do you think?" Randy persisted. "It could happen, don't you think?"

"I'm thinking we'll probably never know," Stephanie said distantly, turning her attention out the window.

"Aw, Steff, you're sure a lot of fun," Randy mumbled and sat back down.

Stephanie could hear her brother settle back in his seat, but she also could feel his frustration and disappointment that no one seemed to want to join in his silly games.

It's time he started to grow up a little, Stephanie thought. *I hope he'll spend the entire five weeks in Mayfair pestering cousin Benjamin and not me. I hope there's something— anything—there that can keep him busy all summer!*

At that precise moment, as if he were reading her thoughts, Randy gave the back of Stephanie's seat a hard, angry kick.

Stephanie knew better than to acknowledge his reaction. That would only make things worse. She knew that, even though her brother was little, he was like a shark—if he smelled even a drop of blood, he'd move in for the kill.

So Stephanie pressed her forehead against the scratched and slightly yellowed Plexiglas window and let her gaze wander out into the vastness of the sky. For the last hour, there had been a solid white cloud cover just above the plane, like an intricately textured white ceiling.

Suddenly, a hole opened in the clouds, and the brightness of the unfiltered sunlight struck Stephanie directly in the eyes. In the brief instant before Stephanie closed her eyes tightly, she noticed the pale full moon, racing alongside the plane in the bright daytime sky.

With her eyes closed, a familiar reddish blackness closed in around her. But in the midst of the blackness behind her eyelids, an image began to form.

It was the figure of a girl, about her own age, dressed in strange clothes, the kind she had seen in history books—the kind that people had worn back in Colonial times.

The girl was sitting with her back against a large old tree, and she appeared to be writing in a small book that lay across her lap. Above the tree was the same pale full moon.

Suddenly, for no apparent reason, the word "Emy" came drifting into Stephanie's thoughts.

Emy?

Stephanie opened her eyes and looked out at the moon, which was hanging so round and large in the sky alongside her. What could it all mean? Her vision of that Colonial girl had lasted less than a second, and it hadn't really been a vision at all, really—it was more of an impression.

The novel she was reading had probably brought it about. Yes, that had to be it, she told herself.

Nevertheless, Stephanie felt another cold shudder wash over her, and then found her eyes being irresistibly drawn back to the full moon outside her window.

"Emy," she whispered as the moon continued to keep pace with the plane.

She frowned, and thought, *Emy? Where could that name have come from? It wasn't in my book.*

Finally, she tore her attention away from the moon and opened her book again. But as she started to read, she couldn't shake the strange uneasiness that lurked in the back of her mind—and the question that kept racing through her mind.

Who the heck is Emy?

Chapter Six

Black's Farm

LUCY MET PRIVATE WEAVER the next morning before first light, and while Lucy was saddling her horse and Weaver was hitching a second horse to a small wagon, Captain Killgrew came walking toward them.

Lucy could tell by her father's slightly hesitant stride that he feared for her safety and wished he hadn't been forced by circumstance to ask her to risk her life, even if it was for America's noble cause.

When he reached the spot where Lucy stood, Captain Killgrew saluted, standing straight and tall, and tried hard to maintain some sort of professional distance, but Lucy could see the look of concern in his eyes.

"Good morning, Private Killgrew," he said, keeping

all emotion out of his voice.

Lucy returned her father's salute, and said, "Good morning, Sir."

Captain Killgrew cleared his throat.

"Are...are you and Private Weaver about ready? Do you have your letter of introduction to Mr. Black, authorizing him to turn over the rifles to you?"

"Yes, Sir," Lucy said, looking her father squarely in the eyes. "And the silver willow trees we've been given to pay Mr. Black for his supplies."

"Good. Very good," said Captain Killgrew.

For a moment, the Captain was silent, but Lucy could see the worry on his face. Then, his features softened somewhat, and Lucy was afraid that he was going to call her his little girl and tell her he couldn't let her go, after all.

But with an obvious effort, Captain Killgrew steeled himself once more.

"Remember, Private Killgrew, your country is counting on you. Pay close attention to the route I laid out for you, and you should be able to avoid any British patrols. But if you should encounter any suspicious riders, I want you and Private Weaver to—"

"With due respect, Sir," Lucy interrupted, using a phrase she had heard her father use once when speaking with Mr. Knox, "I think it's time we were off."

Tom Killgrew closed his eyes for a moment and took a deep breath. He was trying to think of the young girl before him as just another soldier, doing her part to help the Cause—but try as he might, he simply couldn't do it.

"I'll take care, Father—I mean, Captain. I promise. Please, don't worry."

"Listen, Lucy," Tom said, suddenly dropping all pretenses, "for heaven's sake, do be careful."

"I will—Sir," Lucy said with military precision.

Then she saluted, and with some reluctance, but also with a great deal of pride, Tom Killgrew saluted his daughter in return.

Without another word, Lucy turned and climbed aboard her horse.

"You take care of my girl, Private Weaver," the Captain called as Weaver snapped the reins. The wagon jerked into motion behind the old gray horse.

"I will, Sir," said Weaver, saluting as the wagon rattled past the Captain.

Lucy fell in behind the wagon, and Tom Killgrew wiped a tear from his eye as he stood watching his little girl ride away, so bravely, into an uncertain future.

"I love you, daughter," he whispered. "Come back to me, safe and sound."

As they rode away from camp, the realization that she was actually about to head straight into the jaws of potential danger caused Lucy to suddenly feel a quick pang of fear. But as just as quickly as the feeling had washed over her, it was gone. This was an important mission—she knew that—and she must be brave.

Even so, Lucy couldn't bring herself to look back at her father. She knew that he would still be standing there, watching her leave, but she also knew that if she looked back, her courage might fail. So with great effort, she looked straight ahead, gritted her teeth, and kept riding forward.

To her right, at the far edge of the camp, Lucy saw Will Ashley, standing next to a large white oak tree. She smiled—partly because she was pleased to see him, and partly because he was trying so desperately to look as if his being there had nothing to do with an effort to see her. *But how could that be,* she smiled. *Especially after the time they spent together last night.*

As she rode by, she said, "Good morning, Will. Have you come to see me off?"

Will looked quickly at the ground, and Lucy was sure that his cheeks were turning a warm shade of pink.

When Will looked back up, he said, "Well...look, Lucy, I...I...you take care, you understand?"

Then he looked back down at the ground for an instant, but his eyes quickly returned to her, and he said firmly, "And be on the lookout out for Lobsterbacks. They're out there, you know."

"I know," said Lucy. "I'll be careful. And you take care, as well."

She smiled, but her smile was mixed with a look of concern, for she knew that Will would be taking part in the battle for the hills above Boston later that day.

Suddenly, a wave of realization washed over Lucy. *I might never see him again.* The thought presented itself so clearly, so vividly, that it almost seemed to Lucy to be more than just a thought. It seemed to be real somehow, almost as if she had actually spoken the words out loud.

Now, she knew she had to say something to let him know how she felt.

"Will! Do be careful. I...I want to be able to see you again when I come back."

Will nodded his head and smiled—a smile that was warm and friendly. It was one of the things Lucy liked best about him.

"I suppose we both need to be careful," he said. "I'll see you when you get back."

Will waved as Lucy and Private Weaver turned southward, onto the main road. She was leaving a lot behind; she knew that. And she also knew that her life would never be the same again after this day.

For the next six hours, Lucy rode ahead of the wagon

Private Weaver was driving skillfully over and around the ruts that had been left in the dirt road after the last rain. Her job was to keep an eye out for patrolling Lobster-backs. With Boston under siege, it wasn't likely that there would be any patrols in this area, but they could take no chances.

She kept her horse off the dried, hard-packed dirt road as much as possible, preferring to ride on the softer, quieter ground beneath the trees that lined both sides of the road. It was a technique she had learned from her father.

She knew from her father's instructions, and from the detailed map that Mr. Knox had made her memorize the night before, that Mr. Black's farm should be just over the next rise. She slowed her horse and stood up in the saddle to stretch her tired muscles. She looked back and saw that Weaver and the wagon were still plodding along behind her. She wondered briefly if the cart would be big enough to carry the seventy-five flintlocks and a partial load of hay to hide them in.

After a moment, Lucy urged her horse forward. But as she did, she noticed the pungent smell of smoke. It was the same smell she remembered from that day she had entered the burned-out shell of her house a few short weeks ago. It was the same smell that had clung to her clothes and hair for days after that encounter, no matter how many times she washed them.

She hated that smell more than any other smell in the world. It was the smell of death—the smell that had ended her happy, safe life.

Although she hoped against hope, Lucy knew what she would see, even before she reached the top of the hill. But what she saw was still a shock. There, in a clearing, was the smoldering ruin of what used to be Mr. Black's farm.

Quickly, Lucy turned her horse around and signaled

for Private Weaver to stop. She could see no soldiers as she scanned the fields, but she mentally selected several escape routes, just in case any Lobsterbacks should come into view.

She turned her horse northward and joined Private Weaver a short way back down the road.

Before Weaver could say a word, Lucy ordered, "You wait here. I'm going to ride forward and try to draw any British fire. When you're sure it's safe, follow me."

If Private Weaver had any problems taking orders from a thirteen-year-old girl, Lucy didn't give him a chance to voice them. She smacked her horse on its side, causing the animal to bolt forward with a powerful leap. Then, leaving the shelter of the wood and riding quickly down the slope to the open field below, Lucy raced like the wind. She had no intention of becoming an easy target if any British did happen to be about.

The main road to Black's farm was to the south. Lucy and Weaver had come in from the north field, which was like entering from the back door. If the British were watching the farm, Lucy thought, the odds were they would be waiting by the south road.

Nevertheless, the skin at the back of Lucy's neck tingled as she thought about the fact that a British musket ball might hit her at any moment. As she rode, she could see the skeletal remains of the blackened support timbers that used to be Mr. Black's farmhouse stand alone against the cloudy sky. The sickening smell of burning wood filled her nostrils as a black plume of smoke rose into the air. Lucy stayed low in the saddle as she rode quickly past the charred ruins and toward the road.

As she was rounding the front of the house, her eye was drawn to an old well. For a moment, she couldn't understand what had attracted her attention, but then she saw something.

It was a hand. There was someone on the far side of the well! Without quite knowing why, she was certain it was Mr. Black. Lucy rode quickly to the well, dismounted and, taking her pistol from her saddle, ran to investigate.

What she found caused her to gasp.

Black was dead, that was obvious. But the old man's head was being cradled by another man! For a moment, Lucy stood looking down at the black man as he gently swayed back and forth on the ground, his wrinkled face streaked with tears.

Then, as if he hadn't heard Lucy's approach, the man looked up, his eyes filled with fear. In a gravelly voice, he said, "What do you want 'ere?"

Lucy was nearly as afraid as the old black man, but she tried to reassure him, asking softly, "Is that Mr. Black?"

The old black man's face softened somewhat.

"Yes," he said, eyeing Lucy carefully. "This is Adam Black."

"Oh, I'm so sorry," said Lucy. "Was he a friend of yours?"

"He was my friend," the old man said, his voice trembling with emotion. "Adam Black was my best friend—my only friend."

"Did the Redcoats do this?" Lucy asked.

The black man nodded slowly, and then spoke, his words coming in a hollow monotone. "Them Lobsterbacks done all this. There was two of 'em, and some snake of a loyalist they called Coffin. They burned us out, and they killed my only friend."

"Have they been gone long?"

"An hour or so, I reckon," the old man said, his words being drowned out by a fit of coughing.

"I'm sorry, sir. Are you hurt, too?" Lucy asked,

kneeling by the black man's side.

"I guess I'm hurt pretty bad, too," he said.

Lucy could see blood beginning to emerge from the side of the old man's mouth.

"What is your name?" she asked as she stood and began to draw a bucket of water from the well.

"My name's Joshua," he said. "The Redcoats told me I was free. But Mr. Black never owned me. He was just my friend."

Lucy pulled a metal dipper from a peg on the side of the well and dipped it into the bucket.

"Mr. Black made me a free man. He taught me his trade," Joshua said as Lucy again knelt down by his side.

The black man's shirt was covered with blood, but it was hard for Lucy to tell whether it was his or Mr. Black's.

She set her pistol on the ground and lifted the cup of water to Joshua's lips.

"Drink this, and then we'll see how badly you're hurt," she said as Joshua began to drink slowly from the cup.

As the old man drank, Lucy said, "Joshua, where are you hurt?"

"We could see the Redcoats comin' this way, and Coffin, too. We knew there was gonna be trouble, so Mr. Black, he yelled at me to run." Joshua's words were interrupted by another fit of coughing. "Then they shoot Mr. Black. I didn't wanna run then. Instead, I picked up a musket, and I shoot one of them Redcoats dead."

"I probably shouldn't have done it, but I'm glad I did. But Mr. Black, he paid for it. As soon as I shot that one, the other one killed Mr. Black. I think they was plannin' to kill us both, all the time. After I seed Mr. Black go down, I got scared, and then's when I started to run away."

Lucy could see that Joshua was fighting to hold back his tears.

"I knowed I should have gone back to see if'n I could help Mr. Black, but I was scared. I was real scared, and I just started runnin'. And then, all of a sudden, I heard a shot, and then I felt something hit my back, real hard. And I musta passed out right then, because when I woke up, the Redcoats was gone, and the farm was burnt to the ground."

Lucy looked around at the smoldering ruins of Adam Black's farm.

"When I came to, I couldn't stand up, so I crawled back to where Mr. Black was layin', here by the well. I catched him up in my arms, and I ain't moved since—but I'm thinkin' I'm hurt pretty bad, too."

When Joshua had finished drinking, Lucy put the cup down and carefully pulled off the old black man's bloodstained shirt. When she had exposed his wound, she instinctively knew that there was nothing she could do for him. The old man would soon be joining his friend in death.

"Please, Joshua, what I have to ask you is very important," Lucy said, looking into his eyes. My name is Lucy Killgrew, and I've been sent here by my father, Captain Tom Killgrew, to pick up some rifles that you and Mr. Black made for the Patriots' assault on Boston."

Joshua's eyes seemed to brighten at the sound of Captain Killgrew's name.

"Are you Tom Killgrew's girl?" he asked, a puzzled expression of his face.

"Yes, sir, I am," said Lucy.

Joshua studied Lucy's face for a long moment, and then he said, "Yeah, I kin see some of your father around your eyes."

"Thank you, sir," Lucy said, but then she quickly added, "My father sent me here to pick up the rifles. Did the British get them?"

Joshua's eyes began to flutter as he drifted toward unconsciousness. But he strained to speak, saying, "Your father's been here lots of times, girl. I met him, let's see...I think, the first time, he was on his way home from Canada."

The old man then paused for a few seconds, his eyes closed, his breathing labored.

Lucy knew that time was running short. She said softly, but insistently, "My father spoke very kindly of you, too, sir. But the rifles, Joshua. Please, I must know...did the Redcoats get the rifles?"

"He said he wanted some good long rifles, your father did. Then the Redcoats came here. I think they was lookin' for them rifles."

Joshua winced in pain and began to cough again, as Lucy tried to keep the old man conscious by dipping his shirt into the bucket and then applying the cool water to his face.

"They killed Mr. Black, and they burned us out. They called Mr. Black a traitor. But they didn't find nothin'!"

Those words filled Lucy with hope.

"Joshua, are you saying that the British didn't find the rifles?"

She shook the old man slightly, and asked again, "Please, sir, where are they? Do you have them hidden somewhere? Joshua, where are the rifles?"

Lucy heard Private Weaver jumping down from the wagon and moving to where she knelt beside the two old men. Joshua's breathing was becoming more irregular. He had lost a lot of blood. Lucy was surprised he was still alive at all.

Then, feebly, the old man held out a hand and pointed a bony finger to his left. "The well," he said feebly. "We built a special catch-hole in the side of the well. And that fooled 'em...they never found a thing! We fooled 'em—damn Redcoats."

Then, Joshua turned his face toward the sky.

"But now, I guess it's like the Bible say...that ol' Adam and this ol' Joshua, I reckon we found our Jericho. And now, it's time for us both to go—together, like we always been."

The old man shuddered violently, and his body slumped over that of his friend.

For a moment, Lucy was silent, looking into the old man's face, which was now free from pain at last.

But shortly, Private Weaver broke the silence.

"Lucy," he said, "There's nothing more we can for them. We've got to find those rifles."

Lucy shook her head slowly and then stood, looking down into the well.

Without a word, Weaver grabbed onto the rope, jumped over the edge of the well and began to lower himself down into the blackness. She had heard of Colonists hiding things in wells, wrapped in oilcloth and encased in bear fat, but she had never seen the proof.

That proof was only a few moments in coming, however. From a short way down the well shaft, Private Weaver called up, "They're here! I've found the rifles!"

It took almost an hour to bring up all seventy-five rifles and the six casks of black powder that Joshua and Adam Black had hidden in the well.

Lucy was surprised at Private Weaver's energy, for the young man made more than a dozen trips down into the well, each time tying the rope around a bundle of rifles and then returning to the top of the well to help Lucy haul them up.

Then, each time Weaver went back down for more rifles, Lucy would load the bundle of weapons onto the wagon. Before the job was done, both Lucy and Private Weaver were smeared from head to foot in smelly bear fat.

Finally, Private Weaver called up from the well shaft, saying, "Well, that's the last of 'em."

Lucy had to smile, just a little, though she tried to hide it, at the sight of Private Weaver as he poked his filthy face over the top of the well for the last time. But the brightness of his smile was in such contrast to the filthiness of his fat-covered face that Lucy laughed a little, in spite of herself.

Weaver didn't seem to mind. He just extended his hand and said, "When you're done laughing, could you give me a boost out of here, please?"

Just as Lucy reached for the young man's hand, the sound of a musket broke the stillness of the late afternoon, and the smile disappeared off Weaver's face. His arm jerked, and blood splattered Lucy's shirt.

"Weaver!"

"Save the rifles!" Weaver yelled as he tumbled backward into the well.

Lucy heard a splash, but at the same moment, she heard the pounding of approaching horses!

"Stay your ground, girl!" She heard someone yell. "You're under arrest, in the name of the King!"

Lucy dove for the ground next to the well, toward the bodies of the two old men. Lying on the ground, right where she had left it an hour ago, was her primed and loaded pistol. Just as she picked up the pistol, she felt the ground shudder as a lead ball struck, just inches from her elbow.

Lucy grabbed the pistol, rolled over, and then sat up, pointing the weapon in the direction from which the shot had come.

She saw two Redcoats riding quickly toward her, and with them, she saw Lucius Coffin.

Lucy aimed her pistol and fired. The sound was deafening, and white smoke wrapped itself around her head like a scarf. When she could see again, she saw that one of the Lobsterbacks had fallen from his horse. Coffin and the other soldier were reining in horses to tend to their wounded comrade.

But then, Lucy noticed something even more ominous. In the distance, she saw several other soldiers on foot, moving steadily in her direction.

There wasn't time to think. Lucy knew that her obligation was to deliver the rifles to her father. With that single thought fixed in her mind, Lucy jumped aboard the wagon and slapped the reigns against the horse's rump as hard as she could.

"Yah! Giddap!" she screamed, and the horse leaped to a gallop—straight toward Coffin and the soldiers!

It wasn't what Lucy had intended, but it was so unexpected that it turned out to be the best thing she could have done.

The rumbling wagon caused both Coffin's horse and the horse of the remaining Lobsterback to spook, throwing both men to the ground.

As the wagon lumbered by and onto the main road, Lucy heard Coffin yell, "It's her! It's that damned Killgrew girl!"

She looked back and saw both men on the ground, exactly where they'd fallen. But she also saw that their horses hadn't run far and were now standing just a few hundred yards away. She knew that it wouldn't take long for the men to reach them.

Lucy snapped the reins harder, and the wagon lurched as the horse began to move even faster along the rutted road.

Somehow, the added weight of the rifles and powder actually seemed to give the cart a bit more stability. But Lucy knew it wouldn't be long before the chase began in earnest, and if she were caught, the Redcoats would show no mercy.

She quickly decided to turn the wagon off the well-traveled road and into the shelter of the woods. Perhaps she and her precious cargo would be safer out of plain sight.

What Lucy didn't know was that the second Redcoat had broken his arm when he'd been thrown from his frightened horse, which left only Lucius Coffin to follow her.

Neither could she have known that Lucius Coffin had no intention of riding after a Colonial rebel by himself—even if that rebel happened to be a thirteen-year-old girl.

No, Lucius Coffin had decided to tend to the two soldiers and return them to their commands. Then, once he had gathered some reinforcements, he would search for Lucy. After all, he thought, it didn't require the abilities of fortune teller to know where Lucy and her wagonload of rifles were headed.

They would be headed for Boston.

As he knelt over the downed soldiers, Lucius Coffin stared down the empty road toward Boston, his dark, angry mind focused on only one thought: *one day, that girl is going to make a slip, and when she does...*

Chapter Seven

Breed's Hill

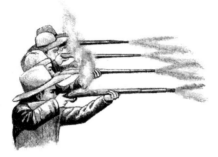

T O THE NORTH OF Boston and across the water was Charleston, and behind the town were two hills, called Bunker Hill and Breed's Hill.

At the exact time Lucy was escaping from Black's farm with her precious cargo, Colonel William Prescott, Captain Tom Killgrew, and 1600 other Americans left the main body of troops and set out to entrench themselves on those two hills.

In just over two hours, the Americans had completed their artillery fortifications atop Breed's Hill. From the top of the hill, Tom looked down at the green water below and the three British war ships moving abreast of the shoreline.

At that moment, British General Gage was livid after

being informed that the rebels had taken both Breeds and Bunker Hills. Gage sent for William Howe.

"How have the Americans been able to outflank our troops?" he screamed as he stood in his Boston headquarters, training a spyglass on the hills across the Charles River.

He knew the answer to his question would have to wait. The most urgent task at hand was the retaking of both Breed's and Bunker Hills, because once the American cannons were in place, Boston and its vital harbor would be vulnerable to an unstoppable barrage.

Tom was watching the harbor from the other side of the river, just as the British began their attack on the newly fortified American positions. He saw clouds of smoke billow from guns on the port sides of three ships, and then, within moments, his ears were assaulted by the muffled sounds of the exploding cannons.

The British were firing! Tom knew that his part in the war had finally begun in earnest.

Multiple explosions began slowly to climb up the sides of the hill as the bombardiers on the British ships slowly corrected their aim. Within minutes the six cannons used for training at Copp's Garrison joined the naval bombardment while British marksmen took up positions from behind gravestones in a nearby cemetery.

The thundering impact of the cannonballs as they struck the ground brought showers of rocks and dirt down upon the Patriots, and the farmers and clerks who made up the American fighting forces were suddenly filled with fear.

For the first time, the Sons of Liberty were looking death squarely in the face.

Nevertheless, as frightened as most of the Americans were, the leaders of the supposedly superior British troops actually believed their situation to be even worse.

"Who told those fools to fire?" screamed General Gage to Sir William Howe, who was standing by his side, watching the battle begin.

"I'm afraid that ends any chance of a surprise attack on their positions, Sir," said Howe calmly. "It would have been better for us if the rebels had been led to believe that we didn't know they were there."

"Well, that's not going to be the case now," said Gage, shaking his head in disbelief. "What do you suggest we do now, Sir William?"

"We must eliminate the American troops quickly, General, and without hesitation. I suggest that, under cover of the naval bombardment, we ferry troops across the river and attack the Americans head on. The last thing we want is for them to have time to place their cannons. We have very little time. We must strike immediately."

"How many men will you need, Sir William?"

"Given the importance of the situation and the position we'll be in should we fail, I may need the entire garrison. But let's begin with a probing assault. Several hundred should be sufficient, Sir."

"But we don't know how many Rebels are up there!" said General Gage, still looking through his spyglass.

"We'll have Generals Clinton and Burgoyne follow with the main body of our force, in the event their assistance becomes necessary. If I know this American rabble, they'll fold after our first musket salvo. Of that, I'm fairly confident, Sir."

"Fairly confident?" Gage scoffed. "Only fairly? May I remind you, Sir William, that it's my head the King will mount on his wall, not yours? And need I remind you what this rabble, as you call them, did to us on our march back from Concord? It is this same American rabble that now has us cut off. I must assure you, my friend, that I value my head more than I do your career!"

"Sir, they had the advantage of surprise during our march from Concord to Boston, and they were well hidden by the terrain. But this time, we know exactly where they are. We have ten thousand men at our disposal, each and every one eager to take on these rebels in a fair fight. As I see it, Sir, our course is clear. We must attack now!"

Gage lowered his spyglass and turned to Howe.

"Very well, Sir William. You may proceed. But understand this: I do not want another fiasco! Is that clear?"

"Quite clear, Sir," said Howe.

American snipers had infiltrated Charlestown and were causing considerable damage. General Burgoyne was furious. He couldn't deal with the fact that American "vermin" had soiled the town, and without a moment's hesitation, he turned the British cannons against Charlestown. By early afternoon, the town was ablaze.

At the same time, more than five thousand British troops made their way across the smoke-covered harbor to begin the attack on the hills behind the burning town.

Earth and rocks continued to shower the ground as the British bombs zeroed in ever closer to the American positions. The Americans hurriedly dug trenches, fortifying themselves against the blasts and preparing for the impending British attack.

But the Rebels, too, had made their presence felt. They had managed to set several strategic parts of Boston ablaze. Smoke from the town had darkened the sky as Colonel Prescott, standing at the top of Breed's Hill and looking down into the harbor, turned to Tom and said, "They'll attack soon, Killgrew. Order your men to the ready."

"Yes, Sir."

"And Tom," the Colonel added, "tell your men to

make every shot count. We may have to hold this position for days, and we haven't a musket ball to spare."

The Colonel's words reminded Tom of his daughter's perilous mission to Black's farm. He had managed to put Lucy out of his mind much of the time since today's battle had begun. But as he thought of her now, he felt his mind becoming numb with fear for his daughter, and he had to shake his head slightly to refocus his thoughts on the problems at hand.

"Have the men fire at fifteen paces, Sir?" Tom asked the Colonel.

That was standard policy for soldiers when conserving shot—to wait until the enemy was within fifteen paces before firing. That policy was summed up by an old saying: "Wait till you see the whites of their eyes."

"That will do, Captain," said the Colonel, again turning to look out across the Charles River.

Then, quite suddenly, the bombardment stopped. An eerie and terrifying silence fell over the hill, and the Rebels strained to see beyond the smoke for any sort of movement by the British.

Then, through a clearing in the smoke, Tom saw long boats and barges approaching Morton's Point below.

"They're coming!" Tom shouted to the Colonel.

"How many?"

Tom peered once again into the black smoke.

"Four...maybe five hundred, Sir."

On the riverbank below, they could see the Redcoats jump from their crafts and assemble on the shore. But they could also see that they outnumbered the British troops in the landing party, which made the Americans feel easier about the battle that was soon to come. As the Rebels looked down at the assembling Redcoats, a change in the wind covered the harbor with an impenetrable blanket of heavy, black smoke, preventing further observation.

Time seemed to pass slowly for the Americans as they waited for the British assault.

"Remember," Tom called to his troops, "hold your fire until you hear my signal!"

The men could see nothing from the hilltop except the thick smoke, and for the moment, all they could do was listen. In the eerie stillness, they could hear the sound of the flames that were consuming the buildings of Charlestown. The dense smoke drifted up toward their fortifications, causing many men to choke and cough. Yet they all knew that the hope of the American cause rested with their skill as marksmen, so each man tried desperately to keep his eyes clear.

Then, they could hear the sound of distant clattering and clanging from the assembling soldiers below, which continued for over an hour. Nerves were as taut as piano wires. The wind began to rise, stirred up by the fires below, but there was nothing the Americans could do but wait.

Then, finally, a new sound filled the air. It was the beat of British drums, faint at first, then growing louder and louder as General Howe led his advance troops toward the Rebel force at the top of Breed's Hill.

As the British troops drew closer, the Americans began to hear the rattle of swords and bayonets. The smoke had cleared the top of the hill but still lay thick mid-way toward the bottom.

The townspeople of Charleston, some carrying picnic lunches, gathered around the northeast shore of the Charles River to watch the battle that was about to begin.

As the Americans watched and waited, the men of the 47th North Lancashires and Royal Marines stepped out of the thick curtain of smoke, marching in tight military formation.

"Hold your fire," Tom reminded his men. "Remember, now, fifteen paces!"

The Americans' morale was high. Tom, and all the others in his command, still believed that the British were attacking with a force of no more than five hundred men. Because of the dense smoke that still hung over the harbor, neither Tom nor anyone else saw the other barges landing—barges that were filled with thousands of additional British troops.

Suddenly, there was a thunder of British muskets, firing in unison. Though the British were still a good thirty paces away, and their weapons were less accurate than the American rifles, one of Tom's men fell in that first volley.

Tom held one hand high, holding back the Rebels' return fire. It was like trying to hold back a raging flood with a single stone. But his men followed his orders—every last one of them.

Deep inside, Tom felt a tremendous pride for these men. He could hear his heart pounding as the British troops, marching in straight lines, began swapping places, each time allowing a new line of soldiers with primed and loaded weapons to move to the front of the column.

When Tom judged the distance to be fifteen paces, he dropped his arm and yelled, "Now, men! Fire at will!"

Instantly, hundreds of Patriot flintlocks fired in unison. For several seconds, the dense smoke from the rifles obstructed Tom's view. But as the smoke thinned, he could see a gaping hole in the British line.

At least fifty Redcoats lay on the ground, dead or dying, and another fifty were limping away, blood flowing from their wounds. The accuracy of the rebel soldiers had taken the British by surprise, and they quickly began to retreat back down the hill, leaving their dead and wounded comrades behind.

The American troops stood and cheered. These farmers and file clerks, trappers and carpenters had sent the mighty British army scurrying for cover, its tail tucked between its legs!

At that moment, the rag-tag American forces were convinced they were unbeatable. But while his men stood, cheering, dancing in circles, and waving their weapons in the air, Tom studied the landscape below. He knew the British would be back.

As he looked down toward the harbor, Tom's heart sank. The wind had shifted, blowing the smoke off the harbor, which revealed dozens of troop barges, each filled with Redcoats. Tom knew that the Rebels may have sent the first wave of British troops fleeing, but the battle had barely begun. Thousands of reinforcements were about to reach the shore, and he knew that soon the Americans would be hopelessly outnumbered.

Tom instantly went into action. He yelled to his men, who were slapping each other on the back and swapping stories of their exploits, and ordered them to begin gathering all guns, powder, and shot from the dead and dying British soldiers.

The grave tone of Tom's voice brought the troops back to reality. They began to sense that perhaps the battle was not over and quickly obeyed.

Over the next hour, six columns of British soldiers marched up Breed's Hill and were cut down by the American forces. By Tom's count, the Americans were killing or wounding five Redcoats for every American that was killed or wounded.

But Tom also knew that his forces were quickly running out of powder and shot. The British, with their superior numbers, could afford to sacrifice their troops. As far as they were concerned, every British soldier that was killed or wounded meant the Americans had used one more musket ball.

Even though it was just past midday, Tom looked up and saw the ghostly image of the moon, skittering through the dense smoke caused by the black powder. For a moment, he wasn't sure why the vision of the moon should make him feel better—but then, he remembered Emy Moon.

Lucy used to tell him that Emy Moon brought good luck. Tom hoped it was true, and in spite of the terrible battle that raged around him, he found himself smiling, thinking of his darling daughter.

We're going to need all the luck we can muster, Emy, he thought.

As they made their final assault, the British reinforcements, their bayonets flashing, stormed the Americans like a tidal wave.

As the Redcoats advanced, Tom loaded the last of his powder into his weapon. The British moving quickly up the hill, firing sporadically at the Americans, many of whom were also out of powder and shot.

Tom knew what the outcome of today's battle would be. Against superior British numbers, the American troops could not withstand this final assault.

How long can we hold up? He wondered. *And why don't our forces on Bunker Hill not come to our aid?*

But the British kept coming, now beginning to overwhelm the American positions. There were a few remaining volleys from both sides, and when the muskets were finally silenced, the fighting became hand-to-hand.

Tom and the other Americans, outnumbered nearly four to one, leapt from their positions to face the swarm of Redcoats. The sound of the battle was terrible. Although there was no more musket fire, the air was filled with the sounds of bayonets, swords, and knives clashing, men cursing, screaming, and dying. Anyone who thought that war was a glamorous and exciting pursuit would learn the horrifying truth this day.

To his left, Tom caught a glimpse of red as a British soldier lunged at him. The attacker was larger than he, but he avoided the fierce jab of the Redcoat's bayonet. He then quickly swung his musket around and used its butt to bring the soldier to the ground. Then they exchanged blows with their fists. Tom gained the advantage by pinning the man down. He didn't see the other soldier move up from behind him, but he did feel the cold blade as it plunged deep into his side.

Tom felt his strength beginning to leave him. His mind began to float outside and above his body. He suddenly felt no connection to himself or to the battle raging around him. Instead, he suddenly felt warm, comfortable, and serene. He watched as that person he vaguely recognized as himself slowly released his grip and slumped onto the body of the Redcoat who had been lying beneath him.

The British soldier quickly rose to his feet and stood beside his comrade. They looked down at the dying American, lying still on the ground.

"Such men as these," the soldier said, "are not the rowdies we were told to expect. These are true fighting men!"

Tom heard the words, but they held no real meaning to him. It wasn't that he didn't understand them. It was just that they had no longer seemed to hold any relevance.

He could feel himself slipping away, and there was a part of him that felt fear. But there was a much bigger part of him that felt as if this was the right thing. It was simply his time, and he knew that it was all right.

Suddenly, the vision of Nancy's face filled his mind. He could see her as clearly as if she were standing right beside him. He reached out to her, to explain to her that everything would be all right, but the words wouldn't come. However, he then he felt a terrible pain, knowing the suffering his beloved wife would go through.

And Lucy...how would his daughter cope? Suddenly, Tom felt a great fear—a fear of dying, of leaving behind those he loved so dearly.

And at that moment, he felt an overpowering urge to fight the darkness, to throw off the soothing blanket of death that was quickly enveloping him. He wanted, more than anything in the world, to hold his dear, sweet wife in his arms once more. We wanted to know and nurture the child—his child—yet to born. He wanted to kiss his precious daughter on top of her soft, flaxen hair one more time. He wanted to tell each of them how deeply he loved them and how much they meant to him. He wanted—

But none of it was to be. No matter how he struggled, there was nothing more he could do. Whatever it was that was about to happen was beyond his control. As he lay bleeding on the ground, the serenity began to return, like a warm woolen blanket on a cold winter night.

Tom slowly began to settle into the warmth. Then suddenly, he looked up and saw a blinding white light, which he instinctively knew was the source of the warmth and comfort he was feeling.

Good-bye, Nancy, he thought. *I cherish every moment we had together. I only pray that my life made some small difference. And Lucy, my dear Lucy, light of my life, if my existence was for no other purpose than to bring you into this world, I die a contented man. Good-bye.*

Chapter Eight

The Old Oak

T HE NEXT MORNING, LUCY awoke with the first light of the morning sun. Her experience with Black, Joshua, Private Weaver, Coffin, and the Redcoats the day before, combined with the long ride, had left her completely exhausted. Even so, she had slept only sporadically next to a knotted old oak, awakening often at the slightest sound.

From her sheltered vantage point, she could see if a rider approached from any direction. The area around her was blanketed with tall grass and wildflowers, whose pungent scent perfumed the air as Lucy ate her breakfast of dried fish and corn biscuits. Only the rush of the gentle wind blowing through the treetops interrupted the sounds of blue jays overhead.

Lucy's legs and arms were stiff and sore. She hugged

her knees close to her chest for a moment, and for the first time in her life, she felt completely alone, and she began to doubt herself. *Should I have fought Coffin and the Redcoats at Black's farm? Should I have stayed with Weaver? Or was it more important to save the rifles and powder?*

As these thoughts ran through Lucy's mind, she suddenly thought she heard her father's voice, so close that she looked around to see if he were standing behind her. The tone of his voice was gentle but firm.

"Trust in yourself, Lucy," she heard her father's voice say. "Trust your instincts, and always believe what your heart tells you."

She smiled as she remembered all the survival skills her father had taught her, from the time she was a little girl. She had always been amazed at how much her father knew about the ways of the natural world, and he had taught his daughter well. Lucy had no fear of surviving in the wilderness—her concerns were with other things like the Redcoats, and the precious rifles in the wagon off to her left.

"The land is God's endowment to us, Lucy," she remembered her father saying. "It can speak to us and tell us many wonderful things. And if you listen and truly understand, you'll never need to be afraid. Show respect for the land, and it'll watch over you and protect you."

Lucy found comfort and strength in her father's words, and at that moment, Lucy could almost feel him putting his strong arms around her, holding her close, letting her know that he would always be with her. The feeling was so strong that she sat perfectly still for a moment, listening and looking.

But she saw nothing but the quiet forest and Weaver's horse, which she had tied to a tree a short distance away last night. Now he was happily eating his fill of the tall grass that was as nearly as tall as his legs.

From the deadly calm in the air, Lucy knew that a storm was approaching and that she'd have to make a choice. She could either try to outrun the storm and deliver the rifles by nightfall, or she could wait out the storm in the relative shelter of the woods. The practical side of her told her to wait. But another part of her knew how desperately her father and the other men needed the rifles and powder.

As she weighed her options, she suddenly heard the distant sound of riders approaching from the north. She settled back into the shadows and watched as two riders appeared at the fork in the road. As they swung into view and stopped their horses, Lucy's heart nearly stopped beating. There at the crossroads, surveying the trail in both directions, were Lucius Coffin and a British soldier.

Suddenly, Lucy became acutely aware of every sound around her. Her breathing sounded like the north wind on a cold winter's eve. She was sure Coffin could hear the pounding of her heart. She desperately wished she had hidden the wagon more securely. If the muskets fell into enemy hands, she would never be able to live with herself. She wasn't afraid to die; she was only afraid that she would fail her father.

All she could do at that moment was keep as still as possible and pray that Coffin and the Redcoat would take the fork that branched eastward onto Newgate Road, away from her and her precious cargo.

Please, Emy, she thought, *let them take the road to the east.*

Lucy watched as both men stood up in the stirrups, looking around for tracks while their tired horses heaved and blew from the long hard ride. She could see Coffin carefully weighing the possibilities as to what direction she might have taken.

Then, Coffin reined his horse to the east, and Lucy let out a huge sigh of relief as Coffin and the Redcoat rode off on Newgate Road.

Although she was relieved, Lucy knew they would probably be back when they found no fresh wagon tracks and realized the error of their decision. Now, her own decision had been made for her. It was too dangerous now for her to be on the road, so she'd have to find a place to hide the rifles.

She could only hope that if the weapons did not arrive soon, her father would send someone looking for her. For just a moment, she allowed herself the tiny luxury of hoping that he would send handsome young William Ashley.

Until someone came to help, she would just have to find a hiding place for the rifles.

"It's far better to be late than to be captured," she told herself as she stood and began scanning the area around her.

Lucy walked a few yards deeper into the woods, until she came upon a small hill. She could hear the sound of rushing water coming from somewhere nearby. A short way up the hill, she found an opening. It was a cave that extended into the hillside some fifteen feet. An animal, a bear, most likely, had obviously used it recently, but the owner didn't seem to be at home at the moment.

She looked up and saw a large red spruce at the crest of the hill, standing alone like a beacon.

"This will be perfect," she said to herself.

Lucy hurried back to the wagon, but she knew that it was too wide to drive through the thick stand of trees that stood between her campsite and the cave. Therefore, she began to remove the weapons, several at a time, and set them on the ground beside the oak tree.

When all the rifles were unloaded, Lucy hitched the horse back up to the wagon traces and gently led him out to the road. Then she took off her hat and gave the horse a hard swat on the haunches, causing him to bolt and scurry down the road, the empty wagon rattling behind.

She watched the wagon disappear around a bend in the road and then returned to her task.

The small cave was far enough from the road to make her feel comfortable that the Redcoats wouldn't find the muskets but not so far away as to make the task of moving the rifles there impossible. Lucy spent most of the morning carrying the weapons and munitions from the oak to their temporary hiding place.

When she'd finished, she stood at the opening of the cave and then, after some thought, she also tossed the bag containing the four hundred newly minted Willow Trees into the darkness. Then she began to cover the cave entrance with mud, stones, and branches. By mid-afternoon, the cave opening was completely closed and blended well with the rest of the hillside.

Exhausted from her labor, Lucy then went back to her observation site near the old oak tree to wait for the help she hoped would soon be on the way. To help pass the time, she began to write about the adventures of the last two days in her diary, including a few vague references to the location of the coins and the seventy-five rifles, each still wrapped in oil cloth and encased in bear grease.

Her only fear was that the British—or Lucius Coffin—would get hold of her diary. So as a precaution, she bundled the diary, quill, and ink into a leftover piece of oilcloth. To her delight, she discovered a small hollow beneath the roots of the old oak tree, and she shoved the bundle as far back into this secure, dry recess as she could.

It had been a long day, and just as night finally closed around Lucy, so, too, did the storm that she had felt coming that morning. Rain fell heavily on the land but softly upon Lucy, since the branches above offered some protection from the downpour. Lucy had never felt as tired as she did on that night, nor had her muscles ever been as sore as they were at that moment.

And she had never felt more alone.

She tried to sleep, but no matter how hard she tried, she couldn't shake the feeling of being all alone in this wilderness, without the comfort of a blanket, fire, friends, or family. She could hear small animals moving in the darkness and rain. She was miserably cold, wet, and uncomfortable.

Even though sleep did not come easily, when it did come, her night was filled with vague but disturbing night-mares. In this most unsettling dream, she saw her father standing before her, silent and smiling, his face pale white, a sadness and pain in his eyes like she had never seen before.

When she awoke from that terrible dream, she stared into the blackness of the night for a long time, filled with the awful certainty that her father was dead. She couldn't explain it, but the feeling was so powerful, and so real, that she couldn't stop the tears from rolling down her face.

It was well past sun up before the rain stopped, and the clouds began to thin. As Lucy sat, considering her next move, she heard a twig snap in the woods behind her. She'd spent enough time in the woods to know that it was not an animal. It was a human who had made the sound—a human who was trying *not* to be heard.

With her heart pounding, she reached for her Fowler

and then stood up slowly and carefully, staying in the shadows, just as her father had taught her to do years ago.

The sound was hard to track and almost seemed to be coming from more than one spot. The forest was dark and damp as she slowly made her way toward a small clearing. From her vantage point at the edge of the trees, she could see small streams of steam beginning to rise from the ground.

Lucy stared into the clearing, as silent as a thought, looking for any sign of movement, but she saw nothing. Then, just as she was about to turn back, she heard the familiar clicks of musket hammers being pulled back. She was frozen with fear, and for a moment, her body refused to move. There was no sound as she slowly and cautiously turned her head in the direction of the sound.

☆ ☆ ☆

The following day, six Connecticut volunteers, fresh from the battle of Breed's Hill, were dispatched to search for Lucy, Private Weaver, and the missing weapons.

Among those assigned to conduct the search was Will Ashley.

Not wishing to be seen by British patrols, the six men kept to the woods, just off the main road. Will had spent so much time on these back roads in the last two months that he knew every wagon rut and pothole.

Suddenly, Will raised his hand, and the other men instantly pulled their horses to a stop and strained to see what had caught Will's attention.

About a hundred yards off the road was an empty and abandoned wagon, its horse casually munching the wild flowers that grew in profusion along the sides of road.

As the Rebel patrol rode forward, Will recognized the horse as the one he'd watched Private Weaver hitch to the wagon before he and Lucy had left camp.

Will's heart sank, but he refused to give up hope. Without a word, he dismounted and walked carefully toward the wagon.

Will's companions remained on their horses. They each knew the thoughts that were swirling through Will's mind.

Finally one of them said, "Where do ya think they are, Will?"

"I don't know, but one thing's for sure, they've got to be along this road somewhere."

Will tied a length of rope to the horse's rigging, freed him from the hitch, then mounted his own horse and began to move down the road once more. The other men followed behind, searching the woods for any sign of Lucy or Private Weaver.

All the while, Will tried not to think, trying not to let any negative thoughts enter his mind.

"We'll soon be at Newgate road," he said. "Maybe we should split up at the fork."

As they rode by the old, knotted oak where Lucy had been hiding, something caused Will to hesitate. He stopped his horse and stared at the tree as if it were speaking to him. Then, without a word, he dismounted and slowly approached the tree.

As they watched Will walk into the woods, his companions looked at each other and shrugged.

Will had no idea what had compelled him to examine this old oak tree, but as he approached its base, he could clearly see that someone had been there—and recently. The leaves were matted and pressed into the soft earth. Footprints were clearly visible.

Suddenly, Will's heart began to race and his spirits soared.

"Lucy!" he yelled. "Lucy!"

Will's companions quickly dismounted and joined their comrade. Will showed them the small footprints, footprints that were clearly smaller than a man's, and then they split up and began searching the woods.

Will followed what appeared to be Lucy's tracks, which skirted around the darker edge of the trees and headed deeper into the woods. The path she had been taking was not the easiest route, and Will began to fear the worst. It appeared to his trained eye that Lucy was trying to hide from someone or something.

Within a few minutes, Will had followed the tracks to the edge of the small clearing. The sun was shining brightly, and the flowers were thick and sweet-smelling. But on the ground in front of him, his worst fears were realized. He could clearly see where Lucy's footprints had been joined by those of at least three men, and no matter how desperately he wanted to believe otherwise, Will Ashley was forced to admit that Lucy Killgrew had been taken prisoner.

Chapter Nine

Escape to Oblivion

FOUR DAYS LATER, THE weather began to grow warm and humid. Gray clouds were forming overhead as twenty-five British soldiers advanced slowly along the narrow road.

Walking ahead of the troops were Lucy Killgrew and seven other captured Rebels. Riding at the front of the column were two mounted officers and Lucius Coffin.

Lucy's wrists were bound with leather strapping, which was attached at the other end to a young lieutenant's saddle. The British knew Lucy was a headstrong and troublesome girl—Coffin had made sure of that, and he made sure that her tether was good and tight, to insure her "cooperation."

As the column moved forward, Coffin turned back in his saddle and looked at Lucy, his lips curling up in an evil smile.

Lucy refused to allow her captors, and especially Coffin, to see her exhaustion, and she was determined not let anyone see her cry. She wouldn't let them see her weaken. She would need her strength for her escape, when the time came.

At least they didn't find the rifles, she thought, with some satisfaction.

With her arms outstretched by the tugging of the horse in front of her, Lucy lowered her head, and then struggled to wipe her brow on her sleeve. As she was pulled along, she searched the edges of the road, looking for a familiar landmark. The pain on her wrists was becoming nearly unbearable, yet she noticed that the constant pulling on the strapping was slowly stretching the leather, causing the binding to loosen around her wrists.

Slowly, trying not to let any of the soldiers see, Lucy pried her wrists apart, again and again, each time stretching leather a little bit more. After many attempts, she relaxed her wrists for a moment, and found that the binding was now so loose that she could pull it half way over her wrist!

A spark of hope rose in her heart as she considered her next move.

In the distance, a rumble of thunder broke Lucy's concentration, drawing her attention to the gathering storm. Within moments, droplets of rain began falling on the column as they continued walking down the road.

The binding around her wrist became moist as the rain began to fall in earnest. The soaked leather binding became softer against her skin and even more pliable. Lucy quickened her pace slightly, relieving all tension on her bindings. The steady rainfall had given the soldiers something else to think about while she pulled and pried, twisting her small hands until suddenly, she was free!

Lucy stole a quick glance behind and saw the rest of the column of Redcoats, now walking with their heads lowered to avoid the driving rain. She continued walking, holding her binding in her hands to avoid letting her captors know she was free.

Up ahead, the other mounted soldier, a haughty young Lieutenant, looked down at Lucy from his well-groomed steed. But she refused to look at him, afraid that her eyes might give her away. Instead, she looked at the ground, holding tightly to her bindings, waiting for her chance to make her escape. The officer then turned back forward, saying nothing.

Lucy looked up again, careful to show no emotion.

But inside, she cried, "Please, Emy, help me."

At that moment, a bolt of lightning struck the wet ground, no more than fifty feet from the head of the column. Lucy had never seen lightning strike so close. Her hair stood straight out from her head in all directions, and she could feel a jolt ripple up through the soles of her shoes.

It was all the riders at the head of the column could do to keep the horses from bolting. As frightened as she was, Lucy seized this moment of confusion. With the incredibly loud roar of thunder still crashing around them, Lucy ripped the bindings from her wrists, shouted, and lunged forward, giving the leather strip a whip-like slash against the hindquarters of the Lieutenant's horse. The animal bolted, throwing the stunned officer off. As he fell, he also knocked Coffin from his horse, and both animals began to race away. As they bolted, the third horse reared, throwing the corporal to the ground.

During the commotion, Lucy saw her chance, and ran into the forest at the side of the road. Once in the woods, she ran like she had never run before, never looking back.

In the confusion of the column, Coffin and the officers were getting back on their feet, and order was being restored in the ranks. In a moment, they realized Lucy was gone.

"Shall I order the men to pursue her, Sir?" the corporal asked the lieutenant, who was busy brushing the mud from his uniform.

The officer looked into the woods for a moment and then looked up at the blackening sky.

"No," he said, "That Yankee girl won't last the night in those woods. Let the rain and Indians have her, and then let the wild animals take what's left. We've got our orders, and we don't have time to go looking for one girl."

Lucius Coffin couldn't believe what he was hearing. He couldn't bear the thought that Lucy was about to elude him a third time.

He shouted, "No, by thunder!"

He ran to the side of the road, waving his musket in the air.

"Lucy Killgrew, you'll not escape me again!"

He raised his musket to his shoulder and fired blindly into the woods.

The lieutenant rushed to Coffin's side, grabbing him by the shoulder and whirling him around.

"Coffin! What are you doing?"

"You can't let that girl go!" screamed Coffin. "I'm telling you, she's dangerous!"

"And I'm telling you," the lieutenant shouted in return, "we have our orders, and we're not going to chase through the woods in search of one girl!"

Coffin turned and stared at the lieutenant, his face flushed with rage and frustration.

"But, lieutenant," Coffin began, but the officer cut him off.

"Corporal," he said, "Order the men to fire a volley into the woods. If the girl's determined to run, let's give her something to run *from.*"

The corporal quickly assembled the troops and ordered them to prime and load their muskets. Then he lifted his sword and gave the order to fire. With a huge explosion, the entire company fired in unison, sending a volley of shot ripping into the forest.

As she ran, Lucy heard the thunder of the rifles behind her. But she never slowed her pace. She raced between pine trees, sometimes feeling the sting of wet pine needles as low-hanging branches scraped across her arms as she covered her face.

She ran blindly for what seemed like miles, until exhaustion finally overtook her. Then she staggered and stumbled, grabbing hold of a large white pine for support. She leaned against the tree, trying to catch her breath as the rain continued to pour down all around her.

Her heavy breathing and the sound of her heartbeat were the only sounds she could hear. Long moments went by, and her breathing began to slow. She looked around at the gathering darkness. She was free, but this certainly was not home.

Lucy wrapped her arms around herself, trying to retain what little warmth she could, and for the first time in days, Lucy Killgrew began to weep.

Feeling more alone than ever, she inched her way down the trunk and sat huddled at the base of the old pine tree. She was tired, frightened, and hungry. Nevertheless, exhaustion finally overtook her, and she fell asleep.

When she awoke, the morning sky was gray and cloudy, and a gentle mist from low-lying clouds hung in the air. Shivering from the cold, she stood up and surveyed her surroundings. Her muscles felt as stiff as cold glass.

Slowly, she massaged her arms, trying to bring some warmth and feeling back into them. She peered into the forest but could see nothing out of the ordinary. Yet, she couldn't shake a feeling of uneasiness. Had she really escaped, or were the Redcoats looking for her, even now?

Lucy continued to scan the woods but saw and heard nothing unusual. She wasn't sure of the reason, but somehow, she sensed that she was not alone.

Then, suddenly, there was crash off to her right, and Lucius Coffin came running out from between two pines about twenty-five yards away, a pistol in one hand and a knife in the other.

Lucy screamed and turned to run, but her cold muscles refused to comply. She instead, fell to the ground as Coffin, his eyes full of fury, closed the distance between them.

Lucy knew this was the end. Coffin would finally have his revenge, and there was nothing she could do about it. Just as she was struggling to her feet, Coffin was upon her, his hand reaching high to drive the knife into her chest.

Lucy could see the rage in Coffin's face as he began to lunge forward, the knife flashing against the gray sky. But just as he began to move his arm toward her, Coffin's body suddenly stiffened, he grunted, and his eyes filled with pain and surprise. Then he fell forward, his entire weight falling onto Lucy's body.

For a moment, Lucy was dazed. But then she pushed Coffin's body away, and as she struggled out from underneath, she saw an arrow sticking out of the dead man's back.

Lucy rose and, ignoring the pain in her muscles, quickly ran into the thick forest.

She had escaped the Redcoats and Coffin and was now being pursued by a lone Huron.

She ran and ran, never giving a thought to direction, until she finally approached a small clearing. This was not good. She knew enough about the ways of the woods to know that it wouldn't be safe to run out into the open.

Instead, she ran along the edge of the clearing, staying under the cover of the forest. But as she ran, her foot caught on a root, and Lucy fell to the ground like a sack of flour, her head striking a large stone.

She heard a soft, dull *thud* and felt a sharp pain in her temple as her head hit the stone, but out of instinct, she instantly rose to her feet and again attempted to run. But she had only gone a few feet when a searing pain began to surge through her head. She could feel blood trickling down the side of her face, and waves of blackness began to cloud her vision.

Her eyes seemed unable to focus clearly. She staggered from tree to tree, finally stumbling to the edge of the clearing. She knew she needed to stay in protection of the woods, but just as she turned to move back into the forest, her legs buckled beneath her, and she fell again.

But this time, her mind began to drift away, toward the darkness that seemed to be swirling all around her. Blackness began to fall over her eyes like a curtain as she lay helpless on the forest floor. Then, just before she slipped into unconsciousness, Lucy saw the sky disappear, blocked out by the shadow of a huge Indian.

Chapter Ten

Mayfair

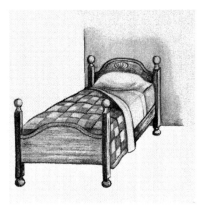

EVERY YEAR FOR THE last one hundred years, *The Chronicle*, Mayfair's local newspaper, had published an annual Almanac. By all accounts, the weather this summer was supposed to be an even mixture of sun and rain, and on this particular day, the sun had just begun to burn off the light morning clouds that hovered over the tiny town.

Clank, clunk, clank, clunk.

Everyone on Billy Schmidt's paper route knew their paper was on its way, judging by the sound of his pedal as it hit his bicycle's chain guard. The birds were singing in the trees as the ten-year-old boy, delivering the morning edition of *The Chronicle*, made his way down the street.

The town of Mayfair was not much more than a two-lane through street, with a dozen or so smaller roads crisscrossing Main Street at various points. There was Hale Avenue, Miller's Lane, and MacAllister Way; all but a few of the roads had been named after the founding families who had settled the town centuries ago.

Clank, clunk, clank, clunk.

One by one, newspapers slid along stone walkways, leading to white, wooden, single-family homes that stood proudly amid lush green lawns. Almost all of Mayfair was like that, and while much of the rest of the country was rushing headlong into a new century, Mayfair seemed comfortably content to remain much like it had been in the 1950s.

Large oak trees, growing along the narrow sidewalks, offered cooling shade against the summer sun, as well as a kind of stark beauty during the harsh winter months.

Along Main Street, the shops and businesses were getting ready for another working day. The owner of the Mayfair Market lowered the awnings over the windows of the store, while other merchants were also out in front of their establishments, sweeping and hosing off the side-walks. The green shades inside the windows of the Farmer's Bank of Mayfair lifted, letting in the bright golden rays of the morning sun.

Sheriff Washington drove by and waved to Mr. Greene, who was out in front of his post office raising the flag.

On the corner, across the street from the post office, was a tree that everyone called Lover's Oak. Its trunk proudly bore the initials of dozens of young lovers, past and present, now preserved for all time in the bark of the massive old tree.

Clank, clunk, clank, clunk.

Billy and his old red Dakota Flyer were almost finished

with the route when the boy heard the engines above him. He looked up, just as the plane lowered its landing gear. Although Billy didn't know it, Randy and Stephanie MacAllister were aboard the small plane, on the last leg of their flight from California to Mayfair.

Neither Stephanie nor Randy said a word as they looked out the windows of the twin-engine plane. The nearer they got to Mayfair, the more subdued they both became. Even Randy was not looking forward to spending five weeks cooped up in Nowhere Hicksville.

Both children were feeling as if this summer was some kind of punishment for all the small misdeeds they'd gotten away with over the course of their lives. They felt as if the cosmic wheel of fate had finally caught up with them—and with a vengeance.

South of Main Street, near the city limits, were a number of older homes. That would be the area where Stephanie and Randy would spend their summer.

To the east and west of that group of homes stood fields of tall grass, its green and yellow stalks reaching for the sun, swaying gracefully in the morning breeze.

Just north of Mayfair was Hudson's Forest, where little had changed since Colonial times. Somehow, those primal woods had been spared the heavy hand of man, and the birds and animals that lived there still foraged and fought, lived and died, exactly as they had for thousands of years.

The sun was well over the horizon, and the last of the low-lying fog was quickly dissipating as the small plane finally touched down onto the well-tended runway.

Stephanie and Randy looked through the windows and expressed their great disappointment as the aircraft made its way toward the tiny red brick terminal.

When the plane had come to a complete stop, and the

engines had shut down, the brother and sister began to collect their belongings.

Once they'd climbed down the steps that had been wheeled to the side of the plane and then walked toward the terminal, Stephanie and Randy could see their grandmother, Betty MacAllister, waiting, along with their aunt, Susan Durham, who'd also brought along her children, Benjamin and Alexandra.

Eleven-and-a-half-year-old Randy was a typical Californian. Much to his mother's horror, he always wore his favorite faded blue denims with the knee cut out of each leg and multicolored short-sleeved shirts. He wore his hair short and spiked, and his worn running shoes were always tied loosely. He was tall, blond, and good-looking, and he never went anywhere without a portable radio headset, which he wore either around his neck or over his ears.

Randy wasn't happy at the prospect of having to "do time" in Mayfair, but his fertile and inventive mind was already giving thought to the possibility of new adventures.

Stephanie was thirteen and, like her brother, had no desire to be in Mayfair for the summer. She was more reserved than her brother, and less adventuresome. She therefore, didn't take well to change. She was, however, intelligent, and she knew that, no matter how boring it might get, summer wouldn't last forever. She'd simply do whatever she had to do to, just to get through the next five weeks—with as little hassle as possible. Then she could return to California and the real world.

Stephanie was also tall—taller than her brother, though he was gaining fast. Her large hazel eyes and attractive smile had already attracted several boys back home. She always dressed well and liked spending time with her friends at the malls and gallerias. She was slightly heavier than most of her friends, but her daily exercise routine kept her healthy and athletic. She sighed, pushed back her long auburn hair and prepared to face the worst summer vacation of her life.

Randy walked slightly ahead of Stephanie as they neared the terminal.

He looked back at his sister and said, "It's show time, Steff!"

Then, as she watched Randy disappear inside the terminal door, she heard someone shout, "There he is! Randolph, sweetie pie, you made it!"

Randy, with a pitiful look on his face, turned and looked at Stephanie as she stepped inside the door. His face reminded Stephanie of the look she'd seen on the face of a gopher her father had caught in the trap last summer.

At the same time, Stephanie felt as if that same look was probably etched into her face, as well.

Let's get it over with, she thought. *Try to smile.*

Stephanie hadn't seen either her grandmother or aunt since she was about six, but she had no doubt whatsoever that the colorfully dressed older woman in her mid-sixties rushing toward them was Grandma Betty, and the younger woman in her wake was Aunt Susan.

The horn-rimmed glasses her grandmother wore were quite noticeable, since they far exceeded the width of her face. With every step, they slipped a little farther down the bridge of her nose. Then, without a thought, her hand went up and pushed the glasses back into place.

As Grandma Betty ran forward, waving and pushing up her glasses, she called out happily, "Yoo-hoo! Stephanie! Randy!"

Stephanie wanted to melt into the asphalt. She couldn't remember the last time she had been this embarrassed.

Her grandmother's hair was snow-white and tied up in

a bun on top of her head. She wore a simple but definitely colorful dress and carried a large handbag with the strap anchored securely in the crook of her arm.

Betty MacAllister was well known in Mayfair. She had taught elementary school for more than forty years, and most of the townspeople, young and old, referred to her as "Miss Betty."

Stephanie watched with muted dread as her grandmother tried to hug the life out of Randy. For his part, Randy stood as still and as limp as a rag doll, waiting for the ordeal to end. Stephanie knew her turn was next. It was a little like waiting in line for an execution. Suddenly, a pair of small hands startled Stephanie, grabbing her skirt from behind.

"Hi, cuz. I'm Alexandra, but you can call me Mouse. Everyone else does. I'm eight years old."

Alexandra stood about four feet tall. She was thin, wiry and wore a mischievous smile. Her hair was ash-blonde and thick with curls that twisted and intertwined down her back. Her small nose was covered with tiny freckles and, since she was missing her two front baby teeth, her speech had a heavy lisp.

"So, you're from California, huh? I'd like to go there sometime. Maybe we could share your room, if I did, huh?"

"Mouse, how many times have I told you not to run ahead of me?" said Susan, running to catch up with the little girl.

Without warning, Grandma Betty spun Stephanie around and gave her a huge hug, saying, "Oh, it's good to see you again, Stephanie dear. It's been such a long time!"

"You probably don't even remember me," said Susan, spinning Stephanie back around and also giving her a hug.

"But I remember you. My, my, you're gorgeous!"

"Aunt Susan," replied Stephanie, smiling as if she remembered her well.

"That's right," said Susan proudly. "What a memory this girl has!"

After Stephanie had recovered from the dizziness of all the spinning, she studied her aunt Susan. The resemblance between Susan and Stephanie's father was remarkable. Aunt Susan was an attractive woman, in her early thirties, with short dark hair that was neatly brushed straight back into a ponytail. She had a slight tan that highlighted a thin gold chain around her neck. She was dressed in slacks and a white blouse.

"You guys are staying here all summer! Isn't that great?" said Alexandra.

Stephanie didn't know this child, but she was already starting to dislike her. Undaunted, Alexandra stared up at Stephanie with a wide grin and sparkling green eyes.

"Yes, well…"

Susan interrupted Stephanie's answer, reaching around and pulling a shy boy, about Stephanie's age, out from behind her back.

"There's someone else here I'd like you two to meet," Susan said. "Randy, Stephanie, this is your cousin, Benjamin."

"Ben," the boy said, looking at his cousins shyly.

Ben had never been outside of Mayfair and was truly a country boy, both in the way he dressed and the way he acted. He'd just turned thirteen but was an inch or so taller than Stephanie. He was thinner than Randy but more muscular, and his brown hair was cut short—but he was similar to Randy in some ways. He also liked to wear jeans, although he preferred to have the knees intact. He also wore short-sleeved shirts, but his were plaid.

Unlike Randy, though, he liked his running shoes laced up tightly.

Susan grabbed Alexandra firmly and said, "And I guess you've met this little terror—she's your cousin Alexandra."

Randy walked over to Ben and shook his hand.

"Hi," said Randy as he looked at Ben's plaid shirt. "Nice shirt. It looks a little like Kansas from the air."

Stephanie gave Randy a warning nudge, since keeping her bratty brother in line was one of the promises she'd made to her mother.

"Hi," said Ben, looking at Randy's pants. "Nice pants. Did you have a rough flight?"

Little Alexandra, wiggling free of her mother's grasp, stepped up to Randy and looked up at him with her hands on her hips.

"Isn't anyone going to say hi to me?" she demanded. "How's it going, Randolph?" she said, thrusting out her hand and shaking Randy's vigorously.

Randy quickly pulled his hand away and then leaned down slightly, so he could look Alexandra directly in the eyes.

"It's Randy, not Randolph," he said firmly. "And I'm fine. How are you doing, Moose?"

"It's not Moose, it's Mouse!" Alexandra said loudly. Then she smiled and said, "And I'm fine, too!"

With a smug little grin, Alexandra turned her attention to Stephanie.

Before the little girl could say anything, Stephanie leaned over and gave her a hug, saying, "Hello, Alexandra."

"Well," said Susan, "Let's get your bags; we can't stand around the airport all day."

Everyone shared the chore of carrying the bags. As

they walked toward the car, Alexandra walked close beside Stephanie.

"Was the plane ride fun, Stephanie?" asked the little girl. "Did you get sick or anything? I bet if I went up in a plane, I'd barf—and I bet Ben would bar—"

"That's enough, Mouse," said Grandma Betty.

Evidently, this was normal behavior for Alexandra, thought Stephanie.

"Yeah, you little dope," said Ben. "Besides, how do you know what I'd do?"

"Oh, yeah?" said Alexandra. "What about that time on the Ferris wheel when you—"

"Mouse! You're going to get it!" Ben said, becoming increasingly embarrassed.

Alexandra seemed to have no fear of Ben, especially with both her mother and grandmother standing next to her. Besides, she knew her brother really loved her, in spite of everything. At least, that's what her mother had always told her.

"That's enough, both of you!" said Susan firmly. "You don't want to give Randy and Stephanie a bad impression now, do you?"

Stephanie thought *a bad impression? How could it get any worse?*

"I've got a whole bunch of Barbie dolls," Alexandra said, tugging at Stephanie's skirt. "We can play Barbies all summer! Pretty great, huh?"

So I was wrong, Stephanie thought, working hard to keep a smile on her face. *I guess it can get worse. A lot worse...*

☆ ☆ ☆

The ride to Grandma Betty's house was, for the most part, uneventful. The big city children couldn't seem to gather enough interest to ask any questions about the area or the landmarks they passed along the road, although they were both relieved to learn that they'd be staying with their grandmother and not their aunt. At least, they'd been spared the horrifying prospect of listening to Ben and Alexandra argue twenty-four hours a day for the next five weeks.

The car finally slowed and came to a stop with a squeak.

"Here we are!" said Grandma. "Be it ever so humble."

"We're going to let you kids settle in," Aunt Susan said. "Ben and Alexandra can come by and show you around town tomorrow."

Randy and Stephanie slowly walked toward their new summer home. Stephanie hung back slightly from her brother and Grandmother while she studied the small, white Cape Cod-style home. The little house looked as if it had been lifted right out of a storybook. The windows on the first floor were bordered on each side with blue shutters, and underneath each window was a light pastel-green flower box. In each box, a variety of flowers were in full bloom.

"Stephanie," her Grandmother said, looking back, "are you coming, dear?"

"Coming, Grandma," Stephanie said, as she began walking toward the house.

When she reached the front door, Grandma Betty paused and began to rummage around in her large purse. After a few moments, she smiled as she pulled out a large key ring.

"Here we are!" She slipped a key into the lock and then turned the knob and swung the door open.

"I don't suppose this is what you're used to in California," she said, "but I hope you'll like it here."

As Stephanie and Randy walked in, Grandma Betty said, "Just leave your bags at the foot of the stairs. I'll show you your bedrooms later."

The living room was filled with a heavy, pillow-filled sofa and several large chairs that took up much of the room. But it was the beautiful, antique cherry wood cabinet, filled with fine, delicate porcelain pieces, which dominated the room. Stephanie's first thought was that she could never be comfortable in a room like this.

"On the left is the den," Grandma Betty said, ushering the children through the house.

The den contained less-formal furniture, a television, and a bookcase, which was filled with books of all sizes and descriptions. Near the large, well-worn sofa, amid the soft yellow rays of the sun that poured in through the parted window curtains, was their late grandfather's favorite armchair. Its threadbare armrests had held many children over the years. As Stephanie looked at the armchair, her heart suddenly began to beat a little faster and a smile spread across her face.

"I've seen that chair," she said excitedly. "I have a picture of my father when he was a little boy—and he was sitting right there."

Then Stephanie caught herself, saying, "This is a little weird."

"You should remember that chair. When you were a little baby," said Grandma Betty, "you used to fall asleep in your grandfather's arms while he sat in that chair."

Stephanie suddenly felt her legs carrying her forward as if they had a mind of her own. They carried her up to the wall, which was covered with framed photos, behind her grandfather's chair. Some of the photos were fairly new (there was one of her and Randy that had been taken at Knott's Berry Farm only a couple of months ago) and some were old and faded. Stephanie reached out her hand as if to touch the glass of the old photo of her grandfather as a young man. He was so young, standing proudly and wearing a military uniform.

Her gaze moved from picture to picture, next pausing on what was obviously a wedding portrait of her grandfather and Grandma Betty. As was the custom back then, neither one of them was smiling.

As her eyes moved to the next frame, a cold chill seemed to shoot through her body like an electric spark. She suddenly had a hard time breathing. Her heart began to pound, and it made no sense. After all, it was only a picture of...*herself*!

At the same time, she knew that it couldn't possibly have been a picture of her. It was an ancient black-and-white photo, more brown than black, actually—and faded and torn in places. The young woman in the photo was wearing a long full dress—a kind that Stephanie had never worn in her life.

"Who..." Stephanie's voice failed.

She swallowed and tried again.

"Who...who is this, Grandma?" Stephanie finally asked, trying to keep the shaking out of her voice.

Grandma Betty stepped forward and peered at the photo intently. "That's your great-grandmother, Gertrude MacAllister, your grandfather's mother."

"She...she looks just like me," Stephanie said quietly. She couldn't seem to take her eyes off the photograph.

"You're a MacAllister," her grandmother said simply. "Blood will tell."

But Grandma Betty's words seemed to fade away as Stephanie continued staring at the old photo. It was if time and space had melted away, and for a long moment, she seemed to be suspended somewhere between the present day and that long ago time she saw in that picture.

Then suddenly, she heard a sound that seemed to come from somewhere far in the distance. She strained to listen, and even as she did, the sound seemed to grow louder. After a few moments, she recognized the sound—it was the sound of a fife and drums, playing some sort of marching tune, like she had heard once in an old Revolutionary War movie.

The noise grew louder and louder, and it was all Stephanie could do not to run to the window and see if a parade of soldiers, dressed in Colonial era uniforms, their muskets and bayonets at the ready, was marching down the streets of Mayfair.

It was a surreal moment, and just as Stephanie was about to give in to the temptation, the noise stopped, and she felt herself being snapped back to the reality of the present.

As Stephanie regained her composure, she could hear Grandma Betty talking.

"...and that old photo is part of your history, Stephanie. That, and all the others, and your grandpa's chair... it's all a part of you—who you are now, and where you come from."

Stephanie had no idea what her grandmother was talking about, or how long she'd been talking. To be polite and to hide the fact that she hadn't really been listening she said, "Yes, Grandma."

"Yes, what?" said Grandma Betty.

"Yes, I think you're right," said Stephanie, still trying to cover her inattention.

"I'm glad to hear you say that," said Grandma Betty. "There aren't a lot of thirteen-year-old girls who have such an appreciation of history.

Oh, that's what she's been talking about, thought

Stephanie. Until a moment ago, she'd had no interest in history, either. But now she found herself wanting to know more about the woman in the old photo, and the invisible thread that somehow seemed to bind the two of them together, across the centuries.

This was something she hadn't expected. For the first time in her life, Stephanie MacAllister began to understand that she was just a tiny thread in the vast tapestry of history—and she would not be who she was today if it hadn't been for each and every other thread that had come before!

"Are you alright, Stephanie, dear?" asked Grandma Betty.

"Yes, Grandma, thank you."

Grandma Betty looked carefully at her granddaughter. It had been a long time since she'd been around teenagers, and she wondered if this was just a normal teenage thing she was witnessing. She decided to let it go.

"Well, if you'll follow me, we'll go out to the kitchen. I imagine you two could use a bite to eat after your long flight," Grandma Betty said, turning to leave the room.

Like a zombie, Stephanie followed Randy and Grandma Betty as the tour of the house continued, but for the next several minutes, she wasn't quite with them. Her mind was still busy, trying to grasp the infinite complexities of the universe that had opened before her just a few moments ago.

As they neared the end of a long hallway, Grandma Betty said, "Up front, on the right, is the dining room, and on the left is the kitchen. Are either of you hungry?"

Randy immediately said yes, but Stephanie told Grandma Betty that she would like to go up to her room.

"Of course, dear," said Grandma Betty. "Your room

is on the right, just at the top of the stairs."

Stephanie climbed the wooden stairs, her mind on autopilot. She hoped it would only be a few more minutes until the world around her once again began to take on real meaning and substance.

When she reached the top of the stairs, she heard Grandma Betty call from downstairs, "Have a nice rest, dear. We'll try to be quiet so you can take a nap and get settled in."

Stephanie turned the handle and pushed the door open gently. The bedroom wasn't overly furnished, but it did seem to contain quality pieces that, by their look, had been in the family for years.

Her room was wallpapered with a yellow floral pattern that had faded over the years. In one corner was a small four-poster bed, and against the opposite wall stood a chest of drawers. The hardwood floor was covered with a circular rug. Under the window was the red steamer trunk that contained her clothes, which had been shipped ahead by her parents.

As Stephanie looked at the sparse, but pleasant, room, an unexpected feeling of contentment and *belonging* settled over her like a warm blanket. It was hard to explain, but it somehow felt as if she had just come home.

"Grandma...it's beautiful! Thank you," Stephanie said softly, even though her grandmother wasn't in the room.

Stephanie walked slowly around the room, walking gingerly as if she was afraid she'd break some sort of magical spell. The feeling that she belonged there caught her off guard. After all, she'd been dreading this day for weeks before she and Randy finally got on the airplane that would take them to Mayfair. It was all so mysterious—and a bit exciting—which was a pleasant surprise.

In spite of herself, she found herself wondering what else might happen over the next five weeks.

Knowing Randy, the only thing he'll want to do is watch TV—or find ways to drive me crazy, thought Stephanie.

Then she noticed something she hadn't noticed while she had been so preoccupied. The room was totally silent—quiet enough to be a little unsettling. Coming from a big city, she definitely wasn't used to such quiet. But even though the silence was a bit eerie, Stephanie walked over and sat on the edge of the bed. The soft mattress yielded gently as she sat down. Then she kicked off her shoes and flopped onto her back, where she felt her head being cradled by a pair of large, fluffy pillows.

Stephanie's eyes became heavy as she lay looking up at the white ceiling. She closed her eyes, trying to absorb everything she'd experienced today. Instantly, images began to appear, swirling out of the reddish blackness behind her eyelids. There was a sound, far away, like a muffled popping sound.

Muskets, she thought idly, without knowing why. But even as her mind was drifting away, a small part of her subconscious asked, "Muskets? Where in the world did *that* come from?"

But she was so tired, and the bed felt so comfortable, so...familiar...that she let her thoughts continue to drift away....

Suddenly, she was dreaming—and yet, she knew she was dreaming—and in her dream, she saw the same old oak tree that she'd seen when she closed her eyes on the plane. The full moon was still caught in the branches of the tree just as before, and sitting beneath the tree was a girl about Stephanie's age, dressed in buckskin, writing something in a small book.

Stephanie sensed that the girl was tired, hungry, and frightened. Then, just as the image began to fade, the young girl raised her head and looked directly into Stephanie's eyes.

There was a look of hope and of pleading in the young girl's eyes. They were asking—no, they were *begging* something of her, but Stephanie couldn't understand what it was.

And then, as quickly as it had come, the image disappeared. For a moment, Stephanie's mind struggled to understand what the girl had wanted, but soon, that desire seemed to fade, as well.

✩ ✩ ✩

"Stephanie, dear...wake up, sleepy head. You don't want to sleep the day away, do you?"

It was her Grandma Betty's voice.

Stephanie slowly awoke and looked up to see her grandmother standing over her.

For a moment, Stephanie wasn't sure if she was really seeing her grandmother or if she was still dreaming.

"Grandma? What time is it?" Stephanie finally asked, slowly sitting up.

"A little after one, dear. I made you some lunch— sandwiches and a cup of nice, hot stew. I hope you like it. Randy already ate. You know how hungry growing boys are."

When Stephanie didn't move or say anything for a few moments, Grandma Betty asked, "Do you just want to rest awhile longer, dear?"

No, I...I was just having a dream, that's all, Grandma. I'm OK. In fact, I am kind of hungry."

Stephanie followed Grandma Betty back downstairs, and as she pushed open the kitchen door, the aroma of homemade stew swirled around her like a warm hug.

The kitchen was perfect. If Stephanie had been asked to design the perfect country kitchen, this is the one she would have created. There was a large white gas stove with a copper vent snaking up through the ceiling. Beside the stove, spaced by a narrow counter, was a white, double door refrigerator. A mosaic of multicolored bits of paper seemed permanently attached to the doors by insect-shaped magnets. A long counter with a double sink stretched across the other wall.

Randy was seated at the table on the right side of the room. The wall behind him contained a large picture window, from which Stephanie could see several houses off to the left and grass-covered fields and forest to the right.

"You have to try this stew, Steff," said Randy. "It's really something!"

Grandmother crossed to the stove where a large white enamel pot, slightly chipped here and there around the rim, was simmering.

"Be a dear, Stephanie, and bring me that bowl there on the table."

"Here you go, Grandma."

"Thank you, dear. Now go and sit and I'll bring you some stew."

Stephanie took a seat facing her brother and watched as her grandmother filled the bowl with piping hot stew.

"Here you go!" said Grandma Betty. Then she added, "Oh dear, it looks like we're in for some rain."

Outside, dark gray clouds were gradually covering the noonday sun.

"It's just as well," said Grandma Betty. "This way, you'll be able to stay indoors and settle in without having the feeling that you might be missing something outside."

When lunch was over, Stephanie carried the dishes to the sink and looked out at the grass in the fields, now swaying with the growing winds.

"Take a look at this Randy," she said, pointing out the window.

Randy walked over and looked outside. "What? I don't see anything."

"Look at the grass. You can see the wind currents in the movement of the grass."

"Fascinating!" he said with a pretend yawn. "Simply... fascinating...."

Then the rain began—lightly at first, then building into a hard downpour. For two kids from Southern California, seeing rain like that was an event. Even so, the rest of the day seemed to pass slowly. That afternoon and evening were spent in discussions with Grandma Betty about California, friends, parents, and school.

Stephanie excused herself early. The rigors of the trip had finally caught up with her, and she was suddenly very tired. Upstairs, she lay in bed, listening to the sound of rain on the roof. She didn't quite understand the strange events of the day, but for the time being, she decided to just let it be—and tomorrow was another day.

Within seconds, she was sound asleep—and if she had any more dreams that night, she didn't remember them when she woke up the next morning.

Chapter Eleven

Gooferville

BRIGHT AND EARLY THE next morning, Ben and
Alexandra came by to take their two cousins on a
tour of Mayfair.

A "shortcut" through the field had long ago been cut
deep by the children of past generations. To Stephanie and
Randy, the field looked like an endless sea of wild grass, but
somehow the route was well marked in Ben's mind. He'd
spent his entire life wandering this area; he knew and loved
every blade of grass.

"And this tree," he said, "is called a tamarack."

As Ben gazed at a group of pines, a rustling noise came
from behind them. He whispered to the others, "Stop where
you are! Look over there."

"Where?" asked Randy.

Ben pointed in the direction of the pines.

"Over there," he said.

The children looked where Ben was pointing. As they watched, straining to see what had caught Ben's eye, a young white-tailed deer suddenly leaped out of the high grass and scurried into the forest. For Stephanie and Randy, who had never seen a deer in the wild before, it was a magical moment.

"Wow!" yelled Randy. "How did you know he was there?"

"It was a she," said Ben. "I just knew, that's all. I could tell by the size, head, and shape."

As the four cousins continued walking, Randy could hear other rustling in the nearby bushes.

"Shhh!" he ordered, pointing toward the woods. "I think I hear another deer!"

Ben smiled and said, "Naw, it's only blue jays, looking for bugs and stuff."

For the next few minutes, hardly a word was spoken. The grass was high and tangled, and it took quite an effort to push through it.

Stephanie noticed that her legs had two or three tiny cuts from the sharp blades of grass. She was getting hot and tired, and the novelty of trudging through the wilderness was beginning to wear thin.

"Is there anything to do in town? Any malls?" she asked, slapping at a bug that had been flying around her head for the past several minutes.

"No, no malls," Ben said. "We do have a theater, though."

"And there's candy at the General Store," Alexandra added. "That's my favorite!"

"Wonderful," Randy said dryly, "a General Store and

one whole movie theater. This summer's gonna just fly by."

"That's what we're all here for—to make sure you never have a dull moment," Ben said under his breath.

"Hey, guys, let's not fight," Stephanie said, wiping the sweat from her brow. "We're stuck here in Gooferville, so let's make the best of it."

The instant the words had left her lips, Stephanie regretted saying them. She looked at Ben, who was looking at the ground with a frown on his face. A silence fell over the group as they walked.

"I'm sorry, Ben," Stephanie said. "I didn't mean that. It's just that this place is so different from where we come from."

"Yeah," Randy continued, oblivious to the fact that he was hurting Ben's feelings, "where we live, they've got running water and electric lights! This place is nothing but trees and farms brought to you in wonderful Smell-o-rama."

Ben stopped and turned to face Randy squarely.

"Listen!" he said. "We happen to live here, and it ain't that bad. Besides, you'll get used to it after a while."

"Randy, shut up," Stephanie said, punching him in the arm. "You're such a dweeb!"

Randy rubbed his arm and looked at Stephanie. He had no idea why she'd punched him.

"It was just a joke," he said. "Geez!"

A few minutes later, the kids crossed the road and walked toward Mayfair Market, the community's grocery store. A wooden sign, with large white double Ms, had hung from the old iron supports above the awning ever since the store first opened, back in the 1920s.

The children stopped in front of the large store windows. For Stephanie, it was like stepping back in time. This store was definitely nothing like the malls back home! In the window, she could see a few faded bolts of cloth, with a blue and white flower design. There was a box of some brand of laundry detergent Stephanie had never heard of. She saw an old, rusty two-man saw, a flashlight, a lantern, and several old-fashioned wooden rattraps.

She sighed deeply and tried to keep smiling, but it was getting tougher and tougher. Life in Mayfair—if you could call this living—wasn't going to be easy.

Alexandra stopped to wave at the clerks inside.

"Hi, Thelma! Hi, Judy!" she yelled.

Both women stopped what they were doing and waved back, big smiles on their faces.

"Hey, Mouse!" they said, in unison.

It was such a simple thing; waving and greeting each other, but it made Stephanie stop and think. It was very different from what she was used to, but that didn't make it strange or odd. Maybe there was something to small town life, after all. Maybe it would be nice to be in a place where people knew you by name. In the midst of that thought, her mind added, *of course, having at least one mall wouldn't hurt...*

"Do you two know everyone in town?" Stephanie asked.

"Sure," said Ben. "Don't you know everyone where you live?"

"No!" said Stephanie. "Do you mean that you know every single person in this town? What, is everyone related or something?"

"No," Ben smiled. "I guess it's just called small town living. At least, that's what my dad calls it."

"Where is Uncle Joe?" asked Randy. "He wasn't at the airfield yesterday."

"My daddy drives big rugs," said Alexandra proudly.

"That's big rigs, you moron," Ben said. "He drives a truck for a week or so, and then comes home to rest for another week or so."

"Don't you guys mind him being gone so long?" asked Stephanie.

"Not really. He actually has more time with us now than when he did when he worked in town. We have lots of fun together, dirt biking and swimming in the summer, and doing other things in the wintertime."

"Yeah, we do all kinds of neat stuff together," said Alexandra.

"Dad should be home in a few days," said Ben. "Then you guys can meet him." He looked up at the big clock over the Mayfair Bank and added, "Hey, it's almost lunch time!

"Yeah," Alexandra said, "and if we're late for lunch, Mom will give our lunch to Willie."

"Who's Willie?" Randy asked.

"He's our dog," replied Alexandra.

Stephanie, who loved animals said, "You should have brought him along."

"It isn't like Willie to want to go anywhere," said Ben. "He's pretty lazy."

"Yeah, he is pretty lazy, but he's also pretty funny sometimes," said Alexandra.

"Yeah," said Ben. "He drools a lot, and we don't bring him on long drives 'cause he tends to get the winds."

"The winds?" asked Stephanie.

"He farts!" said Alexandra, stifling a chuckle.

"Trust me, you don't want this dog tagging along," said Ben.

"And I have a skunk named Felix," said Alexandra.

"Yeah," said Ben. "But you've to be careful around him. He ain't fixed."

"We got to keep him far away from the house 'cause he's a real stinker sometimes," said Alexandra, holding her freckled nose in mock disdain.

"So far, he hasn't 'let go' on us, though," said Ben.

"Come on," said Randy. "We'd better get back."

"Why don't you guys come over and eat at our house?" asked Alexandra.

"Because I think Grandma Betty wants us to eat with her. She wants to spend as much time as she can with us," said Stephanie.

Once they'd crossed the field and then picked off the foxtails and leaves that clung to their hair and clothes, the children went back to their separate homes.

When Stephanie and Randy arrived back at Grandma Betty's, she greeted them each with a hug and a kiss.

"Come on, you two, sit down. I made a nice lunch for you."

As they sat down to eat, the phone on the wall near the table rang loudly.

"Oh dear, who can that be?" asked Grandma Betty as she picked up the receiver.

She raised the receiver to her ear and said, "Hello? Oh, hold on for a moment, will you, please?"

Cupping the receiver with her hand, she looked at the children and said, "Help yourself to the chicken—and there's lemonade in the icebox."

As Stephanie and Randy began to eat, Grandma Betty began to talk into the receiver. "Hello. Yes. Uh, huh. I see. No, no, I'll take care of it. That's fine. Bye, bye, now."

"That was Susan on the phone," Grandma Betty said. "You should know that Alexandra can't keep a secret for even a minute, and as soon as she got home, she told Susan that you two didn't seem too happy here in Mayfair. She says you called it 'Gooferville'. Is that right?"

Although Stephanie and Randy had been busy with lunch, they stopped eating and looked at their grandmother.

Grandma Betty said, "Look, I know that this is way different from Southern California and it's not easy being plopped down in the middle of somewhere totally new."

Stephanie felt bad about what she had said during their walk, and said softly, "Well, Grandma, it is very different, that's for sure."

As Stephanie struggled with what to say next, Randy added, "Ben and Mouse took us through some fields and then into town. It is pretty small around here, Grandma, and honestly, I don't see how people can spend their whole lives here."

Grandma Betty sighed, and said, "I can't argue about that. It is small here, but home is really what you make it. No matter where they live, people adapt to their environment, and just as rural living is difficult for you to understand, city living is just as hard for most of us in Mayfair to try to imagine."

Randy wiped his mouth with the napkin and said, "Well, we're here, and we should try to make the most of it. We're all going to go out again after lunch!"

"That's the spirit, Randy," said Grandma Betty. "You know, watching you use that napkin reminds me of something your grandfather used to tell me. His ancestors have lived in these parts for more than three hundred years, and according to him, the early settlers, no matter how poor, always had to have a good supply of linen napkins because they used to eat with their fingers."

"Didn't they have knives and forks back then?" asked Randy.

"Some folks may have used something sort of like a fork, with one or two prongs, but they didn't have anything that resembles what we have today," Grandma Betty said, picking up a fork and turning it slowly in her hands.

Betty was pleased to see that both children were listening intently.

"Did you know that meals were served on wooden plates, called trenchers, and that two or more people usually ate off the same plate?" she said with a smile. "And children often ate standing up at the far end of the table."

"You mean they ate with their fingers—off the same plate?" Stephanie remarked. "That's gross!"

"I think it's cool," said Randy.

Suddenly, there was a loud banging at the door. They all got up, but before anyone could get to the door, it flung open and Alexandra strode through, headed straight for the cookie jar.

Yanking out a fistful of homemade peanut butter cookies she said, "Hi, guys. Hello, Grandma."

"Hello, Mouse," said Grandma Betty with a smile.

"Where's Ben?" asked Randy.

"He's getting some stuff together," Alexandra replied as she stuffed a whole cookie into her mouth. "Come on! We've gotta get goin'."

Stephanie was halfway out the door before she turned and said, "Thanks for lunch, Grandma; it was really good."

"Yeah, thanks Grandma," said Randy.

"I want you all to be careful in those woods and don't stay out too long!" Grandma Betty called from the doorway as she watched the children sprint toward the fields.

She watched until they were out of sight, and then closed the door and turned back into the house.

She walked into the den and sat in her husband's old chair. Ever since he had died, more than five years ago, Betty found herself sitting in his chair whenever she had some serious thinking to do. She knew it was silly, but there was something special about that old, faded chair. Every time she sat in it, she felt a feeling of comfort, and she could be totally at peace.

She liked to believe there was still a part of her husband among the springs and woven into the fabric. The thought always gave her a warm feeling. She'd never made even one important decision in the last five years without first sitting in that chair and thinking it through.

Her problem at that moment was what to do about the children. Was there something she could do to make them happier during their stay? After all, she knew that five weeks was an awfully long time to be unhappy.

Ben was waiting on the other side of the big field. He was carrying a large, red toolbox, which was slightly dented in places and scratched at the corners.

"Hey, guys," he said with a wide grin. "Do you want to see the fort I built in the woods?"

"A fort? You're kidding, right?" said Stephanie.

"Cool!" said Randy. "You've really got a fort?"

"Well, you guys can go to the fort if you want to, but I think I'm going to go look around town," Stephanie said, shaking her head slightly.

What is it with boys and forts, she thought. *They're about the dumbest things in the world!*

"Oh, come on, Steff, please come with us," said Alexandra. "It won't be any fun for me if you don't come. I'll be the only girl!"

Stephanie started to object but quickly changed her mind. There would be five whole weeks to explore the town, and going to see Ben's fort would at least take up a large part of the afternoon.

"All right, I'll come along," said Stephanie.

"Oh, good!" said Alexandra, taking Stephanie's hand as the four cousins began walking toward the woods.

"Where is the fort?" asked Randy.

"It's by a big old tree over on the army land," Alexandra said. "You'll love it! There's lots of places to hide there."

"Army land? What's that?" asked Randy.

"The military owns a lot of land around here, and there's lots of great trees and hills and other stuff for us to play around on," said Ben. "Sometimes I go there with my dirt bike."

"You got a dirt bike, too?" Randy asked, growing more excited.

"Yeah. In fact, I've got two of 'em," Ben answered with pride. "You wanna ride sometime?"

"You bet I do!" Randy yelled. "Let's go ride them now!"

Ben frowned.

"Sorry, we can't. My dad won't let anyone ride 'em till he's checked 'em out. That's a rule."

"Aw, come on, Ben," Randy whined. "Just for a little while."

Ben looked at Randy and said firmly. "No, sorry, I can't. It's a rule. If my dad found out, he'd take the bikes away and ground me. Come on. Let's go to the fort for now, and when my dad gets back, we can all ride the bikes, OK?"

"Aw—" Randy started to complain, but Stephanie nudged him in the ribs with her finger.

"Forget it, Randy. Ben says you can't ride today. So you guys go ahead and find the fort."

Then Stephanie looked at Ben and asked, "Are you sure it's all right to go on the army land? Don't they care?"

"No one's ever stopped us before," replied Ben.

Chapter Twelve

Sergeant Hacker

WITH ALL THE BASE closings worldwide, Sergeant Hacker should have been grateful for his transfer to the new Mayfair Army Storage Depot, but all he could think was how this move would affect his business.

The sergeant's business had little to do with the military—at least, not in an official, legal, or moral way. The sergeant's business had to do with stealing military supplies and then selling them to the highest bidder—and it was very lucrative.

That is, it had been lucrative while he was stationed in San Diego, where he'd had buyers lined up for whatever he could grab—anything from office supplies to an armored personnel carrier.

It had been a sweetheart of a business, and all of it pure profit.

But now, who knew? It was possible that Mayfair might turn out to be better than San Diego. After all, it would certainly be a much larger potential pool of merchandise, since several smaller facilities on the East coast were being shut down and all their supplies being consolidated in the new Mayfair depot. It was just possible that Mayfair could prove to be a gold mine for someone of his talent and drive.

But in the short run, it had been frustrating for Hacker. He had to work his way into the system all over again. He had to find new buyers, merchandise drop-off points, places to drop money, and new money-laundering schemes. It was a lot of work.

Of course, once he finally got it all set up, Hacker knew it would all be worth the effort he had put into it. Still, there was the short run to consider.

He had house payments to continue making on his place in Malibu and his condo on Maui, not to mention the payments on the Jag and the Porsche. Just to tread water, Hacker's income had to be in the neighborhood of twelve grand a month.

Hacker took a scrap of paper from his pocket and looked at a phone number he had scribbled on a piece of paper. He hated having to call a potential buyer that he'd never met before. After all, he knew that a person just couldn't be too careful in this business.

He looked at the number for a long time, trying to decide what to do. Even though the number had been given to him by the biggest private gun collector on the West Coast, a man with enough armament in his basement to supply a sizable army, Hacker was still hesitant.

What if the guy on this paper was a Fed? Hacker knew it was a risk, but he was used to weighing risks very carefully—and his track record spoke for itself.

Finally, Hacker pursed his lips, picked up the phone, and dialed the number.

"Hello," a slightly accented voice said. "Ram's Head Collectibles. How may I serve you?"

"Look, you don't know me, but your name was given to me by a mutual friend—a Mr. Wyeth...Wilson Wyeth."

There was a pause on the other end of the phone.

"Wyeth? Wyeth? No, I don't believe I know that name, but how may I help you?"

This guy is smooth, thought Hacker. He had paused just long enough to let Hacker know that he *did* know the name, yet if the call was being recorded, no one could prove it.

It was a move that made Hacker feel a bit more at ease.

"Well, I just thought I'd call and introduce myself, so to speak. I occasionally, uh, come across certain items that might appeal to *collectors* such as yourself."

"I see," the voice on the other end of the line said, "and what type of business are you in, Mr. ..."

"Procurement—military, mostly, but sometimes civilian. It depends on the customer. I've just begun working out of the new Mayfair depot. As for names, well, you can call me Mr. Smith, for now. You see, I don't make friends easily."

There was a long pause on the other end of the phone line.

"I see, Mr. Smith," the voice finally said. "And do you have any items at the present time that you think might be of interest to a collector such as myself?"

Hacker was getting tired of this cat and mouse game, but he knew he had to keep playing along. You could never be positive who you were dealing with or who was listening in on your conversation.

"I thought it might be more productive for us both if you gave me some idea of the types of collectibles you're interested in. Then, if I run across anything, we could talk."

"Yes, yes. I can see how that might prove to be most effective. Did you say you were at the new Mayfair Depot?"

"Uh, yeah, that's right. They're expanding, and within a year, this should be the biggest storage facility on the East Coast. Now what types of things are you interested in, if you don't mind my asking?"

Hacker's patience was wearing thin. He was used to dealing with people who stated their business in the fewest words possible, so he could get on with his business, but this guy was taking his own sweet time.

"My name is Mr. Rios, and perhaps we can do some business. Tell me, do you know the story of the Willow Tree sixpence?"

"What?" Hacker was no longer amused. He raised his voice and said, "Look, just tell me the kinds of things you're interested in, and—"

"Please, Mr. Smith. If the story about the Willow Tree sixpence is true, you and I stand to make a great deal of money. And it will all be strictly legal, I might add."

"Legal?"

"Well, mostly legal."

The voice now had recaptured Hacker's attention.

"How much money would we be talking about?"

"If the story is only *half* true, perhaps ten million dollars."

Hacker wet his lips. He knew that getting a share of a ten million deal would set him up for quite a while.

"I'm listening," he said.

"Some years back," Rios began, "I came into possession of some papers that quite possibly were written by General William Prescott sometime near the start of the Revolutionary War. Although I haven't been able to fully authenticate the papers as of this moment, I have reason to believe that they're genuine. In any event, the papers mention something about a shipment of rifles. The soldiers who were sent to retrieve those rifles were also given a bag containing four hundred newly minted Willow Tree sixpence coins. According to the papers, those soldiers were never heard from again, and the whereabouts of the coins is not known to this day."

There was another long pause while Hacker frowned. What kind of game was this clown playing, anyway?

"That's all very interesting," he said, "But what does that have to do with me?"

"According to the papers," Rios continued, seeming not to notice Hacker's irritation, "an empty wagon was found on what is now military land in Mayfair. I have researched the records, and there is no mention of the British having gotten hold of the weapons. Therefore, it is entirely possible that the weapons and the coins were hidden somewhere together—possibly somewhere on what is now your base of operations."

"And you say those coins are worth a bundle?" Hacker said halfheartedly. After all, what did this clown expect him to do, dig up the whole base, looking for a handful of old coins?

"Mr. Smith, each one of those coins would be worth in the neighborhood of, say, forty-five thousand dollars."

Hacker quickly did the math in his head. Four hundred coins at forty-five grand a pop. This guy wasn't talking ten million—he was talking closer to eighteen million dollars!

After another pause, Rios said, "Do you think you might be able to locate the coins, Mr. Smith? If you can, I can assure you that I have buyers ready to take delivery."

"It's a big base, Mr. Rios," said Hacker. "I wouldn't know where to begin."

"That's a pity, Mr. Smith," said Rios. "Still, if you would keep your eyes and ears open, it could be worth a great deal to both of us, yes?"

"Yeah, sure," said Hacker, "but isn't there anything else you'd be interested in right away—as a collector, I mean?"

"Well, there are a few things," Rios said. "I'm always in the market for computers. And missiles."

"Missiles?"

"TOW missiles, Stinger missiles—that sort of thing."

Hacker finally smiled. *Now you're talkin' my language,* he thought with relish.

Then he said, "Thank you, Mr. Rios, I'll see what I can do."

Chapter Thirteen

L.K.

THE CHILDREN WALKED NORTH along a narrow pathway that cut between the field and the forest.

"My dad said that, at one time, this used to be the main road to Boston and all around these parts," said Ben.

"Even British soldiers during the 'revelluson'!" said Alexandra.

"Is that true?" asked Stephanie.

"Sure," said Ben, "but if you don't believe my dad, just ask Grandma Betty. She used to be a teacher, and she knows all about that kind of stuff."

"You mean the kind of stuff we learned in school—stuff about Concord and Lexington and places like that?"

said Randy. "You mean all that stuff really happened?"

"Of course it happened, Einstein," said Ben. "You think they just make up stuff so they can put it in books? A lot of that stuff happened right around here."

"I wonder if there are any skeletons buried around here?" said Randy.

"If you find any, they're all yours!" said Stephanie.

"You mean real live skeltons?" said Alexandra, her eyes lighting up. "Maybe we should bring Willie along to help dig. He's good at that!"

"Right," Randy laughed. "Real *live* skeletons. You're such a dufus."

"I am not a dufus!" Alexandra said, crossing her arms. "I'm gonna tell Grandma that you called me a name!"

"Dufus isn't a name, squirrel-breath. It's more like a description," said Ben. "And I hate to say it, but it does kinda fit. Live with it."

"Will you guys leave her alone?" said Stephanie. Then she added, "When are we gonna get to this fort of yours, anyway?"

"It's just over there," Ben said, pointing off to his left. "There's the big old oak."

The high grass began to thin out as the cousins approached to the edge of the forest.

"Where's this government land you were talking about?" asked Randy.

"I think we're on government land right now," Ben answered indifferently. "I heard somewhere that they're gonna build some kind of big warehouse or something here pretty soon."

Stephanie began to feel a slight tingling sensation as they neared the woods. She wasn't sure exactly what it was, but somehow, she sensed that there was something unusual about this area. Every nerve in her body seemed like it was beginning to tingle. She quickly looked at her companions, hoping they were feeling the same thing, but she saw nothing unusual in their faces.

Why? she wondered. *Why am I feeling these things?*

"My dad says this forest hasn't changed a bit for hundreds of years," said Ben.

"Your dad sure knows a lot about this place," said Randy.

"I used to get tired listening to him, but now that I'm older, I find that, between him and what I learn at school, it's all more interesting to me than it used to be."

"Grandma knows lots of stuff, too," said Alexandra, still holding Stephanie's hand.

"Well, there it is." Ben said proudly, pointing to the old oak tree and the fort he and Alexandra had been working on for several weeks. "Isn't it a beaut?"

But Stephanie wasn't listening. She was busy trying to make sense of what was happening in her own mind. Suddenly, the name *Emy Moon* sprang into her thoughts. Although she'd heard that phrase in her mind before, she still had no idea what it could mean.

As they moved closer, Stephanie realized that she had seen the tree before—not once, but twice. The first time was on the plane ride to Mayfair, and the second was in a dream. It was the exact same tree, of that she was positive. Every branch, every knot was the same. The difference was that the last time she had seen the tree, there had been a young Colonial girl sitting under its branches, writing in a book.

Stephanie could hardly believe she wasn't dreaming now, but this was real—weird, but definitely real. She walked up to the oak tree and placed her hands on its bark, feeling its texture, trying to absorb whatever the tree had to offer.

Without understanding why, Stephanie somehow knew that her life was in some way tied up with this tree, though how it was all connected, she had no idea.

As if in partial answer, Stephanie suddenly felt herself wrapped in a blanket of ice-cold air, sending a chill throughout her body. Then, as quickly as it had come, it was gone.

Stephanie looked at the others, who were now busy rummaging through Ben's toolbox, getting ready to go to work.

"Did you guys feel that?" she asked.

"Feel what?" asked Ben, glancing up from the toolbox.

"That cold," she said.

"Cold! Are you kidding? It's a thousand degrees out here," said Randy, looking first at his sister and then at the fort, which had six walls, each moving out from the center in a different direction.

"So this is your fort," he said, looking over at Ben. "Still needs a little work, huh?"

"Yeah, but I think we can get it all finished by the end of summer," said Ben.

Ben looked at Randy and then pointed to the fort.

"You see, it's going to be shaped like a star when it's done. It may not look like much now, but just you wait— it'll be great when it's finished."

"How about you, Steff?" asked Randy. "Are you going to help?"

"Uh, no, I don't think so. Not right now," she replied. "You guys go ahead and get started. I think I'll just look around for a while."

"OK, you guys," said Ben, pulling out a small axe from the toolbox, "let's start gathering up more wood. We need to add another wall."

Randy walked over to a small tree and began to tug at a branch.

"Hold it!" shouted Ben. "You can only take branches and bark off the dead trees, not the living ones!"

"Why?" asked Randy.

"It's just a rule, OK? My dad made it up. There's no reason to kill living trees when there are plenty of dead branches around," he replied. "Besides, it's a whole lot easier. Look over there," he continued, pointing toward the ground a few feet away. "There's a whole dead tree lying right there. Take the axe and start hacking off the big branches."

Randy grabbed Ben's axe and said, "Thank you, Smokey Bear."

"Here, Mouse," said Ben, "you take this shovel and make an outline of where the new wall will go."

Alexandra obeyed, taking the spade and scraping a line along the ground.

Stephanie continued examining the oak, first wrapping her arms around its trunk as far as they would go. The tree was so large that her arms couldn't reach halfway around.

As she shuffled around the base of the tree, she heard a small sound from just under her feet. She looked down and noticed that she was standing on an almost solid platform of uplifted roots. She bent down to investigate.

Under the matted roots was a hollow area filled with centuries of dead leaves, and, to her surprise, a small, furry animal that was looking up at her with bright, shiny eyes!

Before she could make a sound, the tiny animal bounded up through a hole in the matted roots and darted away. About thirty feet away, it leapt onto the trunk of another tree and scurried upward, until it was lost in the shadows.

"What was that?" Stephanie asked.

Ben, who had glanced up momentarily when the small creature had first scurried out of its hiding place, said, "It was just a chipmunk. There's lots of them around here."

Although Randy and her cousins went back to their work on the fort, Stephanie again bent down and gingerly poked her finger into the hole where the chipmunk had been hiding. She found nothing, but she was still curious, so she picked up a small twig and began poking it in the hole.

Suddenly, as she moved the stick around inside the hole, Stephanie felt the twig hit something. She poked at the same spot, and the twig hit something again. After a few moments, she could tell that whatever the twig was hitting was mainly flat, and it wasn't hard enough to be a rock.

Then, without warning, another blanket of cold swirled around her.

She pulled the twig out of the hole and wrapped her arms around herself to ward off the chill. This was too strange, and she found herself beginning to feel frightened, but she knew better than to say anything to Randy or Ben—and talking to little Alexandra would have been a waste of time. She'd just have to figure this thing out herself.

Slowly, she bent back down and, this time, she carefully stuck her hand into the hole. Dry, brittle leaves met her fingers. She wasn't particularly fond of the sensation, and her mind conjured up images of slimy things, crawling all over her hand. Regardless, she forced those thoughts from her mind, gritted her teeth, and dug deeper.

Suddenly, her hand touched something. It was fairly flat; it also had something slightly slimy and cold surrounding it. Stephanie continued exploring the object with her fingers until she had determined that it seemed to be rectangular in shape, about four to six inches on a side, and about two inches thick.

Trying not to think of what kinds of creatures might be living underneath the object, Stephanie worked her fingers underneath and slowly began trying to work it free. She could hear tiny roots snapping as she carefully worked the dirt-covered object toward the surface, finally turning it on its side so she could get it out of the hole between the roots of the oak tree.

After what seemed like a long time she finally brought the object into the sunshine, and looked at it with a mixture of wonder and revulsion. It was filthy and seemed to be covered with some kind of sticky, translucent wrapping, like old waxed paper.

Carefully, Stephanie began removing the wax-like paper covering. As she did, she could see that what she had found was a book of some kind.

"Hey, you guys," she called out, "I think I've found something!"

Alexandra, who was closest, was the first to come charging up. "What have you got there, Steff?" she asked. "Is it a skelton?"

"No. I think it's some kind of book."

Mouse turned away, her interest gone. "Aw, who cares about some dumb book? I thought maybe you found a skelton."

Both Ben and Randy looked at Stephanie's dirt-covered find with mild curiosity, but neither of them seemed too impressed, either.

"What kind of book is it?" Ben asked.

"I don't know," Stephanie said, "but it looks old."

"Maybe it's a map to a pirate treasure," said Randy, a

big smile on his face. "Yo ho, Captain Steff!"

"Very funny," Stephanie said, gingerly rubbing dirt away from the old book.

Randy made a grab for the book. "Here, let me see it."

Stephanie knocked his hand away, smacking Randy's hand a lot harder than she had intended.

Randy cringed, cradling his hand. "Geez, Steff, you didn't have to break my hand. I only wanted to look at it."

"I'm sorry," said Stephanie. "You guys go back to building your fort. I'll let you know when I figure out what this is."

For a moment, no one said anything. Finally, Randy turned away, still babying his hand, and said, "She's right, guys. Let's get back to work."

While the others resumed their building, Stephanie made herself comfortable and began to carefully scratch away the clay that covered the book. As she scraped, the fragile waxy paper began to tear apart.

Seeing Alexandra's canteen nearby, Stephanie had an idea. She walked over and poured a little water on the cover of the book. Then, as she gently rubbed the book with her fingers, the mud began to melt away, and Stephanie could see that she was holding a leather-bound book in her hands.

Her heart began to beat faster. This could be a real find! There was no telling how long this book had been buried, hidden among the roots and leaves.

On the left hand corner of the cover, scorched deeply into the leather, were the initials L. K.

"Ben," Stephanie asked, "do you know anyone around here with the initials L. K.?"

Ben was busy with a saw, cutting away the leaves of a

branch Randy had just handed him. He wasn't interested in Stephanie's book, but he thought for a moment and then said, "Nope."

Stephanie carefully placed the book into her large shirt pocket. She didn't care if it was damp and still covered with a film of mud. Something told her this book was important—too important for her to deal with here and now, with all the others around. She'd look at it later, alone in her room, where she could take her time and do it right.

"Are you really gonna keep that old thing?" asked Alexandra, who had seen Stephanie put the book in her pocket.

"Well, Mouse," said Stephanie with a smile, "Maybe I'm just a pack rat at heart."

"Yeah," said Alexandra, "and who knows, maybe it really is a treasure map."

"Yeah, right," said Ben. "And maybe you're not really a little pest! Bring me the shovel, will you, please?"

Alexandra looked at Stephanie for a moment, then turned and raced back to help her brother.

As the others continued to work, Stephanie sat with her back against the old oak, wondering who L. K. might be. She was dying to open the book, but some inner voice was telling her to wait, and Stephanie decided to listen.

Chapter Fourteen

The Book

SITTING IN THE OLD, familiar armchair, Grandma Betty spent the afternoon going through some old letters that her husband had sent her while he was stationed in the Mediterranean during World War II. Lost in her memories, she didn't hear the children enter the house.

"Hi, Grandma," said Stephanie, as she and the other children walked into the den.

Looking up from her letters, Grandma Betty said, "My goodness, I didn't hear you come in. Back so soon?"

"It's six o'clock, Grandma. Dinner time," said Randy.

Alexandra walked over to the chair and looked carefully at her grandmother.

"Are you OK, Grandma?" she asked.

"I'm fine," Grandma Betty replied, wiping a tear from the corner of her eye. "I was just going through some of your grandpa's old letters. I wish you children could have known him better. Your grandpa was quite a man."

"What was he like?" asked Alexandra.

"Well," said Grandma Betty, carefully settling the letters into her lap, "he was a real family man. By that, I mean he loved his family very much. When each of you children was born, he and I were there. Even if you'd been born on the moon, he'd have insisted on being there. Oh, and he loved the outdoors."

Grandma Betty reached out and touched Alexandra's cheek, her eyes misting over again.

"He loved to go fishing. He and Stephanie's daddy used to fish all the time. I remember one time, I thought I'd fix them a lunch, and when I brought it out to Mugford's Pond, well, there they were, the two of them, both sound asleep in the boat. What a pair they were!"

"How old was Steff's daddy then?" asked Alexandra, slowly pushing aside the letters and climbing onto her grandmother's lap.

Betty looked down at Alexandra and smiled as she gave the little girl a quick hug. "He was just a little older than you are now, little munchkin," she said, tickling the squirming child. "Why, I'll bet you didn't know your grandpa built this house with his own two hands, and most of the furniture, to boot!"

"Grandpa did all that?" asked Randy.

"He sure did. All that and a whole lot more."

Grandma Betty paused again, and then said, "There never was a better husband and father, and you know, just because people die doesn't mean that everything they did in life dies with them."

For a short time, no one spoke—not even Alexandra. Everyone seemed lost in their own thoughts.

Finally, Ben broke the silence.

"Well, we'd better head for home, Grandma. Let's go, Mouse."

"Yeah, we'd better get home before we miss dinner," said Alexandra, climbing off Grandma Betty's lap.

"I know," said Stephanie with a laugh. "If you're late for dinner, your mom will give it to the dog, right?"

"Zactly!" said Alexandra.

Ben and Alexandra kissed their grandmother good-bye and quickly ran out of the room.

Grandma Betty smiled, amazed at how well Susan had her children trained. Then she smiled again, thinking of how Alexandra seemed to be the spitting image of her mother at that age.

"Grandma, would Aunt Susan really give their dinner to the dog?" asked Randy.

"They like to think so," said Grandma Betty with a chuckle. A moment later, she stopped smiling and gave Stephanie and Randy a questioning look.

"Are you two enjoying your vacation so far?"

"Sure, Grandma," said Randy.

"How about you, Stephanie?"

"Well, to be honest, I had my doubts about the whole thing—until this afternoon."

"This afternoon, dear? What happened this afternoon?"

"Can I watch TV, Grandma?" interrupted Randy.

"Of course, dear," she said. "Now tell me about your day, Stephanie."

Randy turned on the television and flipped quickly through the channels, cranking up the volume. "Oh, man. You need cable, Grandma. There's no MTV."

"No MTV," said Grandma Betty, "And turn it down a little, please."

Randy grimaced slightly but turned down the volume. "OK, Grandma. What's this, the news?"

On the TV screen, an announcer was standing beside

a long row of tractors, earthmovers, and other large equipment.

"...and in less than a week, the first phase of construction will begin on the nation's largest military supply and storage facility, right here in Mayfair—on the site of what is now known as Hudson's Wood."

As Randy switched the channel, Grandma Betty sighed, and then said, "I was hoping they'd forget to show up."

"Why?" asked Stephanie.

"Hudson's Wood has been untouched for centuries, and should be protected. I just hate to see it go. A few of us protested, but I'm afraid we lost the fight."

"Hudson's Wood?" Stephanie wondered aloud as she and Grandma Betty began walking toward the kitchen, leaving Randy on the floor, watching cartoons. "Is that where we were today? Do you know anything about a huge old oak tree?"

"Oh my, yes—and that's one of the most dreadful parts of the whole thing. I've found mention of that oak in papers as far back as 1790, and they'll probably cut it down when they expand the military base. That would be such a shame."

"Yes," Stephanie said, thinking of the old book that she still carried in her pocket. "It would be a shame."

She wasn't quite ready to share her find with anyone yet, not even with Grandma Betty. She couldn't explain it, but she felt as if the book was meant for her alone, and although she was dying to know what was in it, she wanted to be able to look at it for the first time by herself.

"Grandma, do you need me to help with dinner? I'd think I'd like to lay down for a little while, if it's OK with you."

Betty touched Stephanie's forehead with the back of her hand in a reflexive action, built on fifty years of being a mother and grandmother.

"Are you feeling OK, child?" she asked.

Stephanie winced. She hadn't meant to cause her grandmother any concern. All she really wanted was half an hour alone to look at the book.

"I'm fine, Grandma. Honest. I can help with dinner, if you need me, really."

"No dear, I'm just fixing hamburgers. You can help me with the onions and tomatoes later, if you feel up to it. You go ahead and lay down for a while."

"Well, if you're sure."

"I'm sure, dear. You run along upstairs."

As Stephanie turned to go, Grandma Betty said, "Tomorrow, if you'd like, we can go through some old things in the attic. There's no telling what kind of treasures we might find up there."

"OK, Grandma, that would be great," said Stephanie, now making her way up the stairs.

In her room, Stephanie quickly removed the book from her pocket and sat down on the bed. The late afternoon sun was streaming in through her window, making the bed the brightest spot in the room.

She carefully examined the outside of the book again, puzzling over the initials on the cover. Then she lay back on the bed, hugging the book to her chest.

I wonder who L. K. was—a smuggler, or pirate maybe. She let her imagination run wild for several moments.

Then she sat up suddenly as an amazing idea flashed through her mind. *Could L. K. be the girl I saw sitting by the old oak, writing in a book? It's possible! And could this be the very book she was writing in?*

The thought struck her like a thunderbolt, and yet, it was slightly frightening.

This is getting very weird, she thought.

As if on cue, Stephanie was suddenly enveloped in another blanket of cold air. She shivered and held the book close, and the moment she pulled the book to her breast, the coldness evaporated as if it had never existed.

Stephanie looked all around quickly, but there was nothing that could have caused such a strange sensation.

Could this *all be in my mind?* she thought. *Maybe I'm going crazy.*

She pushed those thoughts away as she laid the old book on her bed in front of her and carefully pulled open the covers of the book. She was disappointed to see that the ink had faded over the years, leaving only a few tiny light-brown marks here and there on the first page.

She carefully pulled the delicate pages apart to reveal the next two pages. Again, she saw only faded light-brown smudges. But, by holding the pages up to the light in a certain way, she could just make out what looked like a name.

"Emy."

Stephanie's mouth dropped open and her entire body grew ice cold with fear and astonishment.

Emy?

There was that name again. The same name she'd heard while she was looking at the pale full moon on the airplane and then again in her dream.

There was no doubt about it. This was now *officially* weird!

With slightly trembling fingers, Stephanie carefully pulled back the next page and was thrilled to discover that the words were readable! They were splotchy in places, but they were definitely readable!

Dearest Emy,
Mother and I made soap this day, and I

*pondered as to why we could not use the smell
against the Redcoats. The snows will soon be upon
us. I can feel the cold. Father is in Boston
towne. I hope he comes home soon. Mother says
she wishes his return. Washdays will begin on
the morrow, and all the linen is piled and
ready. I made a likeness of mother at the
bottom of the page.*
Lucy Killgrew
October 17, 1774

Stephanie looked at the bottom of the page. The lines
and curves that once were Lucy's perception of her mother
had long since become indistinguishable. All that remained
was a light brown blur.

"Lucy Killgrew," said Stephanie out loud. "L. K."

"Lucy Killgrew!" she shouted and then clamped her
hand over her mouth, realizing what she had just done.

"Lucy Killgrew!" she whispered excitedly.

She felt like a detective, piecing together long-lost
clues.

"1774! Wow! This is amazing!" she said, looking
again at the delicate words that had been written so long
ago.

She was reading the thoughts and feelings of a girl who
had been dead for more than two hundred years!

Stephanie felt a tingle rush through her body.

"I wonder who Emy is?" she said aloud.

At that moment, Grandma Betty called from the foot
of the stairs, "Stephanie, dear, dinner's ready!"

Stephanie carefully closed the book and slipped it into
her bureau drawer, beneath her socks and underwear. The
rest of her detective work would have to wait until later.

Then she called, "I'm coming, Grandma!"

Chapter Fifteen

Into the Night

STEPHANIE COULD HARDLY KEEP her mind on dinner. All she could think about was the diary, Lucy Killgrew, and the strange realization that somehow she and Lucy were *connected* It was all so bizarre. Her mind couldn't seem to latch onto any one thing, so it just kept spinning, around and around.

Grandma Betty was sure her granddaughter wasn't feeling well, and against Stephanie's feeble protests, she sent Stephanie upstairs to bed right after supper.

Randy was drafted to help with the dishes for the night, and his loud protests were music to Stephanie's ears!

But Stephanie really didn't mind being sent upstairs, although she didn't like the thought of having Grandma Betty worry about her.

In her room, with the door closed, Stephanie was

surrounded by total and complete silence. She removed the book from her bureau drawer and carried it over to the bed.

As she sat down, she glanced at the window and was surprised to see how quickly darkness had fallen. She could hear the chirping of crickets and the croaks of frogs wafting through the air. It was a type of quiet she had never known before.

There was a small gooseneck light next to her bed, and Stephanie craned the lamp so that it shone directly on the book as she gently opened to the page where she had left off before dinner.

The book was almost completely dry now, and the dirt was flaking off freely. There would have been times in Stephanie's life when she would have been horrified to see dirt and mud cascading over her perfectly-made bed, but this was not one of those times. Strangely, she wasn't sure if she would ever care about that sort of thing as much as she used to.

For some reason, she felt as if her outlook on the world was changing in some fundamental way, deep down. She didn't know if it was finding the diary that was causing it or if she was just changing as she got older, but she realized that she simply wasn't the same up-tight girl she'd been until this afternoon.

But why was she wasting time with all these extraneous thoughts?

She turned her attention back to the book. She still found it hard to believe that it had lain hidden beneath that oak tree for more than 200 years—until she had found it!

She—Stephanie MacAllister—found It.

Could it be that all of this was just coincidence? She'd had a vision of Lucy and then found Lucy's book. She had heard the name Emy twice, and then, there it was, on the second page of Lucy's book, in Lucy's own handwriting.

It was just too amazing to be a coincidence. All of this was meant to be. But what could it all mean?

It was too incredible to think about—and she felt there was plenty of time to think about the big picture later. Right now, she just wanted to continue reading Lucy's diary.

She carefully turned to the next page. The words were slightly less splotchy than on the first two she'd read and seemed to be slightly less faded, which was a good sign.

Dearest Emy,
The worst has happened. The British have
burned our beautiful home. Mother and I both
cried. Father is away with the troops. I want
very much to see him. Mother and I have taken
refuge with Mrs. Bigelow. Her husband and son
also serve with the Americans. I feel I must
also do my part, but I know mother will try to
stop me.
Lucy Killgrew
June 5, 1775

Dearest Emy,
Have joined Father at the American camp
outside Boston towne. Everything is very
exciting. A battle is only days away.
There is much tension and excitement
among the people here.
Lucy Killgrew
June 9, 1775

Stephanie stopped reading and looked out the window. She tried to imagine what it must have been like living in Colonial times. She tried to imagine what Lucy Killgrew must have been feeling at that moment. She felt an incredible empathy for that young Colonial girl who had apparently joined the American army to fight the British during the Revolutionary War, and she wondered if she could ever have had the courage to do what Lucy had done.

Stephanie gently turned to the next page of the diary, which was filled with Lucy's fine, clear handwriting.

Dearest Emy,
I believe Jonathan Bigelow and his father are
garrisoned about twenty miles away. I trust
they are well. Will try to learn more of them
soon. Jenny should be proud. I feel guilty
about Jonathan and Will Ashley. It is
confusing, liking two boys. Life in camp is
difficult but very exciting. I feel good I am
doing my part for The Cause.
Lucy Killgrew
June 10, 1775

Dearest Emy,
I can't sleep this night. At first light,
Private Weaver and I are to set out for
Black's Farm to take delivery of the rifles
he has made for The Cause. Father has
impressed upon me how important these rifles
are if we are to defeat the British and gain
control of Boston towne. I fear for Father.

The Battle for the hills may be fierce.
I hope and pray I will return in time to help.
Will Ashley kissed me this night.
I fear for him in the battle as well.
Lucy Killgrew
June 15, 1775

Stephanie stopped reading and looked around. She had the eerie feeling that someone was watching her, and even though her window was on the second floor, she got out of bed, walked over to the window, and looked out.

The moon was full, and the yard below was bathed in soft white light. Stephanie was surprised at how much detail she could make out in just the light of the full moon. She noticed that a slight breeze was rustling the leaves in the tree outside her window, but she saw nothing out of the ordinary. Certainly no one could have been watching her.

But just as she was turning back toward her bed, she glanced outside and saw something amazing. From her vantage point, it looked as if the full moon had become nestled in the branches of the maple tree outside her window!

Instantly, a cold shiver raced through her body, and the name Emy came clearly into her mind. But it was more than just a thought—it was as if someone was whispering the name into her ear, again, and again, "Emy… Emy… Emy…"

Stephanie stared at the incredible illusion for a long moment and then turned away from the window. Her mind was swirling when she settled back into bed, took a deep breath, and began to read.

Emy,
Everything has gone wrong. The British raided
Black's Farm before Private Weaver and I
arrived. We were able to load the long rifles
and powder, but Weaver was wounded and I was
forced to leave him. I pray he is safe.
A storm and the British patrols make
it impossible for me to fulfill my mission
this night. I have hidden the rifles and
powder and Willow Trees some rods north of
the Old Cross Roads Oak, beneath the lone
spruce. I must fulfill my mission by some
means. I shall never rest until the rifles
are delivered into the hands of our soldiers.
I hope and pray that father sends
a party to find me soon. I know my duty and I
shall not fail!
Lucy Killgrew
June 17, 1775

Stephanie carefully turned the brittle page, to learn what happened next, but to her horror, the rest of the pages were empty. She closed the book and again looked out the window. The full moon was framed in the exact center of the window.

Stephanie got up, walked over to the window, and opened it. Then, without thinking, she climbed out of the window and onto a large branch of the tree outside.

For a moment, she tried to convince herself that she didn't know where she was going—but she knew.

She was going out into the night.

She was going out to the Old Oak.

The only thing she wasn't sure of was—why.

Chapter Sixteen

The Meeting

THE NIGHT AIR ITSELF seemed different in Mayfair, thought Stephanie—not at all like the air she was used to in Southern California, and that was especially true on this night!

Somehow, the night itself seemed to be alive. It almost seemed to be breathing. It seemed to have weight, texture, and feeling. It was almost magical—so unlike the concrete and neon nights she'd known all her life in the big city.

Yet a small part of her was frightened. She'd never sneaked out of the house before, she'd never gone anywhere without telling someone where she was going, and she definitely had never crawled out a window onto a tree branch!

But somehow, this didn't seem as crazy as it should have, which was a little strange in itself.

In some unexplainable way, everything that was happening was *magical*. There was no other word for it—magical, because it was unexplainable.

There were so many things that had taken place in the last couple of days that she couldn't and probably would never be able to explain. There was the fact that she had known Emy was the full moon. There was the girl in her dreams, and the book with Lucy Killgrew's Initials on the cover that she now had in her possession.

And last, but definitely most important at this particular moment, there was the fact that she was now sitting on a large tree branch, just outside her second-story window in the middle of the night!

But even as Stephanie thought about all of those unexplainable events, she knew that there was one more still to come.

She knew that she had to go to the Old Oak —tonight.

Slowly she made her way to the ground, and began walking toward the big field that Ben had guided them through earlier that day, but when she reached the edge of the field, she stopped. Even in the full moonlight, everything looked different.

She stared out into the field, looking for the way into the tall grass, which was waving slightly in the gentle night air. After several long moments, she decided that maybe she was acting foolishly. Maybe it would be better to let Ben show her the way another time or two, so she'd be able to find her way in the dark on another night. After all, she had all summer.

She was about to turn back when something happened to change her mind.

It began with the strange blanket of cold air that she'd felt several times today. It swirled around her, enveloping her, almost as if it were hugging her. And then it slipped off her body like a living thing and began flowing into the field, directly in front of her. As the coldness moved forward, Stephanie could actually see the grass parting slightly. It was amazing—and a little scary—but she continued to follow the path through the field, trying not to be too afraid.

She couldn't see or touch the coldness—it always seemed to be just out of reach. It was a little like a breeze, but it was more than that—an energy, a feeling…it was impossible to put into words.

Slowly, taking one cautious step at a time, Stephanie made her way through the field, following the path being made before her. Once, she looked back and saw that the grass behind her was closing back together, blocking any thought she might have of retreat. It was a little like a scene she'd once seen in an old Cecil B. DeMille movie on late night television, showing the parting of the Red Sea for the Israelites during Biblical times.

But as she walked, a strange thing was beginning to happen. With each step, she realized that her fear was decreasing. Of course, it was bizarre—wasn't everything about this situation? But at that moment, she knew for certain that whatever lay ahead would not do her any harm.

In that instant, all her fear was gone. She smiled and picked up the pace. A few moments later, she began to run, trying to see if she could catch up to whatever force was opening the grass ahead of her.

It became like a game. *Let's see who's faster, you or me!* But no matter how fast she ran, the grass continued to part just a few feet in front of her.

She was no longer worried about where she was going. There could be little doubt: she was being led to the Old Oak.

Then, the grass started to become shorter, and she knew that she was nearing the edge of the woods. A moment later, through the moonlit shadows, she saw the Old Oak, and when she looked up, she could see the full moon—Emy Moon—directly above the treetops.

Stephanie made her way carefully toward the Old Oak. Although she had no idea what she'd find once she reached it, she sensed that it would be something that would alter her life.

She stopped about ten feet from the ancient tree and stood looking at it, bathed in the white light of Emy Moon.

For a moment, all was silent. Then the branches of the tree began to sway, even though there seemed to be no wind. Stephanie smiled and watched in fascination.

Then, as quickly as it had started, the swaying stopped, and to her surprise, Stephanie suddenly felt so tired that she could barely stand. She stumbled to the tree, yawning, and slumped down with her back against the Old Oak.

In a heartbeat, she was asleep and began to dream—but she knew she was dreaming, and in her dream, she opened her eyes and stood up.

She was still bathed in the light of Emy Moon and was still standing beneath the boughs of the oak tree—but in her dream, the oak was no longer old. It was tall and strong but not as ancient as before. Its roots weren't raised from the ground as high as they had been, and its branches weren't as thick.

It was then that she realized—this was how the Old Oak would have appeared to Lucy Killgrew, more than two hundred years ago.

In her dream, Stephanie looked down and saw that, in place of her nightgown, she was wearing some kind of soft animal skin. When she rubbed her hand along her thigh, she could feel that the skin was soft, like, like…she struggled for a word.

Buckskin. That was it! She'd never seen or felt buckskin before, but she knew instinctively that it was buckskin that she was wearing in her dream.

Then, in the distance, she heard a muffled sound, a bit like thunder, but too faint to be clear. Then she heard it again. It wasn't thunder—it was the sound of cannons.

Somewhere, not too far away, a battle was in progress. It must have been the battle for Boston towne, as Lucy had called it in her diary. She didn't question how she knew that—she simply accepted it.

She looked down once again, this time rubbing her hands over her arms, trying to make everything feel more real.

Then, without warning, Stephanie began to feel a terrible sense of fear and danger. She wasn't afraid for herself—the fear seemed to be for rifles, for father, for William Ashley, and for all the other brave Americans. And without thinking, she hated the British for forcing her to feel this fear.

The dream seemed to be turning into a nightmare.

Emy, help me! she thought. She could feel her mind being taken over by the feelings of fear and panic. Yet, there was an even greater fear in the back of her mind. *If I don't stop these feelings, I'll lose myself to them entirely!*

The stillness was shattered by an even louder explosion, followed closely by a low, deep, rumble that seemed to roll on forever. Stephanie looked up and saw that the sky had turned cloudy. There was a storm brewing.

I've got to hide the rifles. Lucius Coffin and the Redcoats will be back this way any minute. I can't let them—

Suddenly, Stephanie's mind snapped back to reality. She pounded her right hand against her leg hard enough to cause a bruise. However, nothing seemed to have changed! Even though she was awake, everything around her was still the same!

In an instant, she understood. She was no longer Stephanie MacAllister. Somehow, she had been transported back in time—back to the year 1775—and she'd been placed inside the mind and body of Lucy Killgrew!

It was incredible, but she was experiencing the things that Lucy had experienced on that fateful day in 1775. She was feeling the things that Lucy had felt. She was feeling the fear and panic that Lucy had felt—as incredible as it seemed, she *was* Lucy.

No! This couldn't be happening. Stephanie closed her eyes tightly and tried to regain control. She was not Lucy Killgrew—she was Stephanie MacAllister, living more than 200 years in the future!

"I'm Stephanie...I'm Stephanie," she said again and again, her eyes tightly shut.

When she felt a bit calmer, she opened her eyes and got an even greater shock. In front of her, standing only a few feet away, she saw a girl, approximately her own age.

For a moment, they just stood, looking into each other's eyes. The girl was dressed in the same buckskin outfit that Stephanie had seen herself wearing in her dream. She had an old-fashioned rifle slung over her shoulder.

There was no doubt: Stephanie knew that the girl before her was Lucy Killgrew.

But as strange as that was, it wasn't the strangest thing about the situation. What made Stephanie's mind begin to spin was the fact that, except for the differences in their clothing, she and Lucy Killgrew looked exactly the same!

It was like looking into a mirror. They had the same

round face, the same eyes, the same nose, the same cheek-bones, the same mouth—even the same dimple in the chin, which was just off-center enough to make them self-conscious about how it made them look. And though their hair was worn differently, it was the same color and the same texture.

A long, uncomfortable silence followed, until Stephanie finally found her voice.

"Lucy?" she whispered. "Lucy Killgrew?"

Then she fell silent, not knowing what else to say.

This time, it was Lucy who broke the silence, saying, "Please, I must complete my mission. The muskets must be delivered."

"Muskets?" Stephanie began to ask, but Lucy didn't seem to hear her.

Instead, she continued pleading, "The long rifles must be delivered to the Americans, or all is lost. Please."

The pain in Lucy's voice nearly broke Stephanie's heart. Instinctively, she reached out to Lucy to comfort her, but in the blink of an eye, the girl was gone.

What seemed to be a moment later, daylight was streaming onto Stephanie's face. She opened her eyes and instantly threw her hands in front of her face, trying to ward off the harsh light of morning. She tried to move and found her back was sore.

Then she realized that she wasn't in her bed, and in an instant, all her senses were alert.

She was sitting with her back against the Old Oak.

Then she heard a voice, coming from somewhere outside the woods.

"Stephanie! Stephanie!"

It sounded like Randy's voice.

She stood, her muscles stiff from sleeping up against the tree all night, but she could already feel herself warming up in the morning sun.

Looking out into the field, she could see the high grass rippling as someone moved quickly toward her.

"Stephanie! Stephanie! Where are you?"

It was definitely Randy's voice.

"Randy?" she called. "I'm over here, by the Old Oak."

A moment later, Randy clambered out of the grass, followed by Ben and a big dog, which Stephanie assumed was Willie.

"Geez, Steff, where've you been? Grandma's been worried to death."

Stephanie sought for a reasonable explanation. So much had happened, most of which she couldn't even explain to herself, that she decided not to try.

"I, uh, I guess I must have fallen asleep," she said lamely, hoping no one would press her for more than that.

"Well, come on back to the house, will you?" Ben said, pulling on the big dog's leash. "Everyone thinks you're lost, or kidnapped, or who knows what."

As they began to walk back toward Grandma Betty's, Stephanie looked back at the Old Oak, and then looked at her brother.

"How'd you know I was here?" she asked.

"We didn't know for sure. But then, we figured that you haven't seen too many places around here since we came, so we thought you might be here."

"And besides," said Ben, "old Willie here followed your trail. Well, sort of. Actually, I had to drag him most of the way."

Stephanie took a deep breath of fresh, clean, country air and smiled.

"Well, what are we waiting for?" she said, breaking out into a run. "I'm starved; I'll race you back!"

"Hey! No fair!" shouted Randy as he dashed after his sister.

Ben watched as Stephanie and Randy sped through the high grass and then looked down at Willie, who was walking by his side, most of his leash dragging limply on the ground.

"California kids are pretty weird, aren't they, boy? I wonder what the heck she was doing—hanging out by that old tree all night long?"

He shrugged his shoulders and picked up his pace.

"Come on, boy, let's go get us some breakfast before Mouse eats it all."

And with a whoop, Ben also began running through the tall grass, dragging Willie behind him.

Chapter Seventeen

Forgotten Treasures

IT WASN'T SURPRISING THAT Stephanie had a lot of explaining to do when she got back home. This was the first time she had ever seen Grandma and Aunt Susan when they were mad—and she hoped it was the last.

There was a time (only yesterday, though it hardly seemed possible) when Stephanie would have been *devastated* by the fact that she had worried everyone. But now, she seemed to be seeing everything in a whole new light.

It wasn't that she didn't care—she did—and she understood that what she had done was wrong. She shouldn't have left the house in the middle of the night without telling someone where she was going and when she'd be back.

She understood all of that, and she knew that her

grandmother and her aunt had a right to be upset. Yet she also knew, without a doubt, that, if given the same set of circumstances, she would do exactly the same thing, all over again.

Maybe this was what people meant when they talked about "situational ethics." All Stephanie knew was that she did what she *had* to do—and yet, there was no way she would ever be able to explain why, or even *what* had happened, to another living soul.

So, even as her angry relatives voiced their displeasure with what she had done, Stephanie felt at ease. No one had gotten hurt, and something miraculous had taken place—right there in Mayfair, even though she couldn't talk about it yet.

Grandma Betty and Aunt Susan were really only angry because they loved her so much—she knew that, and she loved them for feeling that way. But in the end, all she could do was to say she was sorry that she had worried them, and she would try not to worry them again.

When they pressed her for more information about why she had gone out, who she'd met, and why she hadn't come back home, Stephanie had to say, "I don't know," "I didn't meet anyone," (which was technically the truth) and "I fell asleep under the tree" (which was also the truth).

After going round and round for an hour, Grandma Betty finally dropped the subject, made Stephanie and Randy pancakes for breakfast, and then sent Stephanie up to her room to think about what she'd done.

Once in the calm and quiet of her room, Stephanie fell onto the bed, closed her eyes, and did, indeed, think about everything that had happened the night before. Already, parts of it were beginning to jumble together in her mind and were hard to recall clearly.

Yet, her thoughts were interrupted by her Grandma

Betty's voice, calling from outside her door.

"Stephanie, dear, are you awake?"

Stephanie opened her eyes and sat up. How long had she been lying there?

Grandma Betty's voice rang out again.

"It's past lunchtime, dear. I thought you might be hungry, so I brought you a sandwich and a glass of milk."

Stephanie smiled. Grandma Betty really was a kind and considerate lady.

"Thanks, Grandma. Please, come in. What time is it?" she called out.

"It's after twelve. How do you feel, dear?" Grandma Betty asked, opening the door and walking over to the bed.

Stephanie reached out and accepted the plate and the glass. She set the plate on the bed and asked Grandma Betty to sit down, too.

"I feel great! Thanks for letting me take a nap."

She took a big bite of the sandwich and realized how hungry she was. Then she looked at her Grandmother, who was watching her with a look of love and concern in her eyes.

"Grandma," said Stephanie. "I want you to know, I am truly sorry that I worried you like that. Please believe me—I never meant to."

Grandma Betty patted Stephanie's hand and said softly, "It's all right, dear. We'll say no more about it."

Then she leaned forward and said in a soft, conspiratorial tone, "The truth is, you're pretty safe around a little town like Mayfair, anyway—even in the middle of the night."

Then she stood, saying just a bit more firmly, "But I hope that you'll at least let me know if you decide to crawl out a window again, all right?"

She patted Stephanie's hand again, and turned to go.

"You can come down whenever you're ready."

As Grandma Betty walked toward the door, Stephanie called out, "Grandma, remember yesterday, when you said we could look at some old stuff up in the attic?"

Grandma Betty turned around, surprised and pleased.

"Yes, dear, I remember. Why?"

"Well," said Stephanie, "I'd really like to learn about the past. Our past."

"Why, that sounds wonderful, dear," said Grandma Betty. " I think I'd enjoy that. Whenever you're—"

Stephanie stuffed the last bite of sandwich into her mouth (it wasn't ladylike, but she didn't care at the moment) and jumped off the bed.

Her mouth full of sandwich, she said, "Can we do it now?"

☆ ☆ ☆

The air was slightly stuffy as Stephanie followed her grandmother through the door that led to the attic. There were cobwebs hanging from many of the rafters, and everything seemed to be covered with a thin layer of dust. The only place that was tall enough for Stephanie and Grandma Betty to stand up straight was right in the center, where the two sides of the peaked roof joined.

It was a junkman's paradise. There was stuff everywhere—lamps, chairs, other pieces of furniture, and boxes—lots and lots of boxes.

As Stephanie looked around, she noticed that her grandmother had stopped in the middle of the room and placed her hand over her heart.

"Is everything OK, Grandma?"

"Everything is fine, child," she said. "Some day, you'll

understand. Memories are a wonderful thing. Never hide from your memories, even the ones that cause you pain."

Grandma Betty walked over to an old rocking chair and carefully sat down.

"Every single thing in this attic has a story to tell. Feel free to look around all you want and to ask me about anything you find."

Stephanie picked up an old tea kettle made of white enamel. Although it was slightly chipped, the hand-painted blue angels on its sides were still bright and clear.

"How old is this, Grandma?"

"Why, that tea kettle belonged to your—"

"No," Stephanie said, setting the teakettle back down. "I mean, how far back does all of the stuff in the attic go? Is there any stuff here from, say, Revolutionary War times?"

"Oh my," said Grandma Betty. "I'm not sure, but it seems to me that there were one or two trunks your grandpa put up here after his parents died. I'm not sure where they would be—"

As she spoke, Grandma Betty stood and began walking through the clutter, poking into boxes here and there as she walked.

Stephanie still felt reluctant to talk about Lucy Killgrew, though she didn't know why—but she wanted to learn more about the mysterious events that had been taking place.

"Grandma, how far back does our family go in this area? Does it go back to the Revolutionary War?"

Betty stopped poking among the boxes and drawers and looked at Stephanie.

"Oh, my, yes—yes, indeed, child. Many of our relatives fought in the Revolutionary War. There were MacAllisters,

Henrys, Killgrews—"

"Killgrews?" said Stephanie. "We had Killgrews in our family?"

"Yes, there was a line of Killgrews, but the name died out fairly early on."

Stephanie tried to sound casual as she asked the next question, but her heart was in her throat.

"Was there ever a Lucy Killgrew in our family, Grandma?"

There was a pause, and then Grandma Betty said, "Lucy Killgrew? Hmmm, let me see."

She walked back to the old rocker again and sat down. "I suppose she would have been related to Daniel Killgrew. I don't recall the name Lucy Killgrew, exactly, but we could check the old Bible when we go back downstairs."

"Check the Bible?" Stephanie asked.

"The old family Bible, dear. We have a Bible that comes from way back, and it has family records in the front. It goes back a long ways, and I recall mention of a Tom Killgrew. Seems like he had only one girl, but I don't remember the names of his wife and daughter."

Stephanie became very excited.

"Where's the Bible, Grandma? Can we go look for Lucy?"

"Come here, child, and sit by me," said Grandma Betty.

Stephanie walked over and sat on the floor, next to her grandmother.

"Now, I want you to tell me what this is all about," said Grandma Betty. "Why are you suddenly so fired up to learn about our family history? And who's this Lucy Killgrew you keep going on about? Does all this have something to do with why you sneaked out last night and spent the night in the woods?"

With a sigh, Stephanie pulled Lucy's diary from the pocket of her windbreaker.

"I found this yesterday afternoon, Grandma, under the old Oak. You know, the one on the army land."

Grandma Betty took the book from Stephanie's hand and carefully turned several pages. Then she asked, "This book...does it mention Lucy Killgrew?"

"It was *written* by Lucy Killgrew, Grandma—in 1774."

"Oh my!" was all Grandma Betty could say.

For a time, there was silence between them while Stephanie decided whether or not to tell Grandma Betty the entire story. A moment later, she made her decision.

"And there's something else, Grandma. You probably won't believe me, but I want to tell you, anyway."

"I'll believe anything you tell me, child. I promise."

Then, Stephanie began to speak of everything she had experienced starting with the strange sensation while looking at the full moon on the plane and ending with her experience at the Old Oak the night before. When she'd finished, she looked with hope at her grandmother to see if she would in fact believe her incredible story.

To Stephanie's surprise, her grandmother only smiled and then reached over and placed her hand on her cheek, saying, "You've had a remarkable experience, child. And I think we'd better find out everything we can about Lucy Killgrew, don't you?"

"You mean—you believe me?" asked Stephanie. "Even though it sounds so, so—weird?"

Grandma Betty stood and looked at Stephanie, who was sitting cross-legged on the floor in front of the rocker.

"Do you believe it, Stephanie? Do you believe everything that you've seen, and heard, and experienced?"

Stephanie stood and hugged her grandmother. "Yes, Grandma. I believe it all happened, exactly the way I told you. I swear it's all true."

"Then I think we've got some detective work to do," Grandma Betty said, starting for the door. "Come, child, let's not waste any time!"

Stephanie felt like jumping for joy! She'd never expected anyone to believe her. After all, there were times when she could hardly believe herself. But as she followed Grandma Betty toward the ladder that led back downstairs, she suddenly felt the familiar blanket of cold begin to envelope her, and she stopped.

Her eyes were drawn to a dusty corner on the far side of the attic. Stephanie grabbed her grandmother's arm and asked, "Grandma? What's that over there? In the far corner?"

Grandma Betty turned, adjusted her large glasses, and looked where Stephanie was pointing.

"I believe those are some things that your grandpa got from his father's estate. I think he always meant to look through them, but I don't believe he ever did."

Without another word, Stephanie walked over to the corner and lifted up an old tarp that had been placed over a pile of papers, small boxes, and assorted furniture. As she removed the tarp, a cloud of dust swirled up, causing Stephanie to sneeze.

"My, my," said Grandma Betty, walking up behind Stephanie. "It must be thirty years since anyone's touched that!"

"Lucy's in here somewhere, Grandma," Stephanie said, looking at the pile. "I can't explain it, but I just felt her—and there's something in this pile that she wants me to see."

Grandma Betty knelt down beside Stephanie.

"Well, let's see if we can find out what that something might be, dear," she said, waving her hand to clear the dust away from her face.

Stephanie eyes scanned the pile of treasures in front of her.

"Look," she said, "an old wooden cradle!"

"My, it does look very old," said Grandma Betty.

Together, they studied it carefully, noticing the detail of the hand-carved side spindles. The head and foot of the cradle were solid oak. The once smooth surface was now rough and dry.

"Can you tell how old it is?" asked Stephanie.

"No, I can't," Grandma Betty replied. "Just feel how rough it is, though—and how heavy it is. A lot of furniture around these parts was made of oak. The early settlers built just about everything they owned out of oak and pine. But I suppose a person who knew about antiques could tell us how old these pieces are."

"Look at this old chair, Grandma. It looks like a throne."

"Oh, I know what that is. That's called a Wainscot chair. It was made for show more than comfort."

"And look at this table over here, Grandma. It's so narrow."

"That's because most farm homes were so small that when the table wasn't in use, it had to be pushed up against the wall. They made those types of tables narrow so they could save space."

Then Stephanie saw a small chest, pushed up against the wall, its top scratched and charred. The moment she saw the chest, a bell went off inside. She knew instantly that the chest was the reason she'd come up to the attic in the first place.

"That little chest, Grandma—the one that looks like

it's been in a fire. What's in that one?"

Without waiting for a reply, Stephanie reached out and began dragging the chest into the open.

"I have no idea what it might be in it, dear. I imagine it was one of the chests your grandpa inherited from his parents—and there's no telling where they might have gotten it from."

"Let's open it, Grandma," Stephanie said, barely able to contain her excitement.

"All right, dear," said Grandma Betty. "Let's do that right now."

A million thoughts raced through Stephanie's mind as Grandma fiddled with the chest's old-fashioned latch.

Lucy had made me come up here. Lucy had directed me to this chest. I wonder what we'll find in there. Whatever it is, I know it's important.

"Is it locked, Grandma?" she asked.

"Yes, it seems to be," said Grandma Betty, and Stephanie's heart sank.

But her hopes rose again as she saw her grandmother tip the chest over and said, "Look at this, dear. I looks like someone might have taped the key to the bottom. See, there's an envelope attached. Let's hope the key's inside!"

Stephanie fought back the urge to reach out and rip the envelope off the chest. She was determined to maintain some control over her emotions.

Grandma Betty carefully removed tape, freeing the envelope from the bottom of the chest. Even as she opened it, a large, old-fashioned key fell out and made a ringing noise as it hit the floor.

The key was huge. It looked more like a movie prop than a real key, but Grandma Betty picked it up, and the key slipped easily into the lock.

The years had taken their toll on the lock's mechanism, though, and Grandma Betty was forced to twist and turn the key carefully back and forth several times, slowly loosening the rust until, finally, the lock clicked open.

With her Stephanie looking on, Grandma Betty carefully opened the lid of the chest.

There could be anything in there, thought Stephanie... *treasure, a map, more old diaries...*

The tension was almost more than she could stand.

Grandma reached inside the chest and pulled out a dress—an old-fashioned dress that was still in remarkably good shape. Grandma Betty held it up for Stephanie to see.

"Look, Grandma, there's a name written in the neckline," Stephanie said, examining the bodice of the dress closely. "But it's so faded, I don't know if I can make it out."

"Drat these old eyes of mine," Grandma Betty said, tilting her head back and peering through just the bottom half of her large glasses. "I don't think I'm going to be of much help."

Stephanie took the dress out of Grandma Betty's hands, and shifted the dress slightly until a shaft of light struck the name. Even though Stephanie had a very good idea of what she was going to find, it was still came as a shock.

It took Stephanie a moment to get the words out.

"It says, 'Lucy Killgrew'."

"What? What's was the name, child?"

"It says 'Lucy Killgrew', Grandma. This was Lucy Killgrew's dress!"

All Grandma Betty could say was, "Well, I'll be..."

Somehow, finding this dress—with Lucy's name in it, struck Stephanie harder than anything else that had happened so far. Maybe it was because everything else could be explained away as some kind of coincidence or something that Stephanie's overly active imagination had cooked up.

But here, she was holding *proof* that Lucy Killgrew was, indeed, connected to her in some real, tangible way.

For several seconds Stephanie just stared at the dress, her mind reeling. Then, she stood and held the dress up in front of her—it looked as if it would be a perfect fit.

Grandma Betty held her hand up to her cheek in amazement. "Why, child, it looks as if it was made for you!"

As Stephanie turned toward her grandmother, still holding the dress in front of her, she thought, *if only you knew how right you are, Grandma!*

Chapter Eighteen

The First Skirmish

"HOW LONG IS A road, anyway?" Alexandra demanded.

"It's not 'road'; it's 'rod', you little nitwit," said Ben as he led his sister and cousins through the tall grass that led to the Old Oak tree.

Each of them was carrying either a shovel or a pick, and Stephanie had Lucy's diary tucked safely in the pocket of her windbreaker.

Suddenly, Stephanie began to feel a little uneasy. At first, she thought it was just because she didn't really want anyone else to be involved in finding Lucy's rifles. It seemed so special that part of her wanted to keep the whole amazing episode to herself. She also wasn't sure if it was important to Lucy for her to complete her mission without help from anyone else.

But the closer they came to the Old Oak, the more convinced Stephanie became that her uneasiness had nothing to do with either one of those things. There was something that just didn't feel right, but she just couldn't put her finger on it.

Suddenly, an incredible stench surrounded them.

"Phew!" Randy said, holding his nose. "What is that stink?"

"It's Willie," Alexandra answered with a giggle. "Remember? I told you, he farts."

Ben looked sheepish. "Yeah, he does—and that's one good reason why we hardly ever take him anywhere," he said. "Sorry about that."

Stephanie put her fingers to her nose, too, and continued walking, but her mind was elsewhere. She was remembering back to this morning, when she and her grandmother were going through the huge old Bible, looking for any mention of Lucy Killgrew and finding an old sheet of folded paper, tucked into the last few pages of Revelations.

Under the watchful eye of her grandmother, who seemed just as excited as she was, Stephanie had unfolded the paper slowly and carefully.

At first, she hadn't understood what she was looking at. There were dozens of names, each connected by lines. It looked interesting, but it didn't seem to make any sense.

The writing was also very old and had faded, but Grandma Betty had read that paper several times in the past, and she knew just what she was looking at.

"Would you like me to tell you what it says there?" Grandma Betty had asked.

Stephanie had then handed the page to her

grandmother.

"Does it mention Lucy, Grandma?"

"Well, way up here, at the top of the page," Grandma Betty had said, he wrinkled finger pointing to each word as she spoke, "There's a record of Daniel Killgrew's family. The note read:

Register of the Daniel & Mary Killgrew Family
Daniel born February 12, 1776.
Mary born February 27, 1779.
Married April 15, 1801.
By him she hath the following Children:

Name	Born	Died
A son	March 20, 1803	March 20, 1803
Ann Killgrew	September 11, 1805	February 17, 1867

"What about Lucy?" Stephanie had asked. "Does it say anything about Lucy?"

Grandma Betty had looked up and smiled.

"This register doesn't go back that far, dear. I think you've discovered a new branch in the family tree—or at least, a new twig," she said.

But Stephanie hadn't been in the mood for smiling.

Grandma Betty had then continued, saying, "It's possible that Lucy might have been Daniel's mother, but, judging by these dates, it's more likely that she might have been his sister. We'll still have to do a little more digging to find out for sure."

"Steff? Hello? Earth to Steff!" Randy shouted, snapping Stephanie back to the present. "Are you OK, Steff? You're walking like a zombie."

Stephanie realized that she had walked a hundred yards or so through the tall grass without any memory of walking at all.

Wow, she thought. *This thing with Lucy is starting to take over my life.*

She was suddenly glad to have her brother and cousins with her. Maybe together, they could find the rifles and then deliver them to the military. Then, she thought, maybe she could get back on with her real life.

Real life? The very thought of it made her laugh. She suddenly realized she hadn't even thought about a mall in days—and that thought made her chuckle out loud.

"What's so funny?" asked Alexandra, who was walking directly behind Stephanie and trying to put her little feet in Stephanie's footprints the moment Stephanie lifted her foot. "Did Willie fart again?"

"You'll have to forgive my idiot little sister. She loves to say the word 'fart,'" said Ben. "She thinks it's a bad word, and she's getting away with something when she says it."

"I do not," Alexandra said reflexively.

"Do you think we're actually gonna find some treasure?" asked Randy.

"I don't know if I'd call it a treasure, exactly," said Stephanie. "I'm hoping that we're going to find a bunch of old rifles that were hidden during the Revolutionary War."

"Wow!" said Alexandra. "Do we get to shoot 'em? Do I get to shoot one?"

"They're old rifles, Mouse," said Ben. "They probably won't work at all. They're bound to be pretty rusty after two hundred years.

"Yeah, that's true. Maybe they've rusted away to nothing by now," added Randy.

The thought had crossed Stephanie's mind.

"Look, guys, I can't promise anything. I'm not sure what we're going to find or if we're going to find anything at all. I'm kinda learning as I go. But I'd understand if you guys don't want to help," said Stephanie. "I can look for them by myself and let you know if I find anything."

"Oh, no," said Randy. "If you find any treasure, I wanna be there! Besides, it beats breaking my back, working on that fort."

"Hey!" said Ben.

"Sorry, Ben, I didn't mean to say I didn't like helping you with the fort," said Randy. "It's just that—"

"Forget it, Randy. I know what you mean. To tell the truth, I think searching for treasure is better, too," said Ben.

As grass dropped off, and the Old Oak came into view, it was clear that things had changed drastically. The fort was gone!

In its place was a sign, with large black block letters on a white board, that read:

GOVERNMENT PROPERTY
NO TRESPASSING

For a moment, no one said anything. Everyone just looked at each other in amazement.

Then Alexandra, hands on her hips, demanded, "Well, will somebody please tell me what the sign says?"

"It says we can't go here any more," Ben said, shaking his head. "I guess they're gettin' ready to start construction on the new Army stuff."

"What do we do, Steff?" asked Randy.

Stephanie's mind was reeling. Her entire life, she had always followed the rules. She'd never cut school, she'd always told her parents where she was going, she didn't lie, cheat, or steal. If a sign said "KEEP OFF THE GRASS," she kept off the grass.

But this was different. Whether it made sense or not, this was a special situation.

"We keep quiet," she answered softly, holding a finger up to her lips.

"All right, Steff!" Randy said, pleased to see the change in his goody-two-shoes sister. He was tired of always being the "bad" one. No matter what happened from here on, this time he would just be following orders!

"Follow me," Stephanie said, stepping carefully past the sign and moving in the direction of the Old Oak. "And for goodness sake, Mouse, keep *quiet*," she added.

"I didn't say anything!" Mouse protested loudly.

"She said to shut up, you little dip!" Ben hissed. "I can't believe you sometimes, Mouse!"

"And I can't believe *you* sometimes, you big bully!" Alexandra said hotly.

"Will both of you please be quiet!" said Stephanie, looking back over her shoulder. "Come on, let's go."

They moved quickly to the base of the Old Oak and crouched behind some low-lying bushes. Stephanie waited, expecting some sort of sign from Lucy—but nothing happened.

"Well?" said Alexandra. "Where's the pirate treasure we're supposed to be finding?"

Stephanie noticed Willie, who was laying in the shade with his eyes closed, pick up his head and look in the direction of the deep woods, but she thought nothing of it, although she briefly thought she had caught a whiff of cigarette smoke.

Ben began to whisper to Alexandra, "It's not pirate treasure, you little—" but Stephanie cut him off.

"Please, shut up! Both of you, just be quiet for a minute, will you?"

They crouched in silence for what seemed like a very

long time.

Then Randy said, "Look, Steff, either we need to start looking for this treasure of yours, or we need to do something else, OK?"

Stephanie sighed deeply and pulled Lucy's diary from her pocket.

"The only thing that Lucy says in the book is that the rifles are buried some rods north of the Cross Roads Oak, under the lone spruce."

Stephanie looked at Ben.

"Ben, does any of that ring any bells with you?"

Ben shrugged.

"No, sorry—but we could take a look around. That way's north."

"What's a rod?" Alexandra asked.

"A rod is about sixteen and a half feet," Stephanie said. "I asked Grandma about it this morning."

"What's sixteen and a half feet?" Alexandra persisted.

"It's a little higher than your I.Q., squirt," said Ben. "Now shut up and follow me."

Alexandra sniffed in protest but said nothing.

Looking to her left, Stephanie noticed that Willie had again lifted his head and was looking in the same direction he had looked earlier, toward a specific spot in the woods not too far away, but when she looked in that direction, she could see nothing out of the ordinary.

"Do you know what a spruce tree looks like?" Stephanie whispered to Ben. "I hope so."

"Oh, sure," Ben said softly. "That's an easy one. It's the 'lone' part that I'm worried about. We need to find a spruce tree around here that's still standing by itself...after two hundred years."

Stephanie smiled and shook her head in agreement.

"Hey, Ben. You need be quiet," said Alexandra. "Why do you get to talk and I don't?"

Suddenly there was a crashing in the undergrowth, but it came from the opposite direction from the way Willie had been looking.

A loud male voice said, "Sergeant Hacker! Get the hell over here. And you kids! What are you doing here? Can't you read?"

A huge soldier stepped out from the brush and stood, looking at the children.

"Hacker!" he shouted. "Where the hell are you?"

Then he said, "Well, answer me! What are you kids doing here?"

"Uh, nothing, sir," Stephanie said, looking at the ground. She never was a good liar.

"Yeah," said Randy, looking the soldier directly in the eyes. "We, uh, just in the area, and we just thought we'd take a hike."

Stephanie had always known Randy was a much better liar than she was, but this time, all she could do was roll her eyes. Is that the best he can come up with?

"Going for a hike, huh?" the soldier said, looking at the children, one by one. "Do you always take picks and shovels with you when you go for a hike?"

Just then, Willie began to growl, his lips curling back in a snarl.

Ben and Alexandra looked at the dog in surprise. But before anyone could say another word, another soldier, this one bigger, older, and wearing an angry expression, crashed into the clearing from the opposite direction—the direction, Stephanie realized, that Willie had been looking since they had arrived at the Old Oak.

The older soldier looked confused for a moment and then turn to salute the younger soldier, saying,

"Captain."

"Sergeant Hacker, it looks like you've been asleep at your post," the Captain said. "You were ordered to keep all civilians off this land."

"Yes, sir. I'm sorry, sir," said Hacker, first looking apologetically at the Captain and then turning to scowl at the children. "But I'll take care of them right now, sir."

Hacker reached into the gun belt around his waist, drew a pistol, and pointed it menacingly at the children.

"What are you going to do, Hacker? Blow these kids away?" said the Captain.

"No, sir, I—"

The Captain cut him off, saying, "Now put your gun away, Hacker, and let's find out what's going on here."

"Yes, sir," said Hacker, returning the pistol to its holster.

Stephanie could tell by the older soldier's manner and voice that he was just barely able to conceal his contempt for the young Captain. She also felt an immediate dislike of the older soldier.

Hacker was wearing a white helmet, with the letters MP stenciled on it. He had several stripes on his shirtsleeves, three up and two down. Dark sunglasses pressed close to his face, hiding his eyes, and though she didn't know why, Stephanie felt something sinister about that man—something evil—and she knew that this was a man she wanted to avoid.

"What are you kids doin' here?" Hacker shouted, but the Captain cut him off again.

Shaking his head slightly, he looked at Stephanie and said, softly, but firmly, "Kids, this is a restricted area. That's why we have signs posted all over, to keep people out. So from now on, you kids are going to find somewhere else to play, OK?"

The Captain's words were kind, but his voice let Stephanie know that he meant every word he said.

"But what about the treasure? We're looking for some old rifles—" Alexandra demanded, stepping forward with her hands on her hips, looking up at the Captain defiantly.

Ben leaped forward and grabbed his sister, placing his hand over her mouth.

"I'm sorry, Captain," he said, "You'll have to forgive my sister. She's an idiot!"

Alexandra bit Ben's hand, and when he let go of her in pain, she looked at the Captain and said, "I'm not an idiot. And we *are* here to search for treasure! And we know it's around here—by a lone spruce somewhere close to here—because my cousin Stephanie has a map! Show 'em the map, Stephanie!"

Stephanie said nothing, her eyes wide with shock and apprehension.

Fortunately, the Captain must have thought it was all a childish game. All he saw was a bunch of kids pretending to look for pirate treasure. But when Stephanie looked over at Hacker, she couldn't tell that his eyes had narrowed in thought, but somehow knew he was staring at her in a menacing way.

The Captain bent down to look Alexandra in the face.

"I can see you're not an idiot, sweetie. But what's this about a treasure and some lone spruce?"

"Yeah," said Hacker. "And any treasure that might be on this property would belong to the military, anyway."

The Captain looked up at Hacker and said, "I'll handle this, if you please, Sergeant."

Hacker said nothing. He just grunted like an angry bull, waiting for his chance to charge.

"Look, Captain," Stephanie said, "It's all just a game we were playing." Then she leaned forward and whispered to the Captain, "But we didn't want my little cousin to know that. We thought it would be more fun for her if she weren't in on the secret. You know how children are."

The Captain smiled and nodded. He then stood and pointed toward the road.

"Well, kids, real or not, I'm afraid the treasure hunt is now officially over. From now on, you kids are going to have to stay away from here. There's going to be all sorts of big machinery working around here, and we don't want to see anyone get hurt."

The Captain smiled again and looked down at Alexandra.

"But I'll make you a promise, little lady. If we do find any treasure, I promise I'll let you know, OK?"

Then he looked at Hacker and again pointed toward the road.

"Now, Sergeant Hacker, do you think you can escort these kids off the property without any gunplay?"

Barely concealing his anger, Hacker growled, "Yes, sir."

Then he turned back toward the kids and said, "All right, you kids, let's get out of here."

He then stepped behind Stephanie and gave her a shove.

Stephanie looked back and saw the Captain disappearing back into the woods. As soon as the Captain was completely out of sight, Hacker grabbed Stephanie by the arm and whirled her around.

"Now, Miss. What's this about a treasure map?" he demanded, trying to sound casual but making sure everyone knew he meant business.

Stephanie looked up at the menacing big man. Her

heart was pounding.

"What map?" she said, wishing she had learned to be a great liar, like her brother.

"The one your little playmate here told the Captain about. The one that mentions something about old rifles."

Hacker bent forward, and Stephanie could smell the stench of cigarettes on his breath.

"Is it in that book there in your coat?" Hacker said, reaching for Stephanie's windbreaker.

Suddenly, Stephanie's heart stopped pounding and her breathing returned to normal. She was less afraid of this man, now that she knew what he wanted. He seemed to know something about the treasure, and it made her more determined than ever to find Lucy's rifles, no matter what.

Stephanie looked Hacker straight in his face. He reached out to grab her by the shoulders, but she stepped out of his reach, saying defiantly, "If you lay a finger on me, I'll scream, and then the Captain will come back."

For a moment, Hacker's hands seemed frozen in place, only inches away from Stephanie's shoulders. For a moment no one moved, no one made a sound, it was as if time had stopped.

Stephanie's eyes never left Hacker's. Her defiant speech had taken them both by surprise, but the moment the words had left her lips, she had begun to be less afraid. She wondered if Lucy had something to do with it all, but she also wondered how much this evil man actually knew about Lucy's treasure.

A moment later, Hacker apparently reached a decision. His hands shot out and grabbed Stephanie's arms in a vise-like grip. Stephanie was too startled to scream but not too startled to begin kicking her attacker in the shins.

"You let go of me!" she demanded.

The other kids jumped to Stephanie's aid, kicking and biting the big man until he let out a howl and loosened his hold on Stephanie.

The instant she was free, Stephanie yelled, "Come on!"

Willie barked once before Ben yanked on his leash and began pulling him along as all four kids began running through the woods and out into the field.

Hacker stood holding his bruised shins for a moment, but it was a moment too long. He knew that he wasn't as young or as fast as he used to be, and, in a few seconds, all he could see was waving grass, marking the passage of small bodies moving quickly across the field.

But it didn't really matter. He'd scared them badly enough that they wouldn't be back—and he knew that the treasure Rios had talked about was *real*.

And Treasure was somewhere near where he was standing, at this very moment—and he flashed a wicked smile as he looked around. The little girl's mention of lost rifles was just too much of a coincidence—and they had a map!

Hacker hadn't gotten where he was, with his beach houses and Swiss bank accounts, by letting chances like this pass him by.

The older girl had been lying, of that he was sure, and her defiance meant that she knew where those rifles—and the Willow Tree Six Pence coins—were buried.

Eighteen million dollars. Eighteen million dollars, split between himself and Rios.

But then, Hacker had another thought. Why should he split the money with Rios? Rios didn't even know if the rifles and coins really existed! And he definitely knew nothing about this latest development.

How hard could it be to unload four hundred old coins, he thought. He'd unloaded millions of dollars of other merchandise over his career. This shouldn't be any harder than selling a tank or a jeep.

Even if he'd lost the map, this was turning out to be one of the luckiest days of his life! He lit a cigarette, looked around, blew out a huge puff of smoke, and smiled again.

Chapter Nineteen

Tonight's The Night

"WOW, STEFF! I CAN'T believe the way you stood up to that Hacker guy!" Randy said, his smile beaming in the half-light of the garage. "You just might turn out to be an OK sister, after all!"

The cousins had all taken refuge in Ben and Alexandra's garage. The only light in the room was the sunlight that poured in from the windows on the south wall, where Ben was standing, keeping a close eye on the street. The garage doors were locked, in case someone had followed them.

"Yeah," Alexandra said, "That was very cool!"

Ben looked at his little sister, who was sitting on the floor next to Willie, scratching the old dog behind one ear.

Shaking his head in disbelief, Ben said, "You were a big help back there, you little twerp—telling them all about the treasure."

Then he made his voice go up an octave, mocking his little sister's voice, saying, "There is too a treasure—and Stephanie has a map! Show 'em the map, Stephanie!"

Ben then spoke in his normal voice, saying, "It was supposed to be a secret, bonehead!"

"Oh, yeah? How was I supposed to know that?"

"Yeah! Well, you should have just kept your mouth shut!"

"Will you two knock it off?" Stephanie yelled.

She was afraid that Hacker might already know as much as they did, which meant he might find the rifles first, and she just couldn't let that happen—not after everything that she'd experienced. It just wouldn't seem right, somehow. It didn't make sense that Lucy would work so hard to contact her just to have someone else find the rifles.

"Listen, everybody," said Stephanie. "If they're really bringing in the heavy equipment in the next couple days, that means we don't have much time. That means we have to go back and find the rifles before—"

"Wait a minute!" Ben interrupted, turning away from the window to look at his cousin. "Are you saying you want to go back there?"

"Well, yes, but—"

"Are you crazy? Maybe you didn't hear either one of those soldiers tell us to stay out of there. Maybe you didn't see that pistol pointed at our heads! And maybe that the big ugly guy didn't try to tear your shoulders off!"

Stephanie knew Ben was right, of course, but she also knew none of that mattered. She had to find the rifles—it was that simple. She took a deep breath and closed her eyes, hoping that some incredibly brilliant plan would pop into her head. But it didn't.

She opened her eyes and said softly, "Look, all I know is that I'm supposed to find those rifles and deliver them to the American military. Lucy went to a lot of trouble to lead us right to them, and now, I have to help her."

Now it was Randy's turn to shake his head and say, "You think Lucy led you to the rifles? Look, Steff, it was Ben who took us the to Old Oak the first time, and he didn't say anything about any rifles. He's been playing around there for years."

"Yes, but it was Lucy who showed me where to find her diary, and—"

Randy cut her off, saying, "Steff, I know this is important to you, somehow, and it was fun and all, pretending to believe in this ghost girl, but—"

"Listen!" said Stephanie sharply. "None of you have to help me do this! I know it may sound crazy, but it's something I have to do! And I'll go by myself if I have to. It might even be better that way. It would be easier for me to hide if I went back alone."

"Why don't we just wait till all the soldiers go to bed?" said Alexandra.

"Go to bed? What are you talking about, squirt?" said Ben, rolling his eyes. "Soldiers don't have—"

"No, wait. I think Mouse has an idea," said Stephanie. "I'll wait until dark, and then I'll sneak back there. After all, until the base is officially built, there's no need to guard every inch of this huge forest all night long. I'll sneak in, find the rifles, and get out before they even know I'm there."

"Before we're there," said Randy, correcting his sister with a smile.

"That's right," said Ben. "This will be the biggest adventure we've ever had around here, and you can't leave us out of it."

"And if there are really 75 rifles, you're gonna need help carrying them all," said Randy.

"Yeah, and it'll give me an excuse to stay up past my

bedtime," said Mouse, making everyone laugh.

"OK, then," said Stephanie. "Tonight's the night. Here's what we're gonna do. After dinner, we'll all say that we want to go to the movies in town. Then—"

Chapter Twenty

Those Who Ignore History

SERGEANT HACKER WAS HOT and tired and *not* in a good mood. All afternoon, young Captain Jenkins had kept him hopping from one assignment to another; he was starting to feel like he was actually in the army!

He smiled at his own little joke. It was the first time he'd smiled since he'd overheard that little girl spouting off about the rifles. Now he knew those rifles were real—and he knew that the chances were good that, if the rifles were real, the silver willow trees were real, too.

And he knew something else—he wanted those coins, more than he'd ever wanted anything in his life.

But since the encounter with the children, Hacker hadn't had a moment to himself. It was already past four in the afternoon, and he still had a list of things the Captain had given him to do that would take him several days to finish.

He would have to come up with a plan. He lit a cigarette and sat down on the stump of a tree that crews had cut down earlier in the day and began to think.

He looked around and thought about how much he hated this place. Mayfair was the Army's equivalent of Siberia for a guy like him, and it was costing him thousands of dollars a day to be there.

But there was something else that Hacker hated about this place—and it had nothing to do with money. His grandmother had lived in a small town not far from Mayfair, about twenty miles up the coast, and he'd spent several unhappy summers there, more than forty years ago, when he was a kid.

Those summers had been the worst of his life, and to Hacker, spending the summer with his grandmother was almost worse than living in Juvenile Hall—a place he knew all too well! As soon as he arrived, his grandmother laid down a whole slew of rules and regulations, and he was expected to obey them, to the letter.

And there was nothing to do for a city kid like him. He had just sat around and moped, while his poor grandmother tried to figure out what to do with a bored and angry teenage boy.

Sometimes, she'd even tried to interest him in his family's history—as if he really cared. He didn't even like his living relatives, so why should he care about some ancestor who had died a couple hundred years ago? They were probably losers, like every other member of his no-good family.

Hacker blew out a huge cloud of smoke as he sat and thought about those hellish summers and how his poor grandmother tried to relate to him. But as far as he was concerned, the whole thing was just a gigantic waste of time—just like school had been.

Hacker could only shake his head at how ridiculous that thought was. *You want to talk about a waste of time,* he thought. *There's a good one!*

In fact, he'd only gotten one useful thing out of all his years in school. During his senior year, just a week shy of his eighteenth birthday, he and a couple buddies had gotten drunk and decided to break into the high school. He couldn't even remember now what they had planned to take, but they'd gotten caught, and the judge had given him the choice of spending time in adult prison or enlisting in the army.

Not much of a choice!

He'd chosen the army, intending to go AWOL at the first opportunity, but, as fate would have it, he'd gotten assigned to supply detail, and the rest, as they say, was history.

But a very profitable history, he thought with a smile, and that thought made him angry all over again. How was he supposed to continue maintaining his extravagant lifestyle when he was stuck in a backwater hole like Mayfair?

It made him more determined to find out more about those rifles—and the coins that would again put him back on Easy Street.

He found himself and his thoughts drifting back to his grandmother and how hard she tried to interest him in their family history. But he could never see how all that garbage had anything meaningful to do with him. Who cared that his great-great-great-grandfather on his mother's side had fought for the British?

No one—that's who cared. For Hacker, life boiled

down to one simple concept: If there was a way to make money from it, a guy had to grab it, and if there wasn't, a guy shouldn't waste his time on it—period.

And at that moment, Hacker knew he was close to something worth grabbing—worth eighteen million dollars of grabbing, to be exact. Now *that* was something that made a difference—it wasn't just a bunch of dead history, totally worthless to anybody.

A guy didn't need a high school education to figure that one out.

Then, the idea that he'd been waiting for suddenly came to him. Of course! It was so simple. All he had to do was volunteer for night guard duty in the sector with that old oak tree and then wait for the kids to show.

And he knew for certain that those bratty kids *would* be back to look for those rifles. He'd been a kid once, and he knew that they had a map, so finding out if the treasure was really there was something they *had* to do.

And when they show up, he thought, *old Hacker would be there to meet them.*

Chapter Twenty-one

Grandma Betty

THE MOMENT STEPHANIE AND Randy stepped through the door, Grandma Betty pulled Stephanie aside and said, "Stephanie, dear, I've found Lucy!"

Randy looked at his grandmother suspiciously and said, "Oh, no. Not you, too, Grandma? Don't tell me you've been talking to this ghost girl, too!"

"No, of course not," Grandma said with a smile. "I think that Lucy only talks to Stephanie. But I did some checking at the library today, and I had the librarian call over to the main county library. It took most of the morning and half the afternoon, but we finally found a reference to Lucy."

"Oh, that's wonderful, Grandma!" said Stephanie.

212

"What'd you find?"

Grandma took Stephanie's hand and led her to the kitchen. Meanwhile, Randy sauntered into the living room, and a few seconds later, Stephanie could hear the theme music from one of his favorite cartoons, which seemed to reverberate throughout the whole house.

Grandma Betty walked to the kitchen door and called, "Randy, turn the TV down, please!"

It took several seconds, but the volume finally was cut in half—now it only annoying, but not deafening.

"I suppose that's better," said Grandma Betty, sitting down at the table and pulling a small notebook from the pocket of her dress.

She flipped the notebook open and quickly scanned through the pages, looking for a particular section.

"Ah, here we are," she said, adjusting her over-sized glasses with the tip of her index finger. "Lucy Killgrew. Let's see. According to county birth records, Lucy was born on April 27th, 1762."

"Wow!" was all Stephanie could say.

"That's what I said when I saw it!" Grandma Betty said. "Her father was Tom Killgrew, and her mother was Nancy Killgrew. They were listed in the records as farmers, but according to the register, Tom Killgrew was a Captain in the American Army. He was killed while fighting the British during the battle of Breed's Hill."

"Oh, my!" said Stephanie.

"But that's not the most the interesting part," Grandma Betty continued. "Seven months after Tom was killed, Nancy Killgrew gave birth to a son."

"Daniel Killgrew!" Stephanie said softly. "That means that Daniel was Lucy's brother, just like you thought!"

"That's right," said Grandma Betty.

Stephanie looked at the notebook, as if eager to find

more information.

"But whatever happened to Lucy?"

Grandma Betty looked at Stephanie and shook her head.

"No matter how hard we tried, no one could find a death record for Lucy. It was as if she simply disappeared."

"But what about the rifles?" Stephanie said, "Did you find any mention of the rifles?"

"No, dear. They only have birth and death records over there. I'm afraid that unless we can find another of Lucy's diaries, there's no way we can learn any more about the rifles."

Stephanie thought about it a moment and made a decision about something that had been lurking in the back of her mind for a day or so, although she never really wanted to think about it. She was afraid of what might happen. But now she decided she had no choice.

I think I know one way to find out, Stephanie thought grimly. *I just hope I don't lose myself completely in the process!*

✩ ✩ ✩

"Let me get this straight," Captain Jenkins said, leaning back in his chair and rubbing his tired eyes. "You're actually *volunteering* for night patrol?"

The Captain hadn't been sleeping much lately, since he'd been put in charge of setting up this new storage depot. There were a million details to coordinate, and it was the biggest project he'd ever been a part of. Sometimes, he even found himself doubting that he was the right man for the job.

He looked across the table at Sergeant Hacker. Without quite knowing why, he had known that Hacker was trouble from the moment he'd laid eyes on him. That was why he had taken on a second job, a job that involved

Hacker directly, a job that he kept to himself.

Jenkins said, "If you'll pardon my saying so, Sergeant Hacker, you don't seem like the type of soldier who would volunteer for anything."

"With all due respect, sir," Hacker said with false sincerity, "I could use the extra pay."

But Captain Jenkins doubted that very much. He may only be twenty-eight years old, but he'd been in the army long enough to know a con artist when he smelled one—and Sergeant Hacker definitely had all the earmarks. He was slipperier than an eel and about as trustworthy as a rattlesnake—of that, Jenkins had no doubt.

Jenkins was silent for a long moment, surveying Sergeant Hacker closely. Then he said, "Very well, Sergeant, tonight, you'll patrol sector—"

Hacker interrupted Jenkins' orders, saying, "If it's all the same to you, sir, I checked the duty roster, and I saw that there's no patrol listed for sector 27-A tonight."

"27-A?" said Jenkins, looking at a map of the area. It seemed strange that Hacker knew exactly which area he wanted to patrol. As his finger moved over the map, it stopped over area 27-A. Then Jenkins said, "Isn't that where we found those kids today?"

"Yes, sir, it is," Hacker said, sitting forward and trying not to tip his hand. "As I was escorting them off the property this morning I overheard them saying they'd be back tonight. I think they mean to cause trouble, sir. Perhaps some kind of environmental protest to stop construction."

Jenkins leaned back in his chair. What was this con man really up to, he wondered.

"Do you really think they'll come back tonight and cause some trouble?" he asked.

"That's what I thought I heard," Hacker said. "But I

think I can head it off, if you'll give me a chance, sir."

Captain Jenkins looked suspiciously at the Sergeant. Although he didn't know what Hacker's real game was, he decided to let Hacker play it through.

"Very well, Sergeant. Sector 27-A, it is. But Sergeant," he said, sitting forward and looking Hacker squarely in the eyes, "if those kids do show up tonight, I want to know about it—and no rough stuff. Am I understood? That's an order, Sergeant!"

"Of course, sir," Hacker said, standing and giving a salute. "You know I would never dream of harming a child."

Hacker then turned and walked quickly from the office. Captain Jenkins watched him go, an uneasy feeling forming in the pit of his stomach. That man was a pro, and whatever Hacker was up to, the Captain hoped he would be able to handle it.

He shook his head and mumbled, "They don't pay me enough to—"

Then he reached for the phone on his desk and began to dial.

"They definitely don't pay me enough—not by a long shot…"

☆ ☆ ☆

Stephanie tried to talk Randy into going upstairs before supper and taking a nap so he'd be wide-awake that night, but he just gave her a dirty look and continued watching cartoons. She didn't feel like arguing with him.

After she'd returned to her own room, Stephanie carefully pulled open the bottom drawer of her bureau and found what she was looking for, exactly where she had left it.

It was Lucy's dress, the one they'd found in the charred little trunk in the attic. Stephanie hesitated even to touch it. She knew, deep down inside, as clearly as if a voice had spoken to her, that the dress had power, almost as if it had a life of its own.

And she also knew that once she put it on, she would lose herself to Lucy. But what she didn't know, and what frightened her most, was whether she would ever be able to get herself back.

But she decided not to think about it. She knew she had only this night to find the rifles, and the only way to find them was with Lucy's help.

She had to put on Lucy's dress and *become* Lucy Killgrew.

She reached into the bureau and carefully lifted the dress out of the drawer. It was heavier than she remembered. She held it in front of her and looked at her image in the full-length mirror on the back of the closet door. It was amazing to see how much she looked like the girl she had briefly seen that night at the Old Oak.

Things were moving quickly. Stephanie suddenly realized that she and Randy had been in Mayfair for less than a week. In less than seven days, Stephanie's life had been completely turned upside down.

And for all she knew, once she put this dress on, her life would never be her own again.

Her hands were shaking, but she took a deep breath and began to slip the heavy dress over her head. Although she instinctively knew that Lucy would never harm her, this was the scariest—and strangest—thing she'd ever done.

She closed her eyes, and even as the dress fell over her shoulders, she could feel herself beginning to drift away. It was as if the entire world around her was changing...

She began to hear strange sounds, and she could smell the smoke from the fires that burned brightly within the camp. She opened her eyes and knew that she was now Lucy Killgrew—and the year was 1775.

As she grew more accustomed to her surroundings, she saw that she was seated in front of a fire. In the distance, perhaps thirty feet away, she saw blacksmiths pounding on bars of red-hot steel at the makeshift forge. Crickets were singing the same songs they would still be singing in these same fields some two hundred years later.

As the heat from the fire began to diminish, Will Ashley looked at her, and she looked shyly back, feeling her face turning slightly red.

"Lucy, if you're cold, you can use my coat," said Will.

"I am just a little cold," she said. She wasn't really, but she knew that this was the first time a man had offered her his coat, and she couldn't refuse.

As he placed his coat on her shoulders, she asked, "Will, what's it like fighting the British?"

"A little scary," he replied. "At first, you don't hear nothin'. Then they come a-marchin' at you with drums a-poundin'. Those drums make it sound like the devil himself is comin' to getcha."

"Where you from, Will?"

"I spent most my life in the mountains of Virginia, trappin', and I guess I just gradually made my way up north. When I reached Connecticut, I heard they were lookin' for volunteers, so I took up with The Americans, 'cause I'd seen too many people sufferin' during my life. How 'bout you? I hear tell that Captain Killgrew has a farm not too far from here."

"We had a lovely farm until the British burned us out," she replied, suddenly having visions of the day when Coffin and the soldiers came to their home. "My father used to trap around here, all the way up to Canada."

"I don't think I could ever settle down enough to be a farmer," said Will.

"I know it to be hard," said Stephanie. It was getting easier now, and she was beginning to get clearer pictures of Lucy's life and memories in her mind with each passing moment.

"I remember many times back home after the evening meal," she said, just letting the words come. "I would see Father standing in front of the house—just looking off toward the wilderness. There were many times I wanted to run to him, but my mother always held me back. She'd tell me that he was communing with nature at those times, and it was my father's way of keeping in touch with his wandering spirit. Sometimes, I'd just watch my father, trying to imagine where he was in his mind's eye, and what he was doing. The strangest thing was that, after a while, it got to be as if I were there with him, somehow."

She stopped talking and looked at Will shyly.

"Oh my, you must think me awful strange."

"Oh, no, Lucy. I don't think it's strange at all," said Will. "The fact is, it seems to me that women like you and your ma understand men like your pa and me."

She felt her face turning red with embarrassment again, and she looked intently into the fire, avoiding Will's eyes.

But Will continued, saying, "And I was thinkin' that maybe some day, if I ever do settle down..."

Will's voice trailed off, as if he had lost his nerve to continue. But she knew that he hadn't taken his eyes off her.

Slowly, Stephanie turned back toward Will, and he leaned close and gently kissed her. At first, Stephanie pulled away, but then she felt her arms reach up and pull Will's body close to hers. She felt her hand reach behind his head and begin to run its fingers through his long hair. A wild array of new sensations was coursing through her body, unusual feelings that she had never known before.

Suddenly, a log snapped loudly in the fire, returning the two of them to their senses.

For a long time after that, they sat talking in front of the fire, not noticing that the camp was growing quieter with each passing moment. The moon was in its first quarter, and stars blanketed the sky. They didn't kiss again, each one wished that time would stand still so that they could savor this moment forever.

It was an amazing moment, full of such joy and sadness.

Then, something strange began to happen, and for several moments, Stephanie was totally confused. Everything seemed to be swirling in some sort of mist. She could hear babies crying, gunshots being fired, men and women shouting, and...

Suddenly, she found herself back in her bedroom. She was back to Grandma Betty's house, in modern day Mayfair. Glancing out the clock on her dresser, she saw that only an hour had passed since she put on the dress. She looked at herself again in the mirror, again feeling how heavy her coarse garment was.

Likewise, her mind felt heavy and sluggish, as if she'd been awakened too soon from a deep sleep.

My, she thought, *this traveling to the past and becoming one with Lucy might be interesting, but it's draining.*

As she sat, thinking about what she'd just experienced, Stephanie heard a light, but insistent, knocking on her door.

"Stephanie? Stephanie, dear, come on down. It's time for supper."

A moment later, the door opened slowly, and Grandma

Betty stepped gingerly into the room.

"Stephanie? Are you all right?"

When Grandma Betty saw that Stephanie had put on Lucy's dress, she put her hand to her cheek and exclaimed, "Oh, my, child! You look exquisite in that dress!"

After she'd changed back into blue jeans, Stephanie joined Randy and Grandma Betty downstairs at the kitchen table. She looked around and smiled. The kitchen was the friendliest, coziest room in the house, and somehow, the room embodied the very essence of Grandma Betty.

The table was filled with goodies. There was Yankee pot roast, mashed potatoes, green beans from Grandma Betty's garden, fresh-baked bread, and milk that was so cold that it felt like liquid ice!

Stephanie stared at her plate for a moment. Lucy Kill-grew might have eaten a meal exactly like this more than two hundred years ago.

"Stephanie, dear," she heard her grandmother say. "Are you all right? You look rather—"

"Sure, she's fine," said Randy. "In fact, we're gonna go to the movies tonight, Grandma. Ben and the squirt are coming, too."

Grandma Betty kept her eyes on Stephanie, trying to get clues from her face. Then she shook her head slowly and said, "Well, I don't know."

"I feel fine, Grandma, really," said Stephanie, looking into her grandmother's eyes.

But Stephanie could feel Grandma Betty's eyes piercing her soul. She felt her cheeks began to burn, just as they had done during the conversation with Will.

But what she needed to do tonight was important, and she had to do it. Even so, she didn't think she could lie to her Grandmother—even to help Lucy.

As she sat thinking, she felt Randy kick her under

the table as he hissed under his breath, "Don't blow it, Steff!"

Stephanie looked into her grandmother's smiling, sympathetic face.

Grandma Betty plopped another scoop of mashed potatoes onto Stephanie's plate and said, "Have some more potatoes, dear. And, please, do tell me what's really going on."

"Nothing's going on," Randy said—too quickly. "Really, Grandma. We just want to go to the movies. That's all."

But Grandma Betty's eyes never left Stephanie's face.

Patiently, she smiled and said, "Stephanie, dear? Is there anything you'd like to tell me?"

That was too much for Stephanie to bear. She broke down and, through her tears, she told her grandmother everything that had happened—about going to the woods to find Lucy's rifles, about the young Captain and the evil Sergeant, and how she was certain that she *had* to go back tonight to find the rifles.

When Stephanie finished, Grandma Betty sat back in her chair, looking astonished.

Randy leaned over to Stephanie and said softly, "Good going, Steff. Just so you know—the movie thing was working. Now you'll never get the chance to find those rifles!"

Grandma Betty was quiet for what seemed like a long time, carefully thinking over the situation.

Then she shook her head and said, "I'm sorry, dear, but I just can't let you do it."

"But, Grandma," Stephanie protested.

"I can't let you kids go back there by yourselves," Grandma Betty said softly. "If we're going to find those rifles, we're going to do it as a family."

"What?" Stephanie and Randy said at the same time.

"First off," said Grandma Betty, a bit more loudly than before. "I want you to know that it's technically wrong for you to trespass on government property. But—in this particular case, I think it will be all right for us to bend the rules, just a little. After all, you do plan to turn the rifles over to the military anyway, so we won't actually be stealing or anything like that."

Now it was Randy and Stephanie who looked astonished. They couldn't believe what they were hearing. Their parents would never be this cool.

Grandma Betty seemed to be reading their minds, and she held up a finger to emphasize her next point.

"You need to remember that what we're doing is probably wrong in the eyes of the law, and no amount of justification can make it right. That is precisely why I must insist on going with you—because if we're caught, I intend to accept full responsibility."

"But Grandma, I—" said Stephanie.

Grandma Betty held up her hand for silence, saying, "Those are the rules, kids. If you don't want to accept those terms, the whole thing is all off."

"Well, all right, Grandma Betty!" Randy said, clapping his hands. "That is so cool!"

Stephanie studied the look of resolution on her grandmother's face for a long moment. Then she reached out and took Grandma Betty's hand, squeezing it gently.

"Thank you, Grandma. I knew you would understand. This is something I *have* to do."

"I know," said Grandma Betty, softly patting Stephanie's hand. "Believe it or not, I was young once, too!"

Chapter Twenty-two

The Return

"I SUGGEST YOU TRY the squid my friend. It's delicious," said Rios, stabbing a four-inch long tentacle, lifting it to his face, and then sucking it into his mouth like a strand of spaghetti.

Hacker shuddered at the sight, and had to concentrate on the Maine lobster on his plate before he got sick. The very thought of sucking squid made his stomach turn.

"You don't want a piece?" Rios asked, daintily dabbing at his thin black mustache with a white linen napkin.

"Uh, not right this moment, thanks," said Hacker. "Perhaps another time."

And on some other planet, he thought, hoping his distaste didn't show on his face.

"Well, more's the pity," said Rios, smiling and stabbing at another tentacle. "It's your loss, my friend."

Although Hacker saw the smile, it didn't reassure him one bit. He'd never seen anyone smile as much as Rios—or mean it less.

Hacker had gotten a call from Rios at the base only a couple hours ago and had been told to meet him at a restaurant.

They had only met a half hour ago in the restaurant parking lot, but Hacker had distrusted the oily little "antique dealer" the moment he'd seen him step out of his long, black sedan. There was an air of superiority about Rios that made Hacker feel like a loser, and Hacker hated that.

How Rios had known that Hacker was close to the treasure, Hacker had no idea—but he wanted to find out. But Rios knew—there was no doubt about that—and Hacker also got the distinct impression that trying to cheat this man would be a big mistake.

He judged Rios to be in his mid-thirties, about 5' 5", and all of 140 pounds. Although Rios wasn't athletic-looking, there didn't seem to be an ounce of fat on him, which Hacker decided was another good reason to dislike him.

Rios wore his shiny, greased-back black hair a little too long for Hacker's taste. On his left cheek was an old knife scar, which wasn't disfiguring, but clearly visible, and his clothes were impeccable. In fact, Rios was wearing a bright white suit, which had irritated Hacker when he first saw the little man emerge from his car. *So much for being inconspicuous. Why not just send up a couple of flares*, he had thought. *This guy really* is *strange.*

They had sparred all through the ordering of their meals, with Hacker trying not to tip his hand and Rios easily making Hacker feel like a complete loser. For Rios, it was like toying with a very large, and slightly backward, child.

Somehow, without even quite knowing how it had happened, Hacker had revealed his real name. He still wasn't sure how Rios had gotten it out of him, but the little man now referred to him as Hacker or, worse yet, "my friend," as if talking to a seven-year-old.

The only positive things about this whole situation, as far as Hacker was concerned, was that Rios seemed to know exactly what he was talking about—and he definitely wasn't a cop. Other than that, there was an aura of menace about Rios that instantly put Hacker on the defensive.

"Look, Rios," said Hacker, pointing at the little man with his fork, "I've got to be on night patrol in a couple of hours, so what do you say we get down to business?"

Rios looked at the fork and then turned his cold, steel-blue eyes to meet Hacker's. A smile crept across his face, and he said, "You cut me, my friend. Here I've brought you to this excellent restaurant, bought us this incredible supper, including this exquisite vintage wine, I might add, and you don't seem to appreciate any of it."

'Well, I—" said Hacker.

"Surely you must realize that we must eat, drink, and make pleasant conversation before we begin to talk business. After all, we know nothing about each other, and there's no better way to get to know someone than over a fine meal, wouldn't you agree?"

"Uh—" said Hacker.

"Spoken like a gentleman," said Rios, his smile never wavering.

Hacker again felt like a child. This man was good, and he would need to keep his wits about him if he were going to match wits with this character. He decided that this would be his last glass of wine.

Rios seemed to notice that Hacker was only toying with his food. Smiling broadly, he said, "Is there something wrong with your lobster, my friend? Perhaps it was not prepared to your taste? I can get you a new one."

"No, no," said Hacker, "The lobster's fine. It's just that I have to get back to the base pretty soon, and—"

"Ah, yes, you have night guard duty. You mentioned that before," said Rios, who was just finishing his plate of squid.

As he spoke, Rios wiped his mouth and then took a sip of wine.

"More wine, my friend? It's an excellent vintage," he asked picking up the bottle and offering it to Hacker.

"No, thank you," said Hacker, placing his hand over the top of the glass to prevent Rios from refilling it. "I really have to go pretty soon."

Rios sat back and took another sip of wine.

"Are you absolutely certain that no one else on the base knows of your—activities?" Rios asked, looking Hacker straight in the eyes.

Rios' stare made him feel as if he were shrinking in his chair. But he was determined to stay with this strange, intimidating little man. After all, he'd met lots of strange characters over the course of his career, and he'd outlasted them all.

"No one suspects a thing. They've all been to college, and that makes them stupid," said Hacker, chuckling at his own joke.

Rios just smiled and nodded his head slightly, acknowledging Hacker's attempt at humor.

"Let us hope you are right, my friend. It would be a shame to have come this far and not succeed in our mission," said Rios, his eyes narrowing, his voice becoming hard and menacing. "And now, let us talk about the silver willow trees."

Something in the tone of Rios' voice made Hacker sit back. He looked into the little man's face and could almost see death reflected in his cold, steely eyes.

He could feel his confidence starting to waver, but he tried to keep his voice as level as he could, asking, "Willow trees?"

"Oh come, come now, my friend," Rios said softly, a dark, cutting edge to his voice, his eyes never leaving Hacker's, "surely you must remember the willow trees. We discussed them over the phone. They were hidden, along with seventy-five Colonial *rifles*, somewhere in this area."

Hacker was caught off guard.

Rios smiled knowingly and said, "Ah, I see by the look on your face that you do remember our conversation."

Hacker pushed himself away from the table slightly, as if ready to get up from the table, but before he could stand up, Rios shot out a hand and clamped it around Hacker's wrist with an amazing quickness. Hacker winced as Rios tightened his steely grip.

"Just so we understand each other, my friend, you should know that you were observed this afternoon, escorting some children out of Hudson's Wood."

Unbelievable, thought Hacker. *This guy knows everything!*

Hacker's wrist was pinned to the table, and he was unable to move. He looked down at his wrist, which was white from the pressure of Rios' grip, and then at Rios' face. While still smiling, the little man once more applied one more burst of pressure to Hacker's wrist, causing him to wince again. Then he released his grip, and Hacker instantly pulled his wrist close to his body and began rubbing it with his other hand. His mind was racing, but even as he tried to think of something to say, Rios seemed to read his mind.

"There's no use denying. I know everything, my friend," Rios said, calmly reaching out and taking another sip of wine.

Hacker sat, rubbing his hand, feeling like a little child who had been caught being naughty.

"Are you having me followed?" he asked.

"Let us just say that one doesn't reach the level that I've achieved without taking, shall we say, certain precautions, my friend—especially when there is so much at stake."

"Look, Rios—" said Hacker.

"Mr. Rios, if you please, Hacker," Rios said, raising his hand to interrupt.

Hacker grunted and began again, "Look, *Mr.* Rios, that was just a bunch of kids who we caught playing where they weren't supposed to. That's all."

Rios sat back, shaking his head, as if catching a child in a lie. He picked up his wine glass and said, flashing that maddening smile, "That's very interesting, Hacker. And why, do you suppose, were those four children carrying picks and shovels?"

Hacker felt as if the jaws of a trap were closing around him.

"Now how in the hell am I supposed to know that?" he asked. "They were just kids. You know as well as I do that kids do strange things, and sometimes, it don't mean nothin'."

"That is very true," said Rios. "But why, then, did you try to grab the oldest girl?"

Hacker could feel the noose tightening.

"Well, she said something that I didn't like. You know how smart-mouthed kids are today. I was only trying—"

Rios again stopped Hacker in mid-sentence by raising his hand.

"I think not, my friend," he said, sitting forward, setting his wine glass on the table, the smile now gone from his face.

"I think it was something more. I think she had something you wanted—a map, for instance."

Hacker was stunned, but before he could speak, Rios continued.

"I advise you to tell me the truth, Sergeant Hacker, and if I were you, I would do it this minute."

Every muscle in Hacker's body tensed, and his eyes darted toward the door.

"Don't even think about it," said Rios. "As you can see, I have associates at every entrance to the restaurant, and if you will look around, you will see a number of others nearby."

Hacker looked to his right and saw two large men standing in front of the restaurant's main door, arms folded menacingly across their chests. To his left, he saw other large men seated at tables nearby. In fact, as Hacker looked around, sweat beginning to show on his forehead, he could see that there was no one in the entire restaurant except large, steely-eyed men, all now looking directly at him.

"You see, Hacker, each of these men works for me," said Rios, leaning back in his chair once more. "In fact, I own this restaurant. This cuisine was most excellent, was it not? That's why I was sorry to see that you didn't seem to enjoy your lobster or this fine wine."

Hacker was now genuinely frightened. But then he relaxed, knowing he was beaten. If he played along with this little man, he would still get a nine million dollar share of the treasure.

He took one more look around the room, and then looked back at Rios and said, "Well, you've made your point, *Mr.* Rios. Let's talk."

Rios leaned forward, his large smile now returning. He picked up his glass and drained it, then picked up the wine bottle and refilled his glass. This time, when he offered the bottle, Hacker held out his glass, and Rios filled it to the brim.

"I'm glad to see that your taste for fine wine has returned," Rios said genially. "Now we can talk about the silver willow tree coins like gentlemen..."

☆ ☆ ☆

Stephanie didn't know what to feel at that moment. On the one hand, she was grateful for having her grandmother offer to help, but on the other hand, it seemed as if things were getting out of control. Randy, Ben, Alexandra, and Willie were in on this, of course, but now Grandma Betty and Aunt Susan, who was not happy about it at all, would also be there.

"I think this whole thing is just silly," Aunt Susan had said the moment she walked in the door.

But Grandma Betty had stood her ground, even though Susan had scolded her by saying, "Mother, I can't believe you're going along with this! You know, of course, that you're encouraging the kids to break the law."

But Grandma Betty had just smiled sweetly and raised a hand.

"Susan, as I told you on the phone, if you don't want Ben and Alexandra to join us in this adventure, then—"

"Adventure?" Aunt Susan had said, "*Break in* is more like it! And this is the United States government you're talking about, Mother. Maybe we should wait for Joe to get back. He's hauling a load to Scranton right now, but he'll be back in a couple days."

Grandma Betty had smiled patiently and said, "There isn't time for that, Susan. We have got to do this tonight."

"So you're saying that you're going through with this, no matter what I say?"

"Yes, Susan, we are."

Susan had stood in front of her mother, hands on her hips, angry, yet feeling powerless.

"Oh, Mother," she had finally said, stomping her foot like a child, "you're so stubborn!"

"So, does that mean you're coming or staying?" Grandma had asked pleasantly, turning to Stephanie and giving her a wink.

Susan's hands had then dropped to her sides.

"Well, I'm certainly not going to let you go out there alone. Who knows what kind of trouble you're going to get into."

"Good for you!" Grandma Betty said, giving her daughter a hug.

Stephanie hadn't waited to hear any more after that. She'd hurried up the stairs to her bedroom and closed the door behind her.

Now, she felt as if she had just a bit of an idea of what Lucy must have been feeling just before leaving on her secret mission to Black's farm more than two hundred years ago. Of course this was very different. If she were caught, she wasn't going to be killed or thrown in a British prison. Still, there was an air of excitement about it all—and a touch of danger.

Stephanie stared at her oak bureau and knew she was stalling, although she wasn't quite sure why. Then she took a deep breath, walked over to the bureau, and opened the bottom drawer. Lucy's dress was still there.

It was almost an hour later before everyone had finished checking their flashlights, gathering shovels and picks, and making sure that Willie had done his business. With each passing moment, Stephanie was becoming more anxious. She was glad when the entire entourage finally started across the field toward the Old Oak.

The evening had turned chilly, and black clouds occasionally covered the bright, full moon, plunging the world into complete darkness. Then, after the clouds had passed, the field was almost as bright as day.

Stephanie was wearing a long yellow raincoat to protect Lucy's heavy, but fragile, dress from the snagging twigs they would encounter in the woods.

Once she had reached the Old Oak, she wasn't sure exactly what was going to happen. But she hoped that Lucy would lead them to the spot where the rifles were buried. If not...well, she wouldn't allow herself to think about that.

Randy and Ben were arguing about who would lead the group through the field. Ben said that he was the leader, since this was his home, but Randy was tired of playing second fiddle and argued that he knew his way across the field as well as Ben. Alexandra was complaining that Ben got extra pudding for desert, and Grandma Betty and Aunt Susan were busy trying to keep everyone quiet.

But Stephanie found herself paying very little attention to everyone else. The closer she got to the woods, the stranger the world began to look. At first, she just felt a little light-headed, but then, the world began to spin, and she knew it was beginning to happen again.

She could clearly smell the smoke of campfires once more, and in her mind's eye, she could see herself sitting in front of one of those fires, Will Ashley by her side. She was wearing his coat. Even though she wasn't actually cold, she felt her body shudder. Instantly, Will put his arm around her and held her close. It felt wonderful—and it did make her feel warmer!

"Lucy, you've got a chill. Would you like me to stoke up the fire a little?"

"No, Will," she said, "this is fine."

Suddenly, she felt Will's large hand touch her chin and turn her face toward his. She closed her eyes and tilted her head back, as if she'd been kissed a thousand times before.

Will's lips were soft and warm, and in a moment, her body began to tingle in ways she'd never experienced before. It was both exhilarating and frightening. She broke off the kiss and pulled back slightly, looking into Will's eyes. For a moment, there was an exquisite silence between them.

She then saw herself stand, kiss Will lightly on the lips, and walk quickly across the compound toward her tent. Just before entering the tent, she looked back, and the last thing she saw was Will, still seated by the fire, his back to her, gently tossing a small twig into the fire.

"Stephanie, dear."

Grandma Betty's voice brought Stephanie out of her reverie. Again, she was momentarily confused. It took several moments before her mind had fully returned to the present.

"Stephanie, dear, are you all right?" asked Grandma Betty.

"Yes, Grandma, I'm fine," she said, a bit absent-mindedly.

But she was still thinking of the vision she'd just experienced. It had been her first kiss—even though it was really Lucy's kiss and not hers. But in some strange way, she had been there, too, and it was her lips that Will's had touched. It was her body that had felt all tingly and warm.

But no! She had to keep remembering—it wasn't *her* kiss. It had been Lucy's kiss, and it had taken place more than two hundred years ago! She could never forget that she was not Lucy Killgrew—she was Stephanie MacAllister, and she was only trying to help a long-lost relative find some peace.

As Stephanie wrestled with her thoughts, the high grass began to drop away and the Old Oak suddenly loomed darkly before them in the woods just ahead. The clouds had grown thicker, and Emy Moon was barely able to peek through.

Grandma Betty looked up at the clouds and said, "The wind is picking up. I'm not sure this was such a good idea, after all. It could rain any second now. Perhaps we should come back later, when the weather has cleared a little."

"I think that is an excellent idea!" Aunt Susan said.

"No, Grandma, please," said Stephanie. "We have to find the rifles tonight. I don't know why, but I know it has to be tonight. Once those machines start digging, it will be too late. Please, Grandma! Lucy is counting on us."

Although Grandma Betty didn't say a word, Stephanie turned and gave her a hug, saying, "Thank you, Grandma."

"Well, let's just try and be quick about it," Grandma Betty said quietly.

Aunt Susan only sighed in disbelief and muttered, "If this isn't the silliest thing…"

Stephanie felt herself being drawn toward the Old Oak as if she were sleepwalking. It was as if someone else were controlling her feet, making them move, one step at a time. The closer Stephanie came to the Old Oak, the less of her surroundings she seemed to notice. She felt the raincoat slip off her shoulders, just as the first raindrops began to fall, but Stephanie didn't feel the rain. She was beginning to slip away in time.

It was strange, in a way. There was no dividing line, no harsh transition. One instant, she was walking toward the Old Oak in the middle of a rainy night in the present day, and the next instant, she was standing in front of the Oak, blinking at the bright sunshine, in 1775.

She looked toward the road and what would one day be the large field of high grass through which they had just come, but there was no grass now—the area was covered with trees.

The Oak was much younger, and the air smelled differently, but before she had time to dwell on any of that, she heard the thud from behind the tree.

She spun around, and there, lying on the leaf-covered ground, she saw the front end of an old-fashioned rifle. As she stood, staring dumbly at the rifle, a second one dropped, the sound of steel hitting steel piercing the silence.

Slowly and quietly, Stephanie walked around to the other side of the Oak, and behind the tree was a buckskin-clad girl, her back to Stephanie. She was scooping up several rifles that had been leaning against the Oak and beginning to make her way deeper into the woods.

Stephanie didn't need an introduction. She knew instantly who the girl was—it was Lucy Killgrew!

Chapter Twenty-three

The End of the Line

SERGEANT HACKER HAD NO trouble sneaking a mine detector out of supply and into a jeep he'd requisitioned for the evening. After all, "appropriating" government property was how Hacker had made his living for almost forty years, and he was a pro.

He didn't relish having to sweep the entire area north of the Old Oak, searching for a bag of silver coins and a cache of rifles that may or may not actually exist. He'd always heard that treasure hunting was supposed to be easy, especially when you had some idea of where the treasure was located. The problem was, as Hacker has seen many times over the years, the world is a much bigger place in real life than it looks like on a treasure map. What seems like a small area on a map can become a huge piece of ground when you have to search it, foot by foot.

And Hacker hated doing any more work than absolutely necessary. His business was stealing supplies, dropping them at a pick-up point, and letting the buyer do all the real work. Sometimes he just left a door open and turned his back, which was even less work, and always profitable.

But *this*…this looked like it was going to turn out to be actual *work*, and there didn't seem to be any way around it—Rios had made that clear tonight in the restaurant.

The words "north of the Old Oak" could mean that he'd have to comb every square inch of two or three acres—maybe more—and that might take days.

But Rios had made it clear that if he failed to turn up the coins, or if they fell into any other hands, his life would be over. In fact, Rios had seemed to take delight in describing in great detail how easy it would be for a body to disappear in the kitchen of a large restaurant like his and never be seen again.

Hacker also had no doubt that Rios would carry through his threats, and who knew—maybe those coins really were out there, just waiting to be picked up.

Besides saving his life, finding those coins had other rewards, of course. Even split in half, eighteen million dollars was a nice chunk of change.

Hacker threw the jeep into gear and began the twenty-minute ride to Sector 27-A.

Who knows, he though, *maybe those damn kids will already be there. Then all I'll have to do is just take the coins out of their hands. It'll be like stealing candy from a baby.*

☆ ☆ ☆

Stephanie found that she was frightened to move very far away from the Oak. Somehow the Oak was her anchor-point in all this. If she strayed too far from the Oak, she was afraid she might never find her way back to the present. But she knew she had to follow Lucy into the woods, and Lucy would lead her to the rifles. So, taking a deep breath, she pushed away from the tree and began to follow, several yards behind Lucy.

The woods hadn't changed a great deal in two hundred years, and yet they had changed. Over time, even without human intervention, trees grow, they die, they're struck by lightning, and the wind and rain slowly wear away the hills upon which they grow.

Lucy was walking very quickly, as if her mission was very urgent. For a moment, Stephanie was afraid that she had lost track of Lucy and that she herself would be lost in these woods forever.

But then she thought she heard the sound of someone singing, very softly. Although she'd never studied French, Stephanie thought the song sounded like French. She followed the sound and, in a moment, she caught a glimpse of Lucy, walking quickly through a grove of trees off to her left.

Lucy seemed to be following along the edge of a gorge. Down below, hidden by the dense forest, Stephanie could hear the sound of rushing water.

After following the gorge for about fifty yards, they came to a small granite outcropping, where Lucy stopped. Under the outcropping was a small cave, with a single spruce tree growing in front of its entrance. Without hesitation, Lucy bent down and crawled into the cave with her armload of rifles.

Stephanie walked closer, her eyes scanning the cave and the lone tree that stood guard in front of it. She looked all around, searching for some landmark that might still be there two hundred years from now. Stephanie smiled as she heard Lucy's muffled voice continue to sing softly in French from inside the cave.

A few moments later, Lucy crawled back out of the cave and dusted herself off.

When she stood up, her eyes met Stephanie's—but not a word was spoken between them.

Their eyes held contact for a long time, but in that time, their souls seemed to touch in a very real way. Then, with a smile, Lucy turned and started back toward the Old Oak, her beautiful voice again softly singing in French.

Stephanie followed, too numb to think. She just let one foot follow the other…

"Hey, Steff! Are you gonna zone out on us all night, or what?"

It was Randy's voice, sounding tired and irritated.

As Stephanie looked around, she could see that everyone was staring at her. They looked worried.

"So where's the pirate treasure? Did ya get any clues while you were dead?" Alexandra said.

Aunt Susan gave her daughter a quick poke in the ribs, saying, "Will you hush up, please?"

"Stephanie, dear," Grandma Betty said. "Are you all right? You had us worried, child."

Stephanie smiled and said, "Yes, Grandma. I'm fine. In fact, Lucy showed me where the rifles are!"

Then she leaned over to her grandmother and whispered, "She looked straight at me, Grandma. She looked right into my eyes, and now I'm sure that she wants me to complete her mission. Isn't it wonderful?"

"Yes, dear, it truly is," said Grandma Betty, taking hold of Stephanie's hand. "I'd say that is quite wonderful, indeed!"

A light rain was still falling, but only Aunt Susan seemed to mind.

"Look, I'm not sure what this is all about, but I do know that I'd like to get it all over with as soon as possible. I don't feel good about Ben and Alexandra being out in weather like this."

"Oh, Susan," Grandma Betty said with a sigh. "Tell me, when was it exactly that you became such a stick-in-the-mud?"

Not waiting for her daughter's reply, Grandma Betty said, "Now, Stephanie, dear, if you know where the rifles are, I suggest we get going—for everyone's sake!"

"OK, everybody, they're over this way, on the edge of a ravine," said Stephanie.

Far away, there was a flash of lightning, followed a few seconds later by the low rumble of thunder.

☆ ☆ ☆

As Sergeant Hacker made his way toward Sector 27-A, he began to get a strange feeling. It started as an itch on the back of his scalp and then seemed to expand throughout his body. It was a feeling he'd gotten a number of times over the past forty years—and it always meant that he was being watched.

Aw, who cares, he thought. *Let the little snake watch me. If I do find the willow trees, he'll know about it, anyway.*

It was probably better this way, he decided. This way, he'd have witnesses to let Rios know he had done his best, whether he found the coins or not. It might even save him from being ground into hamburger in the kitchen of Rios' fancy restaurant.

At that moment, a flash of lightning lit up the sky. Although it wasn't close, the flash lit up the area just enough for Hacker to be able to make out a group of people walking away from the Old Oak—and they were carrying shovels.

This was perfect! Hacker eased the jeep to a stop and snapped off the headlights.

As he stepped out of the jeep, he considered bringing the mine detector with him, then thought better of it. He'd rather not have anything in his hands, until he was sure about the situation. He pulled up the collar on his coat and pulled his hat low across his face. It was only raining lightly now, but he knew it would be pouring soon.

✩ ✩ ✩

"That must have been Mayfair Gorge you're talking about, Steff," said Ben. "It's just over this way, come on!"

Stephanie relinquished the lead to Ben. Even though Stephanie had "just" been to the cave where the rifles were hidden, it had really been two hundred years ago—and in broad daylight. Now it was dark, cold, and wet, and things were unfamiliar enough to make finding her way difficult.

Mayfair Gorge sloped fifteen or twenty feet to a rocky bottom and was about twenty-five feet wide. Stephanie yelled when she heard the water running from the bottom of the gorge, exactly as she'd heard it when she followed Lucy.

"This is it!" she said. "The rifles are just up ahead! I know it! Come on, everyone, hurry!"

"Kids! Slow down!" Grandma Betty called out as the cousins began to move quickly along the gorge.

"Ben! Alexandra!" Susan yelled, but it was no use. The kids were filled with treasure fever and nothing could slow them down now.

Susan said, "Well, Mother, I hope you're happy. We're trespassing on property the kids were specifically told to stay away from, it's dark, it's starting to rain, and—"

"Susan," said her mother sharply, "as the kids say, chill out, dear. And what if Stephanie is right about this place? Have you thought about that?"

"Oh, Mother," said Susan, "You can't seriously believe that—"

But her words were interrupted by the excited sounds of the children, saying, "Grandma! Aunt Susan! We've found the place! Come on!"

Grandma Betty said, "What was that you were saying, dear?"

When the grownups arrived at the cave, Randy, Ben, and Alexandra were already flailing away with their picks and shovels.

"Hold it! Everybody stop, right now!" Grandma Betty said.

"But Grandma, Stephanie says the treasure's buried right here somewhere," Alexandra protested. "And remember, I get to shoot one of the rifles, 'cause I helped find 'em!"

"There'll be no shooting of any kind, young lady," Aunt Susan said firmly.

"There's no time for that right now. We'd best get back to the business at hand," Grandma Betty said. "This rain is starting to come down harder, and who knows who heard all that commotion you kids just made!"

"You're right, Grandma," said Ben. "I'm sorry. Now, Steff, can you tell us where we need to start digging?"

Stephanie looked up and saw an old, broken tree, just barely alive. There were also several other trees growing around, though, and those trees extended all the way down the slope of the hill. It wasn't at all the way she remembered it, even though she knew in her heart that this was the place.

Stephanie closed her eyes and tried to picture exactly what she had seen when she had watched Lucy hide the rifles, and in moment, it almost seemed as if she had partly opened her eyes again. Before her was an image of the hill, but not the hill that stood before her at that moment. It was a slightly different hill, this one bathed in sunlight.

Stephanie opened her eyes just a little, and to her surprise, it was as if there were now two images of the hill in front of her. One was the hill as it was at this moment, and the other was an image of the hill as it had been, two hundred years ago. Then, it was as if the two images were beginning to overlap, like a pair of superimposed photographic images.

And there, as plain as day, she could see exactly where the rifles were buried.

Thank you, Lucy, Stephanie thought. *I won't let you down. I promise, your mission will soon be completed. I won't fail you. You have my word.*

At last Stephanie opened her eyes all the way. Again, everyone was staring at her expectantly, even Aunt Susan this time. Stephanie pointed her shovel at the base of a small bush.

"Right here," she said. "That's where the cave is. That's where Lucy hid the rifles."

Randy and Ben whooped with joy.

"Come on! Let's start digging!" said Randy, ramming his shovel into the hillside.

While all that had been going on, Sergeant Hacker had been leaning casually against the trunk of a tree no more than thirty yards away. He didn't need to worry about being seen. No one was looking in his direction, and nobody would until after the coins had been found—and then he'd make his move.

Obviously this was meant to be. All he had to do was

sit back and wait for these backwater bounty hunters to hand him a cool eighteen million bucks. Life didn't get any better than this!

He vaguely remembered hearing something about old rifles being connected with the coins somehow, and for some reason these 'hicks' were more interested in the rifles than in the coins. How dumb could these people be?

For a moment, he even toyed with the idea of letting them keep the rifles in exchange for him taking the coins, but he dismissed that idea immediately.

No, he thought, *a professional is judged by how he handles the details.*

He gently patted the gun he wore on his side. He rarely was forced to use violence, but he wasn't above getting rough if it were necessary.

Randy and Ben began bickering over who's turn it was to take the next shovelful of dirt, until suddenly, Stephanie had had enough.

"Stop! You two back up and give me that shovel!" she demanded, snatching a shovel from Randy's hands.

Randy started to complain, but the tone in his sister's voice left no doubt that she meant business.

"Mouse, get back," said Aunt Susan.

"Everybody get back," said Grandma Betty. "Stephanie brought us here, and Stephanie should be the one to uncover the rifles."

This time, no one complained. Instead, they all took a few steps back, giving Stephanie plenty of room to work.

She focused all her attention on the one spot of earth where she knew the rifles were hidden. Then, just as she raised her shovel, a break in the clouds allowed one blazing shaft of moonlight to strike the blade, causing it to shimmer like a torch in the darkness.

"This one's for you, Emy," Stephanie said.

She had never used a shovel in her life but, taking a deep breath, Stephanie plunged it deep into the soft earth.

For several moments, the only sound was that of Stephanie, piercing the ground with her shovel, lifting the dirt out of the hole, and tossing it to the side. And then, there was another sound. It sounded like steel scraping against steel. As the sharp point of her shovel struck the ground, the damp earth around it caved in. Stephanie fell forward as the entrance to the cave gave way.

Only the tip of the shovel handle now showed through the rich black soil.

"We've found it! Lucy, we've found your rifles," whispered Stephanie.

For several seconds no one moved or said a word. But then, as if a dam had been opened, the boys again began digging, opening the entrance to the cave even farther. Grandma Betty grabbed hold of the bush that covered most of the opening with its branches.

"Everybody watch out," she said.

She pulled at the bush, causing clods of dirt to fall into the cave opening with a hollow sound. Stephanie grabbed another part of the bush and she, too, began to pull. Then, Ben, Randy, Alexandra, and even Aunt Susan took hold.

"O.K. now," Grandma Betty said. "On the count of three, everybody pull with all you've got. Ready? One... two...three!"

For a moment, the roots of the bush held fast, but then, the bush gave way, and everyone went tumbling over backward.

By the time they were finished, the opening was about five feet high and a few feet wide. More than anything, Stephanie wanted to be the first one to look into the cave, but she stopped to help her grandmother up.

"Are you O.K., Grandma?" she asked.

Grandma Betty looked at her granddaughter and said, "Are you kidding? I haven't had this much fun in years."

Stephanie hesitated for a moment, and Grandma Betty took her hand.

"Now it's time for you to go inside, child. Go find out what Lucy has been trying to show you."

Stephanie turned toward the cave, half expecting to see Alexandra and the boys clambering in. But Randy was holding the others at bay.

"Listen, Steff. You brought us here, and you should be the first one to go inside."

Stephanie's eyes filled with tears.

She smiled at her brother and said, "Thank you, little brother."

Randy stepped aside, followed by the others. Without a word, Ben handed Stephanie a flashlight. She flicked it on, and in a moment, Stephanie was inside the cave.

She shown the beam back and forth in front of her and was struck by a large number of what looked like long, dirty sticks, strewn around the cave floor.

Then she knew. This was what rifles would look like after being buried for two hundred years. She gasped and then began to cry. She hadn't meant to—but she couldn't help herself.

"What is it, dear?" called Grandma Betty from outside the cave. "Are you all right in there?"

"Oh, Grandma, they're here. Lucy's rifles! They're here!"

Suddenly, there was a mad scramble of bodies squeezing through the entrance to the cave.

Stephanie stood back and let the others look around, their flashlights shining like searchlights in the darkness of the cave. She was happier than she had ever felt in her life, and nothing could spoil this moment.

"Well, ain't this touching," a deep male voice called from the entrance of the cave. "The family, in a warm and fuzzy moment. I've got to hand it to you, kids. You've done great."

Standing in the mouth of the cave was Sergeant Hacker, a gun in one hand and a coiled rope in the other.

Grandma Betty shone her flashlight into Hacker's eyes, and he growled, "Hey, lady, get that light out of my eyes, before I shoot it out!"

Once she had seen his face, Stephanie knew who this evil man was.

"It's you again," she said.

"That's right, kiddo. It's me, big as life and twice as mean."

Everyone fell silent as they began to realize what was happening.

"What are you doing here?" Stephanie finally said. "And why are you pointing that gun at us again?"

Hacker smiled and said, "I think I might ask you the same question, little girl. Seems to me you were told to stay off this base. You're lucky I didn't shoot first and ask questions later."

Hacker took a step forward, holding his gun menacingly in front of his chest, causing everyone to step back.

"Anyway, in this case, I figured it might make my job a little easier," he said, looking around the cave.

Stephanie heard Grandma Betty move slowly behind and place her hand on her shoulder.

Grandma Betty looked at the huge man and said, "And what might that job be, may I ask?"

Hacker looked at Grandma Betty and said, "My job? Well, let's see. I suppose you could say that my job is to rob you. Yeah, that'd sum it up pretty good."

"But why?" Stephanie asked. "These old rifles can't be that valuable."

Hacker laughed until his laughter was choked out by a coughing spell.

"I'm not after those moldy old rifles, girlie. Let's say I'm after something a little more valuable."

He threw the rope on the ground then turned to Alexandra and said gruffly, "Hey, runt, toss me that flashlight."

"No," she said, "I won't."

"Listen, kid, I ain't got time to play games. Give me that light!"

Ben grabbed the flashlight from his sister's hand and tossed it to Hacker.

"Hey!" shouted Alexandra. "That's mine!"

Aunt Susan moved quickly and put her hand on Alexandra's shoulder.

"Would you mind telling us what this is all about?" Grandma Betty asked, stepping between Hacker and the rest of the group.

Hacker played the light around the interior of the cave.

"Keep your shirt on, lady," he said.

He continued shining the light around the cave until he found what he was looking for.

"Bingo!" he said, moving quickly over to the far wall of the cave and bending down to pick something off the ground.

In his excitement, Hacker forgot about the little band of treasure hunters. Everyone looked at each other, unsure of what to do. Should they run? Should they try to grab him? Or should they just stand right where they were?

Their questions became meaningless when, a moment

later, Hacker stood and turned to face his hostages, a huge smile on his face, holding a leather pouch about twice the size of his fist.

"I can't believe it," Hacker said softly. "That oily little lizard was telling the truth."

"What you got there?" said Alexandra defiantly. "If it is in this cave, it's ours, 'cause we found it first!"

Hacker didn't seem to hear Alexandra's protest. Without a word, he carefully opened the drawstring at the top of the bag and reached inside, and when he lifted his hand out, he was holding several pieces of metal, round and shiny.

"What are those?" Stephanie said.

"Let's just call them my retirement," Hacker said, laughing. "Let's just say that a handful of these little beauties equals an island in the South Pacific."

"What are they?" Alexandra insisted.

"They're coins, kid. Very special coins."

Alexandra turned to Ben and said, "You see? I told you it was pirate treasure. I told you that all along!"

"You can have the coins," Grandma Betty said, as Randy moved quietly to her side. "Take whatever you want. Just leave us alone, and we'll go."

Hacker pointed the gun at Betty and smiled.

"You know, I like you, lady. You got guts, and I like that. So I'll tell ya what I'm gonna do. I'm gonna leave you and these brats right here with these old rifles you're so fond of."

"Why? What are you going to do?"

"Well, old lady, I thought we might play a little game. You kids seem to like games, right? It's a little game I call 'Tie Up the Kids and the Loudmouth Lady.' You see, the way I figure it, by the time anyone finds your bodies, I'll be long gone and very, very rich."

Hacker then raised the gun to shoulder height and took aim at Grandma Betty.

"Now," he said, "Take the rope....."

Suddenly, another voice came from the cave entrance.

"I see where you are headed with this, my friend, but I think we should alter the rules, just a little. Now, I suggest that you drop the gun, or you're a dead man."

The small man with slicked-back black hair moved into the cave.

"Rios!" Hacker yelled.

"Hey!" shouted Alexandra, "It's getting crowded in here."

Two large men stood on either side of the cave entrance, each holding a handgun, each pointed directly at Hacker.

"Now, Hacker, if you will be so kind as to drop your weapon, set the bag on the ground, and then step over beside the others."

"What do you mean?" Hacker said, his frightened eyes darting between Rios and his henchmen. "We had a deal, and I held up my part of the bargain."

"Oh, I'm sure you did. In fact, I'm sure you had every intention of taking those coins and bringing them to me," said Rios, his voice dripping with sarcasm.

"Well, of course, I did," said Hacker, his voice shaking. "What makes you think I'm not a man of my word?"

"Oh, my friend, of course, I have no doubt that you're a man of your word. Unfortunately for you, I am not."

There was a momentary pause while Hacker assessed his chances in this situation. He then slowly lowered the gun and dropped it onto the floor of the cave.

"Listen, Rios," Hacker said, "You're gonna need me. What about those missiles you wanted? What about—"

Rios cut him off, saying, "Yes, that is a shame. But now that I have the willow trees, I fear that I'll no longer have any need for missiles, and to use your own words, I think it's time for me to retire. Now, if you will be so kind, please set the bag down next to your weapon."

Hacker eyed the handgun and began to bend slowly to the ground, holding the bag of coins in his left hand. Then there was a blur of motion and the sound of two shots being fired almost simultaneously.

Hacker's body jerked twice as the bullets hit him, and a moment later, the large man was on the ground.

Alexandra screamed. Grandma Betty held Randy and Stephanie close to her sides, as if she could protect them from what would happen next.

Rios' goons turned their weapons toward Grandma Betty, but she stood perfectly still, her eyes fixed on Rios.

"That was uncalled for, young man."

Rios laughed a high-pitched laugh.

"I suggest that you begin to worry about yourself and these children, my dear. You're all going to be dead in a little while, anyway, just like your friend over there, " said Rios, as he entered the cave and began walking toward the place where Hacker and the bag of coins lay on the floor.

At that moment, something snapped inside of Stephanie. She thought about all that Lucy had endured as she fought evil in her own time, and not once had Lucy ever given in—so why should she? This man was going to kill them anyway—he'd just said so—so why should she make it easy for him?

She lunged forward and jumped on Rios' back. Instantly, the other kids dowsed their flashlights, and the room was plunged into utter darkness.

There were the sounds of a struggle, with Rios cursing

and Stephanie screaming in anger and frustration.

That sound lasted only a few moments, however, before the beam of a flashlight split the darkness and shown directly on Stephanie's terrified face. The light came from a flashlight held in Rios' right hand.

His left arm was around Stephanie's throat.

Stephanie struggled, trying to catch her breath.

"That was a very bad mistake, young lady," he said through clenched teeth. "Abrams, catch this!"

Rios tossed the flashlight to one of his huge henchmen. Then, as Abrams shone the light on him, Rios pulled a gun from his shoulder holster.

"No one attacks me and lives," said Rios, pushing the gun hard into Stephanie's right temple.

Suddenly, there was a voice from the entrance of the cave.

"All right, nobody move! Drop your weapons and put your hands in the air!"

Rios was confused, and his arm tightened around Stephanie's neck as he spun to face the cave entrance. Stephanie was yanked off-balance, and she lost her footing, causing Rios to tighten his chokehold even more as he struggled to get her back onto her feet.

"This is Captain Jenkins of the United States Army. You are trespassing on a government facility. You are ordered to drop your weapons this instant. If you do not comply, we will begin firing."

Rios waved his pistol wildly in the direction of the entrance.

"I think not, Captain," Rios yelled, the beam of Abram's flashlight clearly showing the combination of rage and fear on his face.

Rios then swung his gun back into Stephanie's temple and shouted, "I think you should be the ones to throw down your weapons—right now, or the girl dies. Do you hear me, Captain?"

For several long moments, the air was filled with nothing but a desperate silence.

Then suddenly, Rios' henchmen looked at each other, nodded their heads slightly, and threw their guns to the cave floor.

"What are you doing, you fools?" Rios yelled. "Don't you see? We've got the upper hand here. I've got the girl as a hostage!"

"*You* may have a hostage," came Captain Jenkins' voice from outside the cave, "but it's clear that your men have realized that they'll make excellent targets for us."

Jenkins then spoke directly to the henchmen.

"You two in the entrance, put your hands in the air and walk slowly toward the sound of my voice."

Both men instantly complied, and as Abrams raised his hands, the beam of the flashlight suddenly disappeared, again plunging the cave into darkness.

To her right, Stephanie heard a shuffling motion and then heard a ferocious bark. It was Willie, and he seemed to be attacking!

There was a huge explosion and a flash of light as Rios fired his gun in the direction of the sound.

As the gun went off, Alexandra screamed, "Willie!"

Willie yelped in pain, but Stephanie felt Rios' grip loosen slightly as he whirled around to face the charging dog.

"Come on, kids, help me!" Stephanie yelled.

She sank her teeth into Rios' arm, and his scream let the others know where he was in the darkness, and they quickly rushed to Stephanie's aid.

There was another blinding flash, another deafening explosion, and, from that moment on, Stephanie suddenly began to hear everything as if it were coming from somewhere far away.

Although she could still see nothing, she could hear the sounds of scuffling in the darkness. There seemed to be many footsteps, and then a shaft of light streamed in from the cave entrance, showing Rios on the ground, with Randy on one arm, Ben and Mouse on the other, Aunt Susan on his legs, and Grandma Betty sitting proudly on his chest.

"I *told* you that was uncalled for, young man, but you wouldn't listen," she said.

Then, Stephanie's mind began to spin. She could hear the echoes of cannon fire, fifes and drums, and the laughter of children. The thunder of battle and the sobs of a young girl, alone and frightened in the woods, reverberated in her head. The large hands of three colonial loyalists grabbing her and taking her prisoner flashed through her mind. Then, she thought she heard a voice, deep and kind, beginning to cut through the roiling jumble of sounds.

"Are you all right, miss?" the voice said, becoming stronger.

"Miss, are you all right?"

But even though Stephanie heard the words, she couldn't seem to understand their meaning. It was as if they were being spoken in a foreign language.

"Miss? Please, can you hear me? I'm sorry we had to frighten you."

Stephanie opened her eyes and saw the face of Captain Jenkins.

"I...I know you," she said, just before she fainted.

Stephanie remembered very little of what happened after that. Apparently, she and the others were taken to the military base infirmary, and she thought she remembered several policemen asking questions, but the details were sketchy.

She vaguely recalled being loaded into a jeep with Grandma Betty, Aunt Susan, and the others—including Willie, who had only been grazed by Rios' wild shot—and driven home.

And finally, she thought she remembered Grandma Betty helping her upstairs and putting her into bed—but that was all she would remember until she awoke, late the next morning.

Chapter Twenty-Four

The Biggest Surprise of Her Life

WHEN STEPHANIE FINALLY AWOKE and rolled over, the clock on the top of her dresser said it was a little after eleven. She couldn't remember the last time she'd slept that late.

Her whole body seemed to be aching—especially her head.

Reaching up, she could feel a large bandage on her forehead. What was that all about?

For a moment, she was totally confused—but then, she remembered, although large parts of it still made very little sense. Who were those strangers who had forced themselves into her life, choked her, and had even threatened to kill her?

Her first impulse was to pull the covers over her head and wish it all away. The whole thing seemed like some story out of a book that she wouldn't have wanted to read.

But it really *had* happened—all of it.

She looked across the room and saw Lucy's dress, carefully draped over a chair in the corner. Seeing that dress opened the floodgates. Every feeling, every emotion, every memory from the night before came washing over her. Some of it had been wonderful and mysterious—some of it had been a nightmare, more frightening than anything she'd ever experienced or ever hoped to experience.

It was over now—wasn't it?

But as she looked at the dress, she suddenly realized that it was *not* over yet.

There was still one detail yet to be resolved. And to resolve it, she would have to put Lucy's dress on one last time.

As Stephanie lay thinking, there was a light knocking on the door.

"Stephanie? Stephanie, dear, are you awake?"

Grandma Betty quietly opened the door and stuck her head in. She smiled when she saw that Stephanie was awake.

"Good morning, child. We all had quite a scare last night. Poor child, you weren't quite yourself after the awful man shot at you."

"Shot me?" Stephanie said, her hand automatically reaching for the bandage on her forehead.

"Oh, thank goodness he only grazed you, dear, but it was enough to knock you senseless. And I don't mind telling you, child, I was, well, we all were pretty worried there for a while. You didn't seem to know who you were, where you were, or even what century you were in! You went on and on about rifles, Tom and Nancy Killgrew, and some man named Lucius Coffin. None of it made any sense."

"Lucius Coffin?" said Stephanie. "I don't know anyone named Lucius Coffin."

"Well, thank goodness that's all over now," said Grandma Betty, gently stroking Stephanie's hair.

Then Stephanie sat up and asked, "Is everyone all right, Grandma? From last night, I mean."

Grandma Betty smiled reassuringly.

"Everyone's just fine, dear. In fact, they're all waiting to see you downstairs."

"They're waiting for me?"

"Yes, dear. I understand that the army people are removing Lucy's rifles from the cave this morning. And Captain Jenkins says he has something they want to present you, as soon as you're up and about. I promised I'd call and let them know when you felt up to it," said Grandma Betty, her eyes full of love for her granddaughter.

Stephanie had never been so much in the center of attention before. It was a little embarrassing but also kind of nice.

"They want to give me something? Did the Captain say what it was?"

Grandma Betty shook her head.

"No, child. I'm not sure. Charlie—I mean, Captain Jenkins—wouldn't give me any details. Dear me, it's always strange for me to run into kids I used to teach, now all grown up. I can remember little Charlie Jenkins from the eighth grade. He loved to play with guns even way back then! I wasn't surprised that he had become a soldier."

Stephanie smiled and hugged her grandmother. For now, everything was all right.

Half an hour later, Stephanie had showered, dressed, and ran downstairs to the kitchen, where she was now eating Grandma's special French toast, along with several scrambled eggs and a couple pieces of bacon. She couldn't remember ever being this hungry.

Everyone else was there, too—even Aunt Susan. Willie was sleeping just outside the back door.

"Willie's OK," said Alexandra. "It was just a fish wound."

"A *flesh* wound, you little knucklehead!" said Ben.

"You were *awesome* last night, Steff!" Randy said. "I mean *really* awesome!"

"You sure were," Ben added. "I couldn't believe the way you stood up to those guys! What was it like having a gun up against your—"

"Please!" Aunt Susan interrupted. "I don't want to hear any more talk about guns. You know how I've always felt about guns. And I don't think I will ever get over last night!"

Then she took a deep breath and said, "Stephanie, I owe you an apology."

"Steff, can I have a piece of your bacon?" Alexandra said, quickly removing a strip from Stephanie's plate before waiting for a reply.

Stephanie looked at her aunt. She had no idea what Aunt Susan was talking about.

"I didn't believe your story about this Lucy girl, or the rifles, or any of it," Aunt Susan said, her eyes filling with tears. "I...well, I was wrong, and I admit it. And to think that you could have been—"

Aunt Susan broke down at that point and buried her head in her hands. Grandma Betty quickly walked over and put her arms around her daughter.

Stephanie was shocked. She wouldn't have blamed Aunt Susan, or anyone else, for not believing her story. If she hadn't been the one Lucy had chosen to ask for help, she probably wouldn't have believed any of it herself.

But what shocked her most was the fact that a grown-up was apologizing to her. Grown-ups hardly ever apologized to kids.

"That's O.K., Aunt Susan. I understand," said Stephanie, "I can hardly believe most of it myself."

Susan looked at Stephanie with a half smile and said, "I suppose being as close and loving as we are, we never believed that our lives could really be threatened. I guess last night was a reality check. I guess last night we learned that things really do go bump in the night, and that trolls, monsters and evil can exist in many forms."

Grandma Betty nodded then looked at the round, yellow clock on the wall and then stood and smiled at Stephanie.

"I told Captain Jenkins that we'd be there tomorrow. I really think you should go back upstairs and rest a little more—unless you want more French toast, dear."

Stephanie wiped her mouth. "No thanks, Grandma. I couldn't eat another bite."

"But when do we get our pirate treasure?" Alexandra said.

Ben slapped his forehead.

"Listen, squirt. After all we've been through, how many times do I have to tell you, it isn't a pirate treasure? There never was a pirate treasure. You're such a twerp!"

"I'm not a twerp!" Alexandra replied hotly. "Mommy, Ben called me a twerp!"

"All right, you two. Knock it off," said Aunt Susan, wiping her eyes with a tissue Grandma Betty had handed her.

"But, Mom, Ben called me a twerp!"

Stephanie listened to the conversation and smiled. After everything she'd been through, even her cousins' bickering sounded beautiful. She also knew that her entire world had changed in the last week, and she would never look at things the same way again.

✿ ✿ ✿

The next day, everyone had piled into Aunt Susan's station wagon for the fifteen-minute drive to the base. Ben and Randy wanted to walk, cutting across the grass-covered field as they always did, but Grandma Betty was firm.

"We're all going in the car together—as a family—and that is that," she said, and the tone of her voice told everyone that there could be no argument.

As the station wagon pulled onto the base, several soldiers waved the car along, directing the vehicle toward the Old Oak.

"What in the world?" Grandma Betty said from the front seat.

It was an amazing scene, Stephanie thought. It reminded her of a scene from some old science-fiction movie, as the military began surrounding a downed flying saucer.

There were people and vehicles everywhere. Soldiers were running back and forth, shouting orders; two helicopters were sitting in the weed-covered field, the grass blown down flat all around them.

And then, as if by magic, Captain Jenkins appeared out of the mass of swirling bodies, smiling and extending his hand to help Stephanie out of the car.

"Miss MacAllister! Welcome! If you'll please follow me, we have a surprise for you!"

Captain Jenkins then turned to Grandma Betty, Aunt Susan, and the others, who were also climbing out of the station wagon.

"Ladies and gentlemen, if you will kindly walk this way."

Stephanie couldn't believe it. Captain Jenkins had spoken to her first and then had spoken to the adults. She'd never felt so important—and she liked it!

Someone shouted something, and every soldier in the area instantly came to attention.

Stephanie waited for Grandma Betty to reach her side, and whispered, "I'm not sure what's happening here, but I want you with me, Grandma."

Grandma Betty looked down at her granddaughter and smiled.

"I'm right here, child," she said, giving Stephanie a wink and patting her hand.

Led by Captain Jenkins, the group walked through rows of soldiers, past several people in white lab coats, past the Old Oak, which now had a stage-like platform built in front of it. Everything looked so different that, for a moment, Stephanie wondered if she wasn't still delirious or asleep.

As they walked, Stephanie looked up at Captain Jenkins and asked, "Captain, that awful Sergeant Hacker. Did he, is he..."

Captain Jenkins looked down and said, "Dead? No, Sergeant Hacker is in intensive care, but they expect him to pull through. And that's good, because the minute he's out of bed, he's going straight into the stockade—and I expect he'll be there for a long, long time."

"But why?" asked Stephanie.

"Well, the Army's had its eye on him for well over a year now. We suspected he was dealing in stolen government property at his old post; therefore, we transferred him here so that we could watch him operate under new surroundings. And even without what he did to you and your family last night, that business with Rios will give us enough evidence to put Sergeant Hacker away for the rest of his life."

"Rios?" said Stephanie. "Was that the other man's name? The one who was choking me?"

"That's right," said Jenkins. "He told us the whole thing last night—and I can tell you, he was none too happy about being taken down by a couple women, four kids—"

"And a smelly old dog," Alexandra said, making everyone laugh.

Nothing more was said for a few minutes as the group walked along the edge of the gorge until they came to the entrance to the cave, which had been made larger. Several people in white lab coats were busy carefully carrying rifles from the cave.

Even though she had seen Lucy carrying several rifles during one of her "visits," Stephanie had been more interested in Lucy than she had been in the firearms. Consequently, she was surprised to see that the rifles were nearly five feet long and that both the metal barrels and wooden stocks were intricately detailed. It turned out that Mr. Black and Joshua had been more than just gunsmiths—they had been artists.

Stephanie sensed that Captain Jenkins was growing more nervous as they approached the cave entrance. There, standing on a large rock, was a rather hefty man, wearing an impressive uniform with lots of medals and ribbons on it.

Captain Jenkins stopped, sprang to attention, saluted, and said, "Sir!"

The older officer looked at Jenkins and then returned his salute, saying, "Captain."

"Sir, may I introduce the young lady who discovered the rifles? Stephanie MacAllister, this is Brigadier General Andrew Preston."

The older man looked at Stephanie and smiled. He

stepped down from the rock and took Stephanie's hands in his. Then he looked deeply into her eyes before he spoke.

There was a grandfatherly-type kindness as he said, "So you're Stephanie MacAllister? I am honored to meet you, young lady. As the Captain said, I am Brigadier General Andrew Preston."

Then he smiled, winked, and whispered conspiratorially, "But you can call me Andy. Would it be all right for me to call you Stephanie?"

Stephanie was so flustered she couldn't think of anything to say for a moment, but Grandma Betty stepped forward and smoothed things over, as she always did.

"Brigadier, I'm Betty MacAllister. I'm Stephanie's grandmother."

Then she gestured to the others in the group and pointed to each of them as she spoke, saying, "And this is my daughter, Susan Durham. And there we have Susan's children, Ben and Alexandra, and this is Stephanie's brother, Randy."

The Brigadier smiled and nodded to the group.

"I'm pleased to meet all of you," he said.

Then he motioned to Captain Jenkins, who stepped forward.

"Captain, would you mind asking General Rivers to take over here? I'd like to get started with the ceremony as quickly as possible. Does this young lady know why she has been summoned here?"

Captain Jenkins shook his head, "No, sir. I just told her it was a surprise."

"Excellent," said the Brigadier, again smiling at Stephanie and giving her a wink.

Then he held out his hand, and as Stephanie took it, he said, "Young lady, I have a feeling that you're going to like this. Will you follow me, please?"

Together, Stephanie and the Brigadier led the group back toward the Old Oak. As they walked, the Brigadier said, "You know young lady, after you were sent home last night, a lot of people, from the Joint Chiefs on down, didn't get a wink of sleep. Half the lawyers in Washington spent the entire night researching this situation."

Stephanie didn't know what he was talking about, but her concern must have shown, because the Brigadier quickly added, "Oh, please, Stephanie. There's nothing for you to worry about. No, indeed! In fact, I think you're going to be pleasantly surprised!"

Stephanie stole a glance to her right, where Grandma Betty was walking by her side. Grandma Betty looked down, and her smile made Stephanie feel a little less nervous.

Just then, Alexandra said, "Hey, don't forget. I helped find those rifles, too, and so I get to shoot one. Remember? Ben promised!"

"I never promised you could shoot a gun," Ben said. "Honest, Mom, I never said the little twerp could shoot a gun! I swear!"

For some reason, having Ben and Alexandra going at it also helped ease Stephanie's nerves. With all the strange things going on, at least there were some things in the world that were still constant.

When she looked at Randy, however, she saw that he was walking with his head down, looking at the ground. She realized that he hadn't said a word in the last half hour.

But that would have to wait, because, as the group approached the Old Oak, they saw that several hundred people were now gathered in front of the stage.

Most of the people waiting for the ceremony were

soldiers, but there were also a number of civilians, and Stephanie noticed that two TV trucks were parked on the grassy field near the helicopters. Then Stephanie saw two men, balancing portable television cameras on their shoulders, and both cameras were pointed in her direction.

This was getting stranger and stranger, and Stephanie began to hold back.

The Brigadier noticed her hesitation and said softly, "Don't worry, Stephanie. Just try picturing everyone here in only their underwear. That's what I do when I get nervous."

Stephanie laughed out loud then quickly slapped her hand over her mouth. The Brigadier looked at her and laughed out loud, as well, and suddenly, she began to feel at ease.

The Brigadier led the group to the edge of the stage and began to walk up a set of wooden stairs, but Stephanie stopped and said, "Sir, can my family come up on stage, too?"

The Brigadier smiled broadly and said, "You can do anything you want, Stephanie. You are the lady of the hour!"

Stephanie still had no idea what was going on, or why such a big deal was being made of all this, but she was glad it was happening. It would give her a chance to tell everyone about her brave ancestor, Lucy Killgrew, and her important mission, some two hundred years ago.

There were a number of chairs on the stage, and Stephanie sat in the one next to the Brigadier while the others sat in a row behind them. As the Brigadier made some introductory remarks, Stephanie turned around to make sure that Grandma Betty was sitting right behind her.

While she was turned around, Stephanie also grabbed Randy by the wrist and pulled him forward, so she could whisper in his ear.

"I just want to thank you for being my brother," she said. "I couldn't have done this without you."

Randy's face broke into a beaming smile. Whatever problems he had been having with Stephanie's notoriety were apparently gone, and everything was back to normal.

"And now," Stephanie heard the Brigadier say, "I'd like to introduce the young lady who was responsible for making this incredible discovery, Miss Stephanie MacAllister!"

Stephanie's mind went blank. What was happening? Was she supposed to make a speech in front of all these people? She could feel her feet moving toward the microphone, but her mind was reeling. This was almost worse than last night!

Evidently, her fear showed on her face, because just before she reached the microphone, the Brigadier placed his hand reassuringly on her shoulder, leaned close to her ear, and whispered, "Remember: underwear!"

In the midst of her confusion, Stephanie giggled at the comment. She stood in front of the microphone, letting her eyes sweep the audience and then took a deep breath.

She had no idea what she was supposed to say.

"I guess I want to begin by telling you all a little bit about one of the bravest people I've ever known. Her name was Lucy Killgrew. Two hundred years ago she joined the American Revolution and fought for what she knew was right. Part of her duty was to deliver a shipment of rifles to the American forces near Boston in the year 1775.

"Although she wasn't able to deliver the rifles that day, she hid them in order to keep them from falling into enemy hands."

"It was such acts of courage that helped America to

become a free nation, and even though Lucy Killgrew couldn't deliver the rifles to the American Army two hundred years ago, she has now seen to it that her rifles have finally been delivered, and her mission has finally been completed.

"So, in the name of Lucy Killgrew, and on behalf of all the other brave men and women who helped shape our nation when it was new, I would like to present these rifles to the Army of the United States of America."

There was a moment of silence, but then the audience erupted into a deafening chorus of applause and shouting!

Stephanie stood, looking out at the cheering audience. She had no idea where the words for her speech had come from. It was almost as if someone else had given the speech and not her.

And then she had another thought, which hit her like a lightning bolt.

She held up her hands until the cheering died down, and then she added, "Please, there is one more thing I'd like to say, and this is very important. It's about this wonderful old oak tree behind us."

She paused and looked back at the tree.

"This tree was where Lucy Killgrew hid the diary that led me to the rifles, more than two hundred years ago, and if it hadn't been for her diary, we never would have discovered her secret. So, if you please, it would mean *so* much to me—and to Lucy—if this tree could be spared when the base is complete."

Stephanie then looked back at Grandma Betty, who was nodding softly, tears filling her eyes.

She saw Ben pump his fist in the air and say, "Yes!"

Then she looked hopefully at Brigadier Preston and saw that he, too, was smiling. But it wasn't just a friendly smile—it was a smile of congratulations. It was a smile that said, "Well done, young lady."

The Brigadier stood and approached the microphone. He put his hand on Stephanie's shoulder and said, "I hereby designate this tree as 'The Lucy Killgrew Memorial Oak' and declare that it will remain a permanent monument to the bravery of not only Lucy Killgrew but also to the courage of the young woman who learned of its secrets. From this day forward, not one leaf of this tree is to be harmed—now or forever more."

The audience went wild again! It was apparent that there were a lot of people who wanted the Old Oak spared.

Suddenly, now that the adrenalin rush was gone, Stephanie felt her knees beginning to grow weak. But before she collapsed, she felt Grandma Betty's warm embrace surround her, and she leaned on her grandmother as she returned to her seat.

"Way to go, Steff!" said Randy, giving his sister a high five.

"Wow! Great speech!" Ben added.

Aunt Susan said, "That was wonderful, Stephanie!"

Alexandra added, "But when do I get to shoot?"

"I'm so proud of you, Stephanie," her grandmother said, helping Stephanie into her chair and then hugging her tight. "I've never been so proud of anyone in my whole life!"

"Thank you, Grandma," Stephanie said. Then she turned and looked at everyone sitting behind her. "And thank you all. I never could have completed Lucy's mission without your help!"

She was a little startled when she felt the Brigadier's hand on her shoulder once again.

He leaned down and said, "I'm afraid you're not quite

finished yet, Stephanie!"

Stephanie looked at Grandma Betty, who shrugged her shoulders. She stood and followed the Brigadier back to the microphone.

Holding up his hands for quiet, the Brigadier said, "Ladies and gentlemen, as soon as we've completed our business here, the news media will have a chance to photograph the cave where the long rifles were hidden. They'll also will have the opportunity to photograph the rifles themselves, all seventy-five of them.

"But before we do that, I have the extreme pleasure and honor of presenting a very special reward to Miss Stephanie MacAllister."

The Brigadier then turned to Stephanie, smiling reassuringly.

"Stephanie, I'm not sure that you were even aware of it, but when Lucy Killgrew buried those seventy-five badly-needed rifles that day some two hundred years ago, she also buried something else. Buried along with those rifles were four hundred brand new silver coins, known as Willow Trees.

"Prior to the revolution, England would not permit the Colonies to mint their own currency. But the Americans copied a die and minted these coins, anyway, and now, even though they won't be put up for sale, these coins are very valuable. In fact, I had three of this country's leading coin dealers appraise those coins, and they tell me that they are now worth approximately nineteen million dollars on the open market."

There was a collective gasp from the audience. Stephanie looked at the Brigadier, and then looked at Grandma Betty, who looked as shocked as Stephanie felt.

"Even though the coins and the rifles are the property of the United States government, we still would like to show you our appreciation."

The Brigadier then reached into his coat pocket and brought out a piece of paper, which he held out to Stephanie.

"It is my extreme pleasure to present you with this finder's fee, made out in your name, in the amount of fifty thousand dollars, to be placed into your college fund. Congratulations!"

Stephanie didn't even hear the shouting and the applause that came next. She held the piece of paper in her fingers as if it were not real. After all, this couldn't be happening."

Her mind was reeling.

Suddenly, Grandma Betty was again by her side, saying, "Stephanie, dear! I can't believe it! This is wonderful! What will your parents say?"

Randy, Ben, Alexandra, and Aunt Susan were also now standing by her side, hugging her and slapping her on the back. They may have been saying things to her, but she didn't hear them. Cameras were flashing, people were cheering, and microphones were being thrust into her face. Her mind was on overload and could absorb no more.

From that moment on, she had no idea what she did or said—or if she even said anything at all.

Chapter Twenty-Five

Threads

IT WAS AFTER MIDNIGHT before all media people,
local friends, and distant relatives were finally shooed
out the front door by a tired, but happy, Grandma Betty,
who then helped Stephanie drag herself upstairs to bed.
Everyone, it seemed, wanted to congratulate her for
discovering the rifles, saving the Old Oak, and getting all
that money.

But the piece of paper Brigadier Preston had handed
Stephanie while on the stage wasn't a real check, of course.
No money would actually be transferred to Stephanie until
a trust account had been established in her name—and her
parents would have to help set that up.

It had been an exciting and exhausting day, but now it
was finally over, and as Grandma Betty pulled the covers
up, Stephanie savored the feel of the wonderfully cool
sheets.

All she wanted to do was to drift off into a peaceful

sleep. She didn't even want to dream. But before she closed her eyes, her eyes fell once more on Lucy's dress, still carefully draped over the chair, and she remembered that she still had one last, important thing to do.

As tired as she was, Stephanie dragged herself out of bed and looked at the dress. Even though there was a part of her that wanted this all to be over with, there was a part of her that was very sad at the prospect.

A moment later, Stephanie was slipping the heavy dress over her head. She knew she should be used to it by now, but it still surprised her just how heavy the dress actually was. How did girls back then stand wearing such heavy dresses every single day?

As she smoothed the dress around her body, Stephanie closed her eyes and tried to clear her mind.

An instant later, she heard a voice, saying, "Hello, Stephanie."

Stephanie found herself standing beneath the oak. She could tell by the size of the tree that she had once again traveled back in time.

No matter how many times she saw Lucy, she'd never get used to how much she looked like the buckskin-clad girl who was now standing in front of her.

"Lucy?" Stephanie said softly.

"Yes."

"I...I don't know what to say."

"It is I who must talk now, Stephanie. I want to thank you."

"But there's so much I want to say, so much I want to know," said Stephanie.

"You have saved me, Stephanie. I can be at peace now."

"I'm so glad. But I'm going to miss you."

"Our bond is solid and can never be broken, for, just

as I prevented the long rifles from falling into the hands of my enemy, you did the same. And you have delivered them," Lucy said, a radiant smile on her face. "My mission is now complete, thanks to you."

Stephanie looked deep into Lucy's eyes but could think of nothing to say, although it didn't seem to matter. It was as if they could read each other's thoughts. Time seemed to stand still. Perhaps time had no meaning in this place. It was a magical moment, and yet it was tinged with a feeling of sadness, as well. Stephanie felt as if she had found a long-lost twin sister but was about to lose her again, before they'd had the time to know each other well.

Tears filled Stephanie's eyes. Somehow, she knew that the time was growing short.

She forced herself to speak, to ask the final question she needed answered before they said good-bye.

"Lucy, the records...they don't tell what happened to you. Did the British capture you? Were you...?"

"Killed?" Lucy asked, completing Stephanie's thought. "No, I wasn't killed."

Lucy looked deeply into Stephanie's pale blue eyes, as if searching for something she hoped would be hidden there. After a few moments, she smiled—a smile that seemed far older than her thirteen years.

"Come. Let me show you—and be not afraid of anything you see. The circle of life can never be broken and need not be feared."

Lucy turned and motioned for Stephanie to follow. Stephanie had no idea what she was about to see, but she trusted Lucy with all her heart and soul and fell in behind.

There was no sensation of movement, no indication of the passage of time. Yet, suddenly, they were standing in a small room with a large, old-fashioned bed. The mattress and sheets were trimmed with hand-sewn lace. The room itself, like the bed, was plain, with little furniture except for a single high-back wooden chair and small bed table. On the table was a white porcelain pitcher and a wooden drinking cup.

There seemed to be other people in the room, as well, besides Stephanie and Lucy, although no one took the slightest notice of the two girls.

Then, Stephanie's attention was drawn to an old woman, lying on her back on the bed, her mouth open. Time seemed to be standing still, but in Stephanie's mind, one thought kept repeating, like an endless tape loop: "She's me. She's me. She's me."

The woman's face was wrinkled and tanned from a lifetime of hard work. Her skin was leathery and hung in folds, especially on her arms, which were crossed over her chest, which rose and fell with each slow, shallow breath.

There was no doubt that she was an old woman, yet despite the ravages of time, her face had lost little of its inner beauty and strength.

And her face was the face of Stephanie MacAllister.

"Oh, my!"

The sound escaped from Stephanie's constricted throat, sounding like the peep of a tiny bird.

"Is...is that—me?" she finally managed to ask.

Lucy turned her pale brown eyes in Stephanie's direction and said, "No. I am the woman you see."

Stephanie looked at Lucy and then looked again at the old woman on the bed.

Then she looked back to Lucy and said, "You? But...I don't understand."

Lucy drew her face close to Stephanie's, and as their eyes met, she said, "There is nothing to fear. The wheel of life rolls on forever. We cannot alter its path, its speed, or its direction, no matter how hard we may try. You must remember: my death occurred more than a hundred and fifty years ago."

Stephanie stammered, "But why? Why are you showing me this?"

"So you will understand," Lucy said softly. "So you will know why I came back. Why I asked your help. Do you wish to understand fully?"

Stephanie looked deeply into Lucy's eyes—eyes that, except for the color, were almost identical to her own, and said, "Yes, of course."

Lucy stepped back, studying Stephanie's face closely. "Are you willing to join me, in the moments just before my death?"

Lucy turned her head to look at the old woman, and it took a second before Stephanie realized what Lucy was asking. When she did, she was momentarily filled with fear.

"You mean..."

Lucy smiled and said, "Yes. You will become one with me, just before my death. You will see what I see, remember what I remember."

Stephanie looked again at the figure on the bed. The idea of becoming one with that wrinkled body, and actually experiencing the riddle of life's greatest mystery was exciting...yet terrifying at the same time.

Stephanie turned back to Lucy and said, "Yes, I do want to know."

"Thank you," Lucy said. "This means a great deal to me. I believe it will make my life complete. There was so much that I was never able to pass on—but now, I can, through you."

In a heartbeat, Stephanie found herself lying in the bed.

A great weight seemed to be sitting on her chest, making it difficult for her to breathe. It took only a moment to know that she was now a part of Lucy—the old Lucy, dying in this small room, with only a few family members gathered around.

Instantly, her mind was filled with images and memories—Lucy's memories—flashing past like a film montage.

She saw herself being thirteen years old again.

The day was bright and clear, and she could see every detail of the stitching on the moccasin as it silently approached, pressing itself into the soft, moist forest floor. She could see the lifeless face of a Huron lying a short distance away, blood seeping from where an arrow had entered his side.

She wasn't sure why she was lying there. She had no memory. Only the present existed and then a large buckskin clad man stood over her.

She heard the Indian say, "Ah, n'aies pas peur."

His words were clear, but their meaning was murky. She felt the cool, damp earth as she lay there, her cheek pressed against the ground, helpless, alone, and terrified.

The Iroquois knelt down beside her and looked deeply into her eyes. It was as if he were searching for something, deep within her soul.

"Je suis Young John," he said kindly. "Ne bouge pas petite!"

She could feel his gentle hands shift her head slightly and examine the bruise on her temple.

"Vous êtes blessée," he said, with a look of concern.

Then, there was darkness. The next thing she remembered was waking up in an Iroquois camp. An older Indian woman and two young girls were caring for her. She assumed the girls were the older woman's daughters.

She was frightened, more frightened than she had ever been before. But strangely, it wasn't the Indians that were making her so afraid. Although she had no idea what it was, this fear was much deeper than that—something more primal.

The memories continued to wash over Stephanie, like the waves of the incoming tide, one wave overlapping another. Months passed, then years, and she could see herself changing. She dressed differently. Her body had changed, growing and maturing. She had become a young woman—a beautiful young woman.

She remembered taking a long trip northward, to a Mohawk village. For her, this trip had meant the end of one journey and the beginning of another.

She had come to love the tribe that adopted her and to feel as if she were a part of it. They had become her family. But now, she had been told that she must go to Canada with a white man, his wife, their two daughters, and their son.

The man's name was Emile Dufore. He was a trapper, known and trusted by the Indians.

At first, life in Canada was difficult for Lucy, but as time went by, her patchwork of English, Iroquois and French languages gave way to fluent French.

Time and memories continued to flow.

At twenty-two she saw herself standing proud and tall before a priest as she married Simon, the Dufore's handsome son, whom she had grown to love over the years. She looked deeply, joyfully, into his clear blue eyes as he slipped a thin band of gold onto her finger.

She remembered the tearful good-byes and hugs as she and Simon left the forest to begin their new life together in Montreal. After living in the forest most of their lives, she found the big city both exciting and frightening.

The only thing that seemed to mar her happiness was the unexplainable fear she felt each time she saw a Redcoat walking patrol in the city.

Then, she experienced a memory of a room, filled with flowers, and in her arms, a baby—her newborn son. For some reason she couldn't explain, she insisted that they name him Thomas.

But that image quickly faded, and Stephanie felt herself being yanked back into the small room where the old woman on the bed was now laboring to breathe.

Although her vision was cloudy, her gaze swept across the indistinct figures gathered around her as she drew in a sharp breath and called out, "Father? Is that you?"

A lanky man, standing next to the bed, bent low and she could feel his hand gently caress her forehead, tenderly, lovingly.

"Maman. C'est votre fils Thomas."

Stephanie could hear the words, but it was too much work to figure out what they meant. But she knew they were soothing, and just hearing them made her feel better.

"The long rifles," she heard her old voice say in a barely audible tone. She was apparently delirious. "I must deliver the rifles. Father is depending on me."

Her son Thomas bent over her and said, "Maman. Je ne comprends pas Maman!"

She was barely aware of her son looking down at her, a look of worry and sadness filling his face.

She then closed her eyes, which seemed too heavy for her ever to open again. In a moment, she felt her chest grow heavy. It was like nothing she'd ever felt before. It was almost too much effort to breathe. It would be so much easier to give up the fight.

There were only moments left, but was this all? Was

this everything that Lucy wanted her to know?

Then she remembered. *She remembered!*

Suddenly, like an old and forgotten door being opened, she remembered everything from the past—a past that had been so securely locked away but was now there for her to see in all its glory and pain!

Instantly, she could see herself standing next to the oak, picking up the last armload of muskets and carrying them to the cave, where the rest had already been hidden. The only thought in her mind was keeping the rifles out of the hands of the British and then getting them to her father, to Will, and to all the other brave men and boys fighting to make America free.

Nothing must stop her from fulfilling her mission. Without the muskets, her father and the others might not defeat the British. It meant everything to her to deliver those rifles—everything!

Suddenly, she saw her father, Tom, standing before her, his arms outstretched, a look of pride and love on his shining face. She ran to him, a little girl with open arms, crying with the joy. She saw him again bending low in the saddle to avoid an overhanging tree branch the night he came home for her thirteenth birthday.

Then she saw her mother, Nancy, loving, kind, and as beautiful as ever. Her joy was so great that she felt as if she would explode. It almost was more than any one person could bear! Tears of love and joy washed over the years, washing them clean and sparkling bright.

Nothing in life had ever been so sweet, so beautiful, and so perfect.

Then, Stephanie knew that life had given Lucy one final gift in those final moments—the memory of her family.

Then, all was darkness—blessed darkness and a feeling of peace such as Stephanie had never known.

✰ ✰ ✰

With a jolt Stephanie suddenly realized that she was back in her bedroom at Grandma Betty's house. She was still wearing Lucy's dress, but something had changed. The dress wasn't physically different, but something was missing, nonetheless. It was an intangible quality—a spirit—that had been there before, but now was gone. In less time than it takes to relate, Stephanie knew that she would never see Lucy again.

Lucy's spirit had finally been set free.

Slowly, and with a touch of sadness, Stephanie removed the heavy dress, which had been so lovingly given to a little girl more than two hundred years ago, for the last time and laid it carefully on the bed.

"Good-bye, Lucy Killgrew," Stephanie whispered, wiping a tear from her eye. "I'll never forget you—and thank you."

✰ ✰ ✰

Randy and Stephanie's summer in Mayfair was coming to an end.

Since Stephanie was still a celebrity in Mayfair, the good-byes were many and the pace was hectic.

Ben and Alexandra stopped bickering just long enough to give Stephanie several hugs and make the usual promises to write.

Stephanie even gave Willie a special hug and a good-bye scratch.

But the hardest good-bye was the one she had to say to Grandma Betty.

"Thank you for believing in me," she said, hugging her grandmother tightly.

"And thank you for giving me something to believe in," Grandma Betty replied.

They stood holding each other for a long time, until

Grandma Betty finally broke off the embrace and, wiping her eyes, said, "You know, of course, this isn't as bad as you might think. After all, you can afford to visit me every summer, if you want, from now on!"

She was right, of course, and Stephanie hugged her grandmother again, this time even tighter.

"I'll be back, Grandma. I promise," said Stephanie, sniffing back her tears, "on our very next school vacation."

Then she laughed and added, "And who knows? I might even bring Randy with me."

As the tiny plane taxied onto the runway for the trip back to New York, where the connecting flight would whisk both Stephanie and Randy on to Southern California, it seemed like the entire town had turned out to say their final good-byes.

Stephanie felt the vibrations as the small plane gathered speed, preparing to leap into the gathering dusk. She pressed her face against the Plexiglas window and waved to her family, friends, and dozens of well-wishers.

Had it really been only five weeks?

She began reflecting back on everything that had happened during those few short weeks. She had aged a lifetime since then, it seemed.

She smiled, somewhat sadly, knowing that some things would never be the same again, knowing that she had gained something wonderful—but had lost something special, as well.

Suddenly, Randy's voice cut through her thoughts like a dull bayonet.

"Hey, Steff, look at that."

Even though the plane was virtually empty, Randy had taken the seat directly behind hers. With exaggerated slowness, Stephanie turned and looked up, where she saw her brother's face.

"Wanna see what a body looks like after a plane crash?" he said.

Then he grabbed his top lip and pulled it up halfway over his nose, exposing the entire top half of his mouth.

The sight was totally disgusting, and Stephanie could only shake her head and look away, although she couldn't suppress a smile.

"Well, Randy," she said, "it's nice to see how much you've grown up in these past five weeks."

A few seconds later, Stephanie felt Randy kick the back of her seat—hard.

Maybe things haven't changed as much as she had thought.

The loom of history had labored hard, and the weaver's shuttle had whipped back and forth, almost as if it had a mind of its own, weaving together the many and varied threads that make up the fabric of life. Each thread may have been tiny and insignificant within the overall pattern, yet each one added something special to the completeness of the whole.

And somewhere within the darkening forest below, light, brittle leaves were dancing and swirling in the late summer wind. Shrubs and young pine now covered the site where the Killgrew home once stood—a home where, so many years ago, the silhouette of a young Colonial girl had shone through a window and was cast upon the ground by the glow of the warm fire within.

The haunting sound of the wind passing through the arbor corridors seemed to whisper, *"Lucy, come away from the window, dear. It's time for supper."*

And as the small plane banked and climbed, it suddenly broke through a thin layer of clouds and there, shining brightly in Stephanie's eyes, was the moon, now in its first quarter.

At that instant, Stephanie realized that she was carrying something precious back home with her—a cargo of tales that would be told for generations to come.

Stephanie couldn't help but let out a little chuckle at her brother's ongoing antics behind her. With a smile and a deep sense of well-being, she nestled herself in her seat and fell fast asleep.

No more would Lucy be lost to the ages, and for all eternity, there was one thing that would always remain constant. It was the one thing that would always keep Lucy close to her.

It was Lucy's friend and confidant, Emy Moon.

THE END

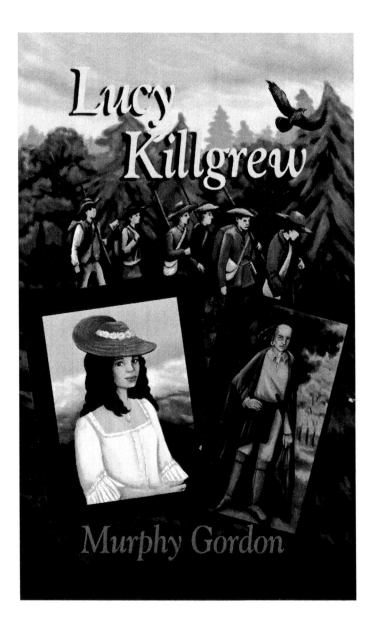

Lucy Killgrew

Murphy Gordon

ATTENTION READERS!!

NOW AVAILABLE – "LUCY KILGREW"

A young colonial hero's adventures continue in this second of a series of books centering on the American Revolution. New villains and new characters come to life in this exciting continuation of "Emy Moon".

"Lucy Killgrew" takes the reader on a fascinating journey of her past just after she disappears. After losing her memory and eventual rescue, she is adopted and taken north by Young John, a Mohawk Iroquois. While she is learning a new life among the Bear Clan, Will Ashley, the young man Lucy befriended has joined Benedict Arnold's march north to invade Canada. Will has decided that he would use the invasion route in his search for Lucy. We learn of the hardships that abound in the invasion attempt as well as discover a new villain also in search of Lucy.

All paths will merge on the Iroquois Nation and dramatically change the lives of all.

Send check or money order to:
Sawmill Publishing
6444 E. Spring St. # 215
Long Beach, CA. 90815

Or save time and order online at
WWW.SAWMILLPUBLISHING.COM

$14.95 Paperback $19.95 Hardcover.